SCOTT ARBUCKLE

Augmented

PRAISE FOR "SCAVENGED" BY SCOTT ARBUCKLE

"⭐⭐⭐⭐⭐ This is top-notch science-fiction." -Renaissance Writer

"⭐⭐⭐⭐⭐ Powerful and captivating...a must read. I highly recommend this book." —Leonard Tillerman, My Writer's Nook

"⭐⭐⭐⭐ Impressive science-fiction...tightly written and full of vivid imagery. Congratulations to Scott Arbuckle for nailing his debut." —Cal P. Logan, author of the "Shattered Fate" series

"⭐⭐⭐⭐⭐ A fantastic, wonderfully crafted sci-fi debut." —Kelly Creagh, author of the "Nevermore" series

"⭐⭐⭐⭐ "An engaging YA sci-fi tale with plenty of action, Scavenged is fast paced, with enough twists and turns to make this a hard book to put down." —Ishmael A. Soledad, author of "Sha'Kert: End of Night"

"⭐⭐⭐⭐ Cleverly balanced...immediately I fell in love with the writing style." —Charleigh Writes, via Reedsy Discovery

"⭐⭐⭐⭐⭐ Well-conceived and artfully described...highly recommended." —Gordon A. Long, author of the "World of Change" series

"⭐⭐⭐⭐⭐ An excellently crafted story...I thoroughly enjoyed the twists and turns in every chapter...and cannot wait for the sequel." —Mel Snyder, author of the "Zepharius" series

First edition

This book was professionally typeset on Reedsy.
Find out more at reedsy.com

Contents

Chapter 1

Detective First Class Harlow marched through the front entrance of the spaceport, nodding at the sector security officers without breaking stride. There was no need to ask them what they'd seen, since the attacker wouldn't be carrying weapons and Harlow had never seen his face. Speaking to the guards here would only cost him time. Harlow was in full tactical gear; the passive scanners screamed as he went through the gate, but the security team scurried to get out of his way. Internal Friend/Foe tags identified him as a Protectorate officer, and the stony gaze beneath his darkened brows identified him as a man not to be trifled with.

The Josiah Corvus Memorial Spaceport had been open less than a week, and the smooth floor was unscuffed, almost slick. Harlow's boots called neat echoes from the high, curved ceilings—this place had the acoustics of marble, although it appeared to be made of plexiglass. Outside, shuttles flitted above the expanse of smooth white pavement, docking at the building's terminals. Farther out on the tract, the colossal cigar-shaped outlines of freighters, and smaller, boxier transport ships, loomed against the desert's empty horizon.

Inside the concourse, the crowds were sparse. Travelers carted their belongings in hard-shell carrying cases, trying not to look excited. Interplanetary trips—the true purpose for the new spaceport—hadn't begun yet, but the prospect of zipping around the globe to other Sanc-

1

tuaries in little more than an hour was nothing short of electrifying.

Humans were not the only travelers present. Here and there, a gaunt, gray-skinned alien shuffled through the concourse. Each of them was perhaps a hundred twenty centimeters tall, with an inverted-teardrop head and huge obsidian almond-shaped eyes. The other commuters deferred to them, consciously or unconsciously giving the right-of-way to the diminutive beings.

New Zaragosa was still rebounding from the shocking events of a few months past: the assassination of an Illuminatus, the city's special liaison to the Greys; a curtailed invasion by the murderous lizardlike alien Lacertas; and the disappearance—some daring heretics even said *destruction*—of the city's guardian angel, a scout-class Grey flying saucer. The creation of this terrestrial space station was not merely practical, but symbolic: a reassertion of the United Corporations Order's supremacy. *We are still in control,* it said, *and the Greys are still with us.*

So an attack by one of Vulpecula's men would have the exact opposite symbolic effect: *No, you're not in control. We're running the show—not you, and not the Greys.* Even if the potential number of casualties was light, a successful strike by the fanatical doctor would have far-reaching implications. For the past six months, Noreen Vulpecula had slipped free of every trap the Protectorate had set for her, vanishing without a trace. Public confidence was at stake—and that pillar of the UCO had recently been shaken. Harlow would not allow it to collapse.

He scanned the faces of the people he passed. One of them was a wolf among sheep. Vassals—the Greys' name for Human citizens—returned his scrutiny with mild curiosity: as a security officer, he raised little interest in the spaceport, but the would-be attacker would spot him right away. Would he panic, and bolt? Harlow didn't think so. The discipline, and zealotry, Vulpecula required of her initiates would hold such a one steady to his mission, even in the face of discovery. Harlow wouldn't be able to pick his adversary out of the crowds based on simple suspicious behavior. Not until it was too late.

He arrived at the security office, and let himself in with his enhanced-access Protectorate keycard. A uniformed guard swiveled in his seat, concern plastered on his features at the sight of a Detective barging in. Harlow frowned. Weren't they expecting him? The spaceport should already be under alert.

"Sir?" the young officer said, rising from his seat. A second guard remained on the stage in a corner of the room, using the augmented-reality grid to access the supernet with an eyepiece, earpiece, and gloves.

Harlow scanned the monitors lining the wide desk and tough, opaque walls. Birds-eye views of the concourse portrayed travelers and employees going about their business. He flicked through the access corridors and off-limits personnel areas, and found nothing unusual. Good—it appeared he wasn't too late. He turned back to the waiting man: McKay, by his badge.

"You should have gotten a Priority One," Harlow said.

Worry tensed the younger man's brow. "No sir," McKay replied. "I'm sorry, sir. What's the situation?"

Harlow zeroed on the officer using the stage. "Hold it right there," he said. "Keep your hands—"

A low groan cut through the building as the lights went out. As one, the monitors went dead and then reset with an error message, rebooting. Blackness swallowed the room for a split second; by instinct, Harlow put his back to the wall and reached for his weapon. The taser, not the pistol; he wanted the suspect alive. Before he could bring his hand up, though, a barreling weight crashed into him, and he caught a vicious punch to the gut. The lights snapped back on in time for Harlow to see the black-clad form of the second Protectorate man flinging the hallway door open. Harlow pushed himself forward, bruised from the debilitating strike, and snatched at the fleeing man's wrist as he went through the doorway. Startling momentum carried him into the hall; the perp was as strong as an ox. Harlow wrenched the man's arm, twisting it to bring him into a controlling position; as they crashed against the wall together in the corridor, Harlow squeezed the dual triggers on the stun gun and jammed the weapon against the suspect's neck.

Blue sparks popped with deafening clacks in the concrete corridor. In the brilliant flash, Harlow caught his first glimpse of the man's face: White, middle-aged, with a neatly trimmed dark goatee and brown eyes that shone with mirth. Ignoring the crippling voltage, the perp lashed out with his free hand and shoved Harlow with such force that his boots left the floor. The opposite wall slammed against his back, and he gasped. The suspect had shrugged off 15 million volts like it was nothing. Harlow rebounded from the wall, aiming a knife-hand strike to the man's throat, but the assailant was gone, streaking down the hall at an astounding pace.

The first security guard rushed past Harlow, giving chase. Harlow recovered and joined the pursuit, sprinting down the corridor while ignoring his aching bruises. The intruder was heading for the concourse, picking up speed like a bird in flight and outdistancing McKay and Harlow with ease. By the time they followed him out the door at the end of the hall, Harlow couldn't be sure of which way the attacker had run.

The lights had only been off for a second in the terminal, and people would attribute it to a power surge or some similar anomaly. Harlow halted at the doorway, again studying the passersby for clues. No one wore an expression of worry or disbelief, staring after a running security guard; the fugitive must have played it cool as soon as he'd gotten to the public area of the spaceport.

The other officer was on his comlink. "McKay here. We got a rogue officer on the run. Was going by the name 'Zubrin' when he was a sleeper. Revoke all security clearance immediately. White male, dark hair and goatee...let's seal the entrances and lock down—"

"No," Harlow cut in, still scrutinizing the area. "No lockdown. That's what he wants. Get these people out of here. Evacuate."

McKay relayed the order, then lifted an eyebrow. "So this is a terrorist attack? Like a bomb?"

"Not a bomb," Harlow said, fitting his rebreather over his face. "A virus."

Concern deepened the young man's features as McKay mimicked the protective action. "We're on channel four, by the way," he said, indicating Harlow's own comlink.

As Harlow made the adjustments to join the security channel, a voice in his ear broke in in midsentence. "—shut tight, sir."

McKay frowned. "Well, get them open."

"Yes, sir. Trying, sir."

Harlow clenched a fist. So far, things were playing right into the attacker's hands. This Zubrin's credentials must have been impressive forgeries. He had intercepted the Protectorate's alert notification using the security grid, and initiated his own selective lockdown before slipping away to carry out the rest of his plan. There was little doubt of what was about to happen if Harlow didn't get in front of the situation somehow.

He assessed his options at lightning speed. The attacker was stronger and faster than his pursuers, and was hidden amongst the vassals in the wide expanse of the spaceport. Roaming the concourse, trusting to luck, would hardly work in his favor, and would only cause a panic as the travelers noticed that the security team had donned their biohazard equipment. With Zubrin having blocked the exits, a stampede would be deadly. How could he anticipate Zubrin's moves, lure him out, and trap him?

"Maybe Zubrin is planning to release the virus into the facility's ventilation system," McKay offered, noticing Harlow's momentary hesitation.

"No, we can rule that out," Harlow said. "He would have stuck to the access corridors, where he can move at full speed and overpower us without anyone seeing. Instead he came to the public concourse. The people around here don't act as though they've seen anything unusual, so he's blending in, not using his augmented potential. He's not here to cause blind chaos—he's a professional on a mission."

"How'd you know he was the terrorist?" the spaceport guard asked.

"You said you hadn't received the Priority One, but Zubrin was right next to you, using the stage. He'd have seen the alert, which means that he disregarded it and didn't tell you about it."

McKay nodded. "He could have killed me when my back was to him in the office. And he didn't take his time with us when you arrived and blew his cover. He must be on a timetable. A professional, like you said."

Harlow looked up to the schedule boards. Arrivals, or Departures? There were a half dozen flights headed in and out of the spaceport in the next thirty minutes.

Then something Harlow himself had just said took on new significance to him.

Zubrin was using the stage...

"There's something he was doing on the supernet," Harlow deduced. "He needs a stage for whatever it is he's trying to do. Check the cafés."

Again, McKay repeated Harlow's orders into his comlink. The detective consulted a map of the spaceport on an overhead monitor, his sharp marengo eyes picking out the coffee shops scattered through the terminal. The closest two were an equal distance from the access corridor where they'd flushed the perp into the public area of the spaceport; those cafés were in opposite directions from where Harlow now stood. Choosing the wrong one would mean backtracking, giving Zubrin all the time he needed to carry out his orders and get away. Then Harlow's mind made another leap.

"There," he said, pointing at the monitor. "He's at Spaced-Out Coffee. Come on."

As they ran, now drawing disconcerted stares from the vassals, McKay asked for a second time how Harlow had known what the suspect was up to.

"The icon for Spaced-Out Coffee was gray on the map—it's closed. But this is the middle of the day. He could have gone there, flashed a badge and shut the place down, and had it all to himself. That's what I would do."

Approaching the café, Harlow saw that it was indeed closed, its steel-and-acrylic security gate lowered and the lights off within. The spaceport facility was brand new, after all; some of the businesses were still under construction, not yet ready for customers. Harlow had pinned his one and only shot on this being a clever ruse from the perp. If Harlow was wrong, there was no doubt the virus would be dispersed and Zubrin would get away.

The nearly-opaque gate and the darkness within obscured Harlow's view into the coffee shop. "Get this thing open," he told McKay, taking cover against the wall at the edge of the doorway. After a moment's debate, he unholstered his weapon—the gun this time, not the taser. Passersby exclaimed and hurried away, dragging their luggage after them. The Protectorate man could only hope people would stay away from here without inciting a full-blown panic. He wished for backup, but the facility's other officers needed to canvass the other coffee shops in case Harlow was wrong here. The junior officer watching his back would have to do.

McKay knelt at the access panel and in moments had the gate rising, announcing their presence to whoever might be inside, but it couldn't be helped. When the bottom had cleared the floor by fifty centimeters, Harlow swung around the corner, hit the ground and rolled under the lifting gate.

There was barely any cover inside; the tables and chairs were wiry and postmodern. He had nowhere to take shelter while his eyes adjusted to the semidarkness. The front counter looked like solid metal, keeping with the space-age theme of the place, but it was several meters ahead and to the left, and an exposed run would put him out in the open. To the right, near the back of the café, several cubicles offered relative privacy for patrons renting stage time. If Zubrin was there, he'd have an entrenched position among the metal walls, and was now impossible to surprise.

Harlow tore a flashbang grenade from his tactical vest, and chucked it toward the cubicles. He turned away, shielding his eyes from the blinding concussion, and then bolted for the protection of the front counter. Behind him, McKay was slipping beneath the security gate, shouting for Zubrin to put his hands up and surrender.

Harlow crouched before the bulky metal counter, and risked a fast glance over the top in the direction of the cubicles. A shadow snaked around one of the portable walls, and several loud bangs shook the room—Zubrin was firing in McKay's direction. Harlow hoped it was just blind-fire for suppression while the perp shook off the disorienting effects of the flashbang; if Zubrin was blindly shooting in the direction of the younger officer's voice, then Harlow hadn't given away his own position at the counter. He still didn't have a firing angle, though.

Harlow pressed the silent alert on his comlink, paging all officers to converge on his position. It was difficult to get a bead on his enemy, but he thought he had it narrowed down to two of the supernet cubicles. He'd have to stay on the offensive; if Zubrin felt trapped, he'd simply disperse the biological weapon. Harlow couldn't give him time to consider that option.

He bounced a second and third flashbang into the two possible hiding spots, and shielded his eyes with a forearm. The twin explosions thundered in the confined space.

Time to move. Harlow rose from concealment and dashed to the rear of the shop. Instead of movement in the stage cubicles, though, he caught the motion of a back door swinging shut. Again Zubrin's reflexes astounded him—the man had apparently sprinted from shelter in the brief second after the grenades were tossed and before they detonated.

Harlow shouldered through the door and blinked in a well-lit concrete corridor. The escapee was up ahead, tearing down a narrow serviceway for employees. Harlow gave chase, legs pumping, lungs burning. He'd never be able to match Zubrin's speed. Then, salvation: three Protectorate officers pushed through a door into the hallway far ahead, coming straight for them. Behind Harlow, McKay crashed through the coffeehouse door they'd just come through. Zubrin was trapped in the corridor with five Protectorate men closing on him from both sides—finally, some decent odds against the superhuman terrorist.

"Hands up!" Harlow called. "Go to your knees, and then all the way down on your stomach!"

Just ahead of Zubrin, a heavy security door on the right read "RESTRICTED ACCESS". The rogue officer swiped his card, but a red light blinked; the administrators had successfully revoked his clearance. The reinforced door opened outward, into the hallway; even with his monstrous strength, it was doubtful that Zubrin could kick it open. Instead, he bashed the steel door with his shoulder, denting the frame. Another slam, and the housing stove inward. He forced his fingers into the gap, prying it outward like a gorilla escaping from a cage.

"Stop!" Harlow shouted, coming forward, raising his pistol. But his backdrop wasn't clear—the other Protectorate men filled the hallway behind Zubrin. The rogue officer was no ordinary suspect; if Harlow fired and missed, he'd surely strike one of the friendlies. But if he didn't shoot, letting Zubrin get away, an untold number of civilians would be at risk.

Just don't miss. Feet apart, both eyes open, shoulders squared, exhale, squeeze, don't jerk, the trigger. But the moment of indecision had cost him—as he fired, the fugitive jerked the door open and Harlow's bullet clanged harmlessly against the steel.

The Detective bolted after the fleeing suspect, through a back hallway, twisting and turning through the administrative section of the spaceport. They raced past offices containing shocked employees, heading deeper into the facility. Zubrin crashed through a set of double doors into a giant room where machinery processed passenger bags.

These 'feedbelts' were the next generation of the outdated 'conveyor belts', using artificial gravity to achieve a similar effect in a fraction of the time. Harlow eyed the fugitive ducking past equipment ramps, outpacing him. There were a million places to hide in this heavily-obscured environment.

No time to think about it—take a risk. You're going to lose him anyway. Harlow vaulted onto the nearest feedbelt and braced himself as the machine zipped him forward at a dizzying pace. He crouched, keeping his center of gravity low, and was still nearly decapitated by another belt that crossed the track overhead. Harlow ducked lower, but kept his eyes and weapon raised. From this raised view of the floor, and the nerve-wracking speed which matched that of Zubrin, he was able to keep an effective tail on the fugitive. Taking a shot was still out of the question, though; firing at a moving target, while moving himself, with the crisscrossing feedbelts offering frequent obstructions, was an exercise in futility.

Instead, Harlow looked ahead, and ducked a second overhanging hazard. They were approaching a loading bay, where a fully-laden tug awaited transfer of its cargo to a spacecraft. Beyond the open bay door, the endless expanse of the runway was separated from the even more boundless desert by a single security fence. If Zubrin got outside, there'd be no outpacing him; he'd disappear in moments.

A desperate scheme sprang into Harlow's mind. Still crouching, he holstered his gun and tensed his body, preparing for the perfect, and only, chance to strike. Then as he neared the end of the feedbelt, Harlow leapt off, shooting into the air in sudden and awkward flight. Airborne, he flailed at a neighboring belt, also terminating at the bay, and closed both hands around its control lever. The sudden arrest nearly tore his arms out of socket, but Harlow wrenched the bar into full operation, sending luggage shooting into the bay like missiles. One hard-shell case collided with Zubrin as he broke out of cover and into the bay, throwing him off balance; a second large package sent him careening off his feet. Crates and packages pounded him, throwing Zubrin against the tug's rear gate, nearly upsetting the cart; still hanging from the lever by one arm, Harlow drew his weapon and fired a single shot at the vehicle's gate release.

An avalanche of heavy luggage buried the rogue officer. Harlow dropped to the concrete floor and hustled to the still-settling mountain of crates and suitcases. Under the burden, Zubrin struggled to free himself; Harlow kicked aside a few bags until the man was partially uncovered and still pinned in place, with only one arm and part of his torso exposed.

Harlow leveled his weapon at Zubrin's face. "No escape, Zubrin. You're under arrest." Behind him, the other Protectorate men were charging into the bay, weapons drawn, forming a perimeter around the makeshift prison. The heavy overhead door rolled shut, blotting out the daylight, barring Zubrin's intended exit. McKay came forward, readying a set of powerbinders.

Zubrin grunted, wedged in tightly. Then he locked eyes with Harlow, and spoke the first and last words the Detective would hear from him:

"Haven't you ever wanted to be more than one man?"

The light in Zubrin's eyes flared and subsided, and he slumped against the cases that pinioned him. Harlow checked for a pulse, and found nothing.

The other officers joined him. This time, McKay did not need to ask what had happened. "Cyanide pill," the junior officer said. "He must have had orders not to be taken alive."

Harlow nodded, his face grim. The Protectorate men kept digging, tossing cases aside to free the fugitive's body. In the corpse's right hand, a yellow canister was clenched.

The man's dying words haunted Harlow.

I am *only one man, Zubrin. How many men like you are out there?*

Chapter 2

He'd grown used to the powerbinders pinning his wrists together, and the chafe of the coarse orange jumpsuit as it bagged against his skin, but the shackles that hobbled his legs were another matter. Auriga took the stairs slowly; the cobalt-titanium chains rattled against the stone floor as he ascended one step at a time. A Protectorate officer gripped his bicep on each side, steering him straight ahead through the tall oak doors and into the packed courtroom. Nearby, a metallic matte-black drone hovered alongside him, its spheroid form bristling with the nubs of holostackers.

Auriga had not been surprised to learn that his trial was recorded and broadcast for the benefit of the good vassals of New Zaragosa. What shocked him was that some entity called 'Trans-Galactic Communications' was doing the same throughout the *galaxy*. It meant that aliens hundreds of light years away were viewing his upcoming sentencing as though it were the season finale of a *telenovela*. Auriga tucked his chin and smiled coyly right into the holostacker. *Muy guapo.* He approached the vacant defendant's table and stood motionless while a claw in the floor pinched the center of his leg chains and retracted with the slack, holding him taut.

The bustling courtroom settled. Spectators found their seats, swapping excited whispers. Protectorate men stood at proud attention, trying not to look smug.

"Now hear this," recited a gray-mustachioed bailiff. "The court of Regent Millard H. Strughold is hereby commenced: Let no assertion waver from the unblemished truth."

A jowly, white-haired and olive-robed man took the bench, locking eyes with Auriga. The Regent leaned forward.

"Martín Auriga, you've been found guilty of murder in the first degree with regard to the death of the Illuminatus Josiah Corvus. You are furthermore found guilty of murder in the second degree with regard to the deaths of no less than twenty-eight Protectorate officers. Guilty of murder in the third degree with regard to the death of one Grey diplomat. And most importantly, you are found guilty of the crime of sedition." The Regent rubbed his hands together with glee, and then clasped them under his chin. "It is, therefore, my solemn privilege to sentence you to die by lethal injection. On the twenty-fourth day of this month, at nine hundred hours, you shall be executed under authority of this court."

"Your honor—"

A bang of the gavel. "The defendant is not permitted to speak. At this point I shall say a few words regarding the nature of Mr. Auriga's crimes, and the repercussions they have had for the Human race."

Auriga rolled his eyes. *Madre de Díos.* As if being sentenced to death wasn't bad enough, he was going to get a lecture on top of it. The UCO wasn't missing the opportunity for a press release while it had, literally, a captive audience.

Strughold cleared his throat, and swiveled to face the holostacker. "The defendant's actions have caused serious harm to the citizens of planet Earth—or Terra, as she is known among other civilizations of the Milky Way—and to those men and women who represent us elsewhere in the galaxy. At this critical moment in history, when the importance of unity has never been stronger, seditious actions such as these threaten our burgeoning place in galactic society.

"I would take this opportunity to reaffirm that the dwindling ranks of the so-called 'Resistance', who oppose the security and unification established by the UCO, are nothing more than short-sighted outlaws who promote anarchy and division for its own sake. These separatists have no place among the civilized species, and are doomed to pay the inevitable price of all isolationists: stagnation, decay, and extinction."

Murmurs of approval and light applause rippled through the room. The Regent warmed to his subject. "Never before has man carried a deeper responsibility upon his shoulders. We, the people of Terra, are now beholden to each other, beholden to the cause of unity and accord with one another. Standing at the threshold of a new age, we needs must put aside the fractured differences of the past, and join hands as one race, one people, with manifest destiny."

The clapping resumed, louder now, and the Regent beamed at his audience. Auriga shifted his weight to a minute degree; the chains held him fast. *Can we move up the date of that execution?* he thought. *It would be better than this.*

"And so," Strughold continued, "we reject those divisive and impertinent iconoclasts who sabotage our march into the future: a future of peace and prosperity for all. A future where we, the people of Terra, will stand shoulder to shoulder with our galactic brethren and claim our true birthright as worthy and honored members of the species of the Imperium."

More cheers and applause echoed from the spectators. Strughold was really laying it on thick. "Let this sentence of death stand, therefore, as an affirmation of life. Let this be a message to all life, everywhere, that the people of Terra are ready to join your wondrous galactic society. Let this be an end to isolation, an end to furtive groping in the darkness. May those primitive and base designs perish alongside the man who is condemned here today!

"And lastly, I should be remiss without a word of friendship and atonement for our gracious allies, the Greys. If I should presume upon myself the honor of speaking for the whole of mankind," here Strughold paused to clear his throat. The audience leaned forward in mute expectation. "We thank you for your unwavering support of Terra, and for your good faith in her people. You have watched over us in the darkest of times—when atavistic barbarians wondered uncomprehendingly at the skies, when civilization was the dimmest of embers in their minds, you bestowed upon us your gifts, and set us on the path to enlightenment. Throughout our many struggles along the way, you have been there to guide us—and this, from the shadows of anonymity, without a thought for your own material gain or advancement.

"And, let us never forget, in our greatest hour of need you were there, to stanch the flood of an enemy such as this world had never known. O grisly and untimely end, that was stayed by your benevolent hand!"

Strughold's voice dropped from a lofty pronouncement to an admonishing growl. "And for all this, some would repay your kindness with treachery. Some would turn their back on salvation, to wallow in prideful ignorance. Let me not hesitate to name the person of whom I speak: a traitor to the United Corporations Order, and to Humanity, Doctor Noreen Vulpecula.

"Like the defendant before us today, that wretched fugitive shall not long escape judgment for her crimes. Mr. Auriga may refuse to give her up, but no matter: as the proverb goes, murder will out. And when she is found, she will share in his fate."

Thunderous applause came in reply. Strughold's tongue rose again, with the masterful inflection of a practiced orator. "Long live the spirit and the memory of Josiah Corvus, Illuminatus and heir to the glorious legacy of Terra reborn!"

Strughold clasped his hands beneath his chin again. A wide smile lifted his fleshy jowls to the sound of raucous cheering. The Regent seemed to forget that Auriga was present, and his eyes shot back to the table in concern when the defendant raised his voice above the crowd.

"Great speech, Your Honor. I think you could be the next Illuminatus, with a speech like that."

Strughold reached for the gavel, but Auriga's next words stopped his hand.

"At least, I hope you do become the Illuminatus, Regent."

Despite himself, the Regent raised an eyebrow. "You do? Why is that?"

Auriga smiled. "Because I'd like to kill two of them in a row."

Strughold's face reddened, and he banged the wooden mallet in the courtroom's flabbergasted hush. "Bailiffs, escort the prisoner back to his cell."

Auriga squared his shoulders as the uniformed men took him by the arm. The claw between his feet released the chain, and he shuffled out from behind the table. Endless sets of angry eyes lined the aisle as the officers led him to the doors, but no sound interrupted the jangling of his chains. The heavy oak doors boomed behind him, and he started down the polished stone staircase one step at a time.

***

They hustled him through the sallyport with gusto. Protectorate men surrounded Auriga, creating a traffic jam in the choking bottle-neck of the prison's entrance into gen-pop. Auriga made eye contact with a few of them, grinning; his overabundance of escort was only partially for the sake of security. Each of them jockeyed for position, trying to be the one to steer Auriga by the arm or open the gates as he passed through. The young guards did their best to remain stone-faced, but the excitement and celebrity of this prisoner fought a fierce battle with their professionalism.

Especially now that he was condemned.

That thought should have wiped the smile off his face, but Auriga

17

whistled a cheerful tune as he waited for the interior portal to open. His perverted prestige hardly stemmed from the fact that he was soon to be executed; under the authoritarian UCO's regime, such things happened all the time, and Auriga had been notorious long before the events of this morning. What commanded the attention of these officers was that their distinctive guest had killed an untold number of Protectorate guards: men just like them. And not only that, but he had butchered who knew how many of the hated and feared Lacertas—the reptilian extraterrestrials that had massacred the people of Terra these past ten years.

To exchange a word or a glance, to observe the movements and mannerisms of this Resistance mogul, to brush against the fabric of an ordinary prison uniform made strange and remarkable by his wearing it, was to brush against the mortality that he had brought to man, and the enemies of man. He was an angel of death, and he was sentenced to die.

Perhaps these Protectorate men wondered at seeing Auriga in the flesh. He supposed that he was shorter than they expected: a hundred and sixty-eight centimeters, but solid and powerfully built. His deep desert tan had faded during his incarceration, and his boyish black locks had been shorn close for prison. Auriga now detected the faintest scattering of silver at his temples, and in the dark stubble on his cheeks and chin: the preliminary hallmarks of an old age that would never come. But his eyes were still stormy and penetrating, and the small, subtle crow's-feet bordering them spoke not of age and weariness, but of experience and certainty.

Auriga continued his merry whistling, leaving the sallyport and stepping into the common area of the prison hall. Ward Two: violent offenders. The metal tables and stools, driven into the cement floor for immobility, were deserted: the inmates had been rounded up and deposited in their cells in preparation for Auriga's arrival. High overhead, caged and suspended from a metal armature, the ancient television was still on, its volume loud enough to compete with the rattle of his chains as Auriga shuffled across the commons to his cell.

"...sends a message to everyone out there that there will be justice, there will be civility and order. I thought the Regent's speech was magnificent, and it serves as an encouraging reminder that the dark times in our history are almost gone."

A guard turned his chunky metal key in the circular housing, and swung the door to the cell open. Two bunks, each with two austere cots, were bolted to opposite walls; three inmates, each with two austere eyes, fastened their attention on Auriga and his escorts.

"Yes, I would agree with that a hundred percent. It's important to remember that the past can be difficult to bury sometimes, but every time something dies that used to pertain to the old ways, that's a step forward, and that can be literal, like with the case of this mass murderer, or it can be figurative..."

Someone behind Auriga released his powerbinders with a neat clacking sound. Jangling with a steady rhythm, Auriga walked to the vacant bunk and stripped it of its blanket and pillow. He gathered a few meager bottles of toiletries into a zip-lock bag, and slung the belongings over one arm. The other inmates nodded at him with silent, stern faces, raising hands in a farewell gesture. He returned to the cell's doorway, and an officer closed and relocked it.

"Figurative, such as the terrorist attack that was thwarted today at the spaceport. Every time one of these attempts is countered by our brave and skilled Protectorate men, it's a clear deterrent. And that terrorist from this morning was killed, and Martín Auriga has been sentenced to capital punishment..."

Cutting across the commons back to the entrance, Auriga turned his eyes upward, to the caged television. The photo of an attractive but severe-looking woman in a white lab coat dominated the screen. He passed under it, out of its view, and heard a final sentence before the sallyport's door clanged shut behind him:

"But the orchestrator of all this, Doctor Noreen Vulpecula, is still at large..."

Chapter 3

An officer led Harlow down the brightly-lit corridor, and banged on a red metal door with his fist.

"Hey, don't get too comfortable in there, prisoner. You got a visitor," the guard said.

Harlow had timed his visit to perfection. Having just been moved into a new cell, Auriga would not have the "home advantage" of surroundings that were familiar to him. Quite the opposite, in fact: the reality of being on Death Row would now be hitting him full-force. The prospect of impending isolation would work in Harlow's favor, as well. The simple fact of having had cellmates on Ward Two would have bolstered camaraderie, giving him strength in numbers, regardless of how well Auriga actually got along with his bunkmates. By contrast, Auriga would now know that his coming days, limited as they were, would be spent alone, thinking of his imminent death.

Harlow had studied the prisoner's file at length. He didn't believe the upcoming execution would bother Auriga, who had nearly died a handful of times already at the hands of Lacertas, Greys, and his fellow man. Auriga wasn't the type to fear death, since it would inevitably come as a companion to his chosen cause. But the zealot in him would rage at a death administered before that cause was realized. A man of action could accept being killed on the battlefield, but wasting away in prison was a different sort of death. Having your enemies give you a last meal and a lecture, and then neatly stick a sterilized needle into you, was so…inglorious for a man like Auriga. Especially since the closure was so one-sided: we are able to zip you up in a body bag all nice and tidy and forget about you the next day, but you will never know if what you gave your life for ended up being worth it. If it ended up being anything at all.

The heavy door swung inward, and Harlow filled the doorframe. His tactical gear was gone, in place of a simple black uniform with the embossed Protectorate insignia. He had checked his weapons at the front security office, but he still needed a subtle symbol of authority to tip the odds in his favor. Outside, a hat, helmet, or tactical mask would perform that function, adding to the officer's stature and impassivity, keeping the suspect off balance; however, these accessories would look out of place when worn by a visiting officer inside a prison. And so Harlow toted a padded folding chair into the cramped cell and set it down in the center of the room.

He didn't sit down yet. Instead, he quietly watched the inmate, who wore a dull orange tank top, facing away while repeating a smooth pull-up motion on the exercise bar mounted to the wall opposite the door. Harlow had instructed that the door remain open, with the guard out of sight; it conveyed the image of choice. Staring at a closed door while Harlow, locked in with him, commenced the grilling, would be more likely to make Auriga clam up. Harlow was convinced that Auriga was inherently a talker, though, and these subtle messages could make all the difference.

Harlow waited while Auriga performed his reps at an unhurried pace. The prisoner wasn't counting out loud, and Harlow hadn't kept track of the number; he'd already been exercising before the officers had opened the cell door, anyway. However, as he watched, Harlow timed the pull-ups at about one every two seconds, and first one minute passed in silence, then two, with Auriga's body moving up and down like clockwork. Over and over, his arms straightened and then bunched, pointing his elbows at the floor, and straightened again in hypnotic rhythm.

Very well—Harlow could keep waiting. He'd portray patience and accommodation, and not take the bait. Auriga was playing his own game, trying to unsettle him with a physical exhibition before one word was spoken. He'd now done around eighty pull-ups since Harlow had arrived; it was astounding. His physical stamina was beyond comprehension, and Auriga was silently telling him that his mental fortitude would be equally inexhaustible.

Finally, after four minutes, Auriga lowered himself to the floor, apparently deciding that the point had been proven. Harlow's first words were critical, and would determine who had won this opening contest—but what might they be? A compliment to flatter his opponent; a joke to ease tension…no, these things would be flimsy and transparent. His opening sentence had to establish him as someone to be taken seriously, someone that it would benefit Auriga to speak with, to work with. The prisoner turned around, and his bluish-gray eyes connected with Harlow's. It was time to begin.

"I could see about getting you some better workout equipment, if you like," Harlow said in a placid tone. There it was: Harlow's skilled opening move contained a reason for Auriga to cooperate, a reminder of Harlow's status, and an unconcerned pitch.

"No, I'm good," Auriga said. "I can do pushups, sit-ups, and pull-ups; that's all I need. And sometimes I meditate, to pass the time."

Touché. Auriga's response had been disciplined and meaningful. Not the *Why, so I can be in better shape when they kill me?* retort he'd been half-expecting. It was a refusal to negotiate—not on the grounds of childish spite, but rather an assertion that Harlow had nothing of value to give.

Very well, then; he would switch to offense.

"You may have heard about the attack at the spaceport this morning," Harlow said, seating himself in the folding chair. His posture was critical: comfortable and relaxed, but not slouching. Shoulders back, attentive, making eye contact. Harlow folded his hands, squelching the anxiety he felt from his vulnerable position—the illusion that Harlow was unassailable was paramount. In truth, he didn't know whether Auriga would assault him or not; the open door could prove tempting, but Harlow had insisted upon it as a way of reading his subject. If Auriga did become threatening, the officer just outside in the hallway would employ a dart gun loaded with carfentanil. Harlow wasn't sure how the elephant tranquilizer would affect the heavily augmented prisoner, but he had vetoed the security guard's customary cattle prod after remembering the taser incident from that morning.

Auriga leaned against the wall near his cot. Good: it was potentially evasive body language, but physically unchallenging. "Yeah, I heard about the spaceport thing," he said. "The actor was killed, right?"

Harlow read through the prisoner's blasé affectation. Although Auriga appeared indifferent, this was a weighted question that presented an opportunity, and a problem. Harlow would have preferred if the news hadn't stated outright that the spaceport attacker had been killed. Although this information was good for public morale, it left Harlow with a hard sell that there were other ways to get the answers he needed than by speaking to Auriga.

Harlow considered a lie: the terrorist had been taken captive, but this information was being hidden from the public. It could pressure Auriga into speaking if he knew that another of Vulpecula's operatives was being questioned. The obvious threat was that the Protectorate was bound to get their information no matter what; whichever prisoner cooperated first would be rewarded, and the one who kept quiet received nothing. Harlow could tell his prisoner that the captured man was already rolling over, and that they knew everything—so Auriga might as well cooperate. However, it was too common a tactic. Pitting two conspirators against each other worked well with cowards, first-time offenders, or men who had something to lose. Auriga was none of these. And with Auriga's willingness to bargain already at a low level, Harlow lacked the leverage of knowing what the prisoner wanted—other than freedom, which was off the table for Death Row inmates. Nor could he credibly promise commutation, after Strughold's lengthy performance that morning. With no bargaining chips as of yet, Harlow would have to trick Auriga into giving up information; therefore, his best option at the moment was to establish rapport by telling the truth.

"Yes," Harlow said. "The operative killed himself rather than allowing us to take him into custody." *Operative*, not *terrorist*. Also, relaying the distinction of how the man had died was important: Harlow conveyed the message that the Protectorate didn't want to kill anyone, but the attacker had chosen this outcome for himself. He scrutinized the condemned man's reaction to these words.

"I see." Auriga seated himself on the bunk, and rolled a cigarillo as he spoke. "Otherwise, you'd be talking to *him* right now, instead of me."

"Probably so. These attacks are becoming more frequent, and more formidable. Dr. Vulpecula is clearly determined to expose the public to this...compound, whatever it is."

"She calls it the 'Perseus Agent'. It's a genetically-engineered virus that heightens the physical and mental abilities of its subjects to superhuman levels. At least, that's what it's supposed to do. Our testing procedures were interrupted that night when you and your buddies marched into the lab through a hole in the wall, and arrested me." Auriga's eyes were teasing and mirthful.

"So these attempts to release the virus on the populace are her way of testing its effectiveness?"

"No, I doubt it," Auriga said. "The doc's had enough time to fine-tune the Agent, and she'd want to do the experimental work in secret. She would consider it a waste of resources to expose the public to a virus that may or may not perform as she intended. I'd say that if she were really trying to distribute it, the Agent must be ready for prime time."

"How does the virus work?"

Auriga grinned. "If I told you that, you'd have a better chance at creating a cure for it."

"So you wanted to see these people become infected with it, too." Harlow forced his voice to remain neutral, fact-seeking, non-accusatory.

"The word 'virus' has negative connotations," Auriga replied. "But there are viruses that actually boost the immune system and fight infectious bacteria. The Seneca Valley Virus attacks malignant tumor cells, and has been used successfully in cancer treatment. And vaccines for a variety of diseases, like smallpox, are simply less dangerous cousins of that illness. By injecting the patient with the live cowpox virus, which is relatively harmless, the body's defense system becomes prepared to fight off the real threat of an invading, hostile illness."

"So your position is that the Perseus Agent is beneficial to its host. Were you...exposed to it, yourself?" Harlow avoided the word 'infected'.

Auriga exhaled twin streams of white smoke from his nostrils. "Nope—I was a guinea pig, all right, but in a different way. The doc used me for a prototype nanobiotic surgery that she intended to undergo herself, when it was perfected." Auriga stood, and turned in a full revolution with his arms outstretched and chin raised. "See? Perfection," he chuckled.

Harlow raised an eyebrow. "That's what you mean by doing the experimental work in secret. So the Agent really is finished, and performing as it's intended."

"You tell me. I didn't get to see the...what did you call him?

'Operative'?" Auriga chuckled again.

For an instant, Harlow relived the memory of Zubrin shoving him so hard his boots lifted off the floor. "Let's say the Perseus Agent really does make people stronger, faster, smarter. Why would Dr. Vulpecula want to do that?"

"I think the better question is, why would the UCO want to stop her?"

A moment passed. Auriga crushed his cigarillo out, his eyes on Harlow the whole time.

"I think it would be dangerous to expose the general public to a catalyst like that," the Protectorate man said after a time. "It would be an unsafe amount of power to give to people who weren't familiar with how to use it. Like giving a loaded gun to a child."

"But instead, you got there and stopped it in time. Good for you, *caballero*. Maybe they'll give you a medal."

Harlow's lips turned in a gentle smile. "Why do you think it was me personally who stopped it? Why not the security at the spaceport itself?"

"Because you're the one who found the doc's secret lab and figured out that her death was staged. You're the one who's been tracking her, trying to figure out her next moves." Auriga flashed straight, white teeth. "You're the one who arrested me. That makes you the UCO's expert on me and the doc. That's why you're here talking to me now, *hombre*."

"All of that is true," Harlow said. "But I don't consider myself an expert on you and Dr. Vulpecula."

"Oh no?"

"No. What I really am is the Order's expert on cult behavior. It's what led me to take a special interest in Dr. Vulpecula."

Auriga snorted derisively. "Ironic."

Harlow arched an eyebrow. "How so?"

27

"How can you take yourself seriously? The UCO is the very definition of a cult."

Harlow returned the prisoner's withering look with one of placidity. "I'd say that Dr. Vulpecula is the quintessential cult leader."

The orange tank top shook with mirth. "Okay, I gotta hear this."

Harlow was in familiar territory. "First of all, she enjoys a legendary status among her acolytes. Her followers regard her as more than Human."

"She is more than Human—but go on."

"Second, she promises salvation for her followers, and predicts catastrophe for the rest. She sells a specific utopia that hinges upon their beliefs and actions."

"I thought you were talking about the UCO, there. What's a Sanctuary if not a specialized utopia for the faithful? Members only, man. If you ain't inside the city walls, you're screwed."

"All right, fair enough. Let's say that's a matter of perspective."

"It sure is," Auriga said. "I'm surrounded by walls, and this ain't no utopia, brother."

Harlow made a mental note of the prisoner's admission, which contradicted the earlier unspoken claim that being imprisoned didn't bother Auriga. It was too soon for an honesty built of actual rapport, so the condemned man was attempting to manipulate Harlow with a show of forthrightness—in effect, an appeal for pity. Auriga had sized him up and decided against confrontation and violence, at least until he saw how this approach would work. Harlow welcomed the attempt at rapport, even if it was weighted with subtext; such a tactic could make Auriga more easily goaded into divulging information that he didn't mean to. The challenge would lay in discerning the right place to push—but not pushing yet. This was their first meeting, after all.

"Moving on," the officer said, "Dr. Vulpecula exhibits a preoccupation with spreading her message, extending her influence, and recruiting new—"

"Allow me to jump in here," Auriga said with a smile. "One of the classic indicators of cult leaders is that they claim to have access to divine revelation, right? Specialized information, coming from higher beings or extraterrestrial sources, that isn't common knowledge among the general public. Doesn't sound like the doc to me, but you know who it does remind me of? Fella by the name of Corvus. When you think about it, an Illuminatus checks an awful lot of these boxes."

"Another indicator might be that the leader promotes a polarizing worldview," Harlow continued. "It's common to find an 'us-versus-them' mentality, along with the insistence that the leader and her followers are above the law. Does that sound like anyone you know?"

"Speaking of that," Auriga said, "the UCO demands that individuality is sacrificed for the benefit of the group. A single, powerful figure is trusted as the final authority—not just in matters of morality, but in every single action the cult takes. Offenders are publicly castigated. You didn't happen to catch my sentencing on Trans-Galactic Communications today, did you?"

"I'm trying to do what I can to understand you and Dr. Vulpecula better."

Auriga smirked. "You sound like such a shrink." He returned to his position under the exercise bar, and rolled his shoulders in a sequence of stretches. He was preparing to work out again, and Harlow was about to lose him.

"That's not intentional."

"Uh huh. Thanks for stopping by, *caballero*. Seeing as how I don't have a lot of time here, pardon me if I don't waste any more of it on you."

"Have you been in contact with her since your incarceration?"

Caught off guard, Auriga folded his arms. "Of course not."

Harlow studied the prisoner, letting the denial hang in the weighted air for a time. Auriga's response was difficult to judge: his defensive posture and straightforward, simple answers sent mixed signals. A subject who crossed his arms over his chest while being interviewed often did so to deflect questions he didn't want to answer: the gesture was essentially like giving oneself a hug, seeking comfort.

It was possible that there was a crack there, some nerve that remained raw at the mention of the doctor's name, or in the condemned man's relation to her. Harlow decided to take a chance.

"No, I suppose not," he said, leaning back in the chair. "I don't believe she'd try to contact you."

The understated jab struck gold: Auriga's features conveyed a flash of relief, and then injury, before the stone mask returned. Harlow pretended not to notice, although his inward elation surged. Auriga possessed some talent for deception, but no one, no matter how skilled, could erase all trace of emotion from his mannerisms. For an instant, Auriga had betrayed comfort at Harlow's dismissal of this line of questioning, and then anguish in some realization that had accompanied it. It suggested that Auriga had expected Vulpecula to get word to him somehow, and was hurt by her not having done so.

The prisoner now erased his momentary folly by affecting an unconcerned sneer, and tucking his thumbs into his waistband with his fingers pointing downward. A masculine and threatening posture, Harlow noted.

"You'd think she didn't know when visiting hours were, eh, *caballero*? Just leaving me in here to rot," Auriga said.

"It's common for a cult leader to withdraw from a follower that has displeased her in some way. It's a form of punishment, withholding her physical presence from someone until they've completed their penance."

The prisoner looked at the ceiling. "Well, nineteen days from now, I'd say it'll be completed."

Harlow didn't move a muscle, even though the stillness made his body scream with discomfort. It was time to play the card he'd hidden up his sleeve from the beginning.

"You know," he said, "my superiors have been considering the idea of a public broadcast for your execution. They believe it would increase the likelihood of Vulpecula attempting a rescue—an attempt that could be anticipated and countered."

Silence coated the cell, chilling and thick like the ocean's depths. Auriga's lips parted in a sad smile as he spoke.

"You can tell them not to waste their time," he said. "None of you know her like I do. She would let me die for sure."

This time, Harlow had no doubt that the prisoner was telling the truth.

Chapter 4

The valley sprawled under a closely cloud-banked sky. Tree-dotted mountains lifted their chalky peaks along either side of the rust-colored highway. Ahead, the wide, faded road sloped away and around a bend, and a painted wooden sign announced the presence of a town as yet unseen.

Lyra Vaughn leaned against the sign and tugged at the heel of one dusty boot until it slid off. She shook it, rattling pebbles out onto the ground. How did they even get in there? The boots fit snugly, all the way up to her calf. She'd traveled in a myriad of ways the last four months: driving when there was a car, gas, and open road—although that trifecta was rare; horseback, when an equine companion could be coaxed to do so; and flying for short distances, when she could spare the energy for such a taxing feat.

And a considerable amount of walking. Always with rocks in her boots.

She read the sign again—"WELCOME TO SPRINGDALE, UTAH"—before putting her back against it and pulling the boot back on. She resumed her hike into the valley, strolling down the center of the desert highway. Before her was another lead, another chance: an opportunity for exultation or bitter disappointment. Lyra resolved to stay sharp, to keep her wits tuned to her surroundings, but the temptation to let her thoughts wander, to relive the mind-bending seconds that had lured her life into a fruitless scavenger hunt, resurfaced.

She remembered the lurching weightlessness of the flying saucer's plummet from the sky. In the demented throne room at the ship's center, she'd been locked in a midair battle of psychic force against Pyxis, the aliens' commander, while Orion tampered with the ship's systems in a desperate bid to spirit them off before it crashed. She recalled the vivid blue blaze of the Vinculum, the control apparatus Orion had constructed, as he used it to commandeer the saucer's biotransporters. It had cast his features in a sapphire glow as he stretched out his hand for her.

She'd flown to him, and gotten a hand on the device—and so had Pyxis. With the three of them locked together in freefall seconds before impact, the Vinculum had activated with a flash...and then what? Try as she might to fit the pieces of those awful moments together, only weird and shadow-haunted phantoms would dare to surface from the blank respite in her thoughts. Again she paged through the half-remembered visions clinging to her mind like ghostly cobwebs. More than fear, she had felt terrible confusion, utter ineptitude. Was that what it felt like to be insane? To be dead?

Her next clear memory was of the canopy of madness being parted before her like a curtain, and stepping through it, as into another room, she had found herself back in the deserts of western Texas—Midland, to be precise: the ruined town where she had escaped the *banditos* on her final mission as a courier. The same rooftop, in fact, where she had been picked up by the Greys for the very first time.

What flight of fancy had closed the circle of her cosmic journey? Was it possible that the ship's hijacked biotransporter had recognized her biological signature, and used its own memory to return her to the place from whence she had come? Orion would know. He would know a lot of things, in fact: like why, after their first kiss, she had awoken from stasis with her psionic powers surging to a level the Greys had never been able to match with surgery.

Lyra had promised Orion another kiss, too: one where they could take their time. She yearned to fulfill that promise. But he was gone, along with Pyxis and any other trace of that doomed saucer. Months had passed while she crisscrossed the midwest, chasing rumors of crash sites and alien outposts, only to find false leads: the same old battered cities and decade-old killing fields. The trail was growing cold, and her hopes now rested on reports of a downed Grey ship here, in what used to be southwestern Utah.

The little valley town moved into view around the bend. Single-story buildings nestled on either side of the road with their backs almost to the mountains. This had been a tourist trap fed by visitors to the nearby Zion National Park: inns, diners, quaint gift shops. Rustic lodges and outdoor supply stores, dominated by the towering rocky peaks standing vigil at the east and west. It was a pleasant scene that yet failed to satisfy: no overgrown brush, no burned buildings or piles of abandoned vehicles...and no six-month-old alien wreckage. So there had been no devastation here during the Great Harvest ten years ago, when the monstrous Lacertas had invaded Earth: the people had likely fled to the park for safety. If they were savvy, some could have survived.

Lyra scanned the still structures lining the highway. Her large gray eyes found no signs of life, but a more accurate means of perception needled her mind. She kept to the center of the road, and when she reached the heart of the little hamlet, she stopped and set her backpack down, then unslung the silver machine pistol from its strap on her shoulder.

Stooping to place the weapon next to her pack, she called, "You can come on out. I'm alone."

Leaves rustled in the wind. Other than that, silence.

Lyra frowned. There was no mistaking her perception; she was certainly not alone. Her defenses surged.

Ka-chunk.

She whirled in the direction of the hollow, metallic sound: a widening net, fired from a cannon, was already upon her. Centimeters away from her body, it broke against her mental barrier, and coalesced into shimmering particles of dust. The multicolored cinders washed around Lyra as if around the outer edge of an invisible bubble, and scattered across the roadway.

Thok.

Lyra turned her head, sensing more than seeing the flash of the dart rocketing to her. The needle's path glanced away at an unnatural angle, and the projectile bloomed into a congeries of streaming stripes that settled to the pavement like ticker-tape in a hero's welcome parade.

She examined the roofs of the low buildings, suspecting them as the origin of the attacks. Yes: shapes now skulked amongst the billboards and façades: perhaps ten that she could see, and surely more that she couldn't. She saw the barrels of weapons, but further volleys were withheld; her assailants now seemed to recognize the futility of such an act when Lyra was plainly aware of their presence.

She struggled to assess her options, wishing for her companions. Auriga, a one-man army, would jeer and then engage them all. Orion would utilize his skills and his surroundings to gain the advantage against a numerous and entrenched enemy. But Lyra's mind filled with questions: who was she up against, and what did they want with her?

These queries bore fruit, however, as she focused on the silhouettes creeping on the buildings' roofs. Reaching her thoughts out to probe at them, she found their minds unguarded. Lyra found no singular, complete assertions in the myriad collection of her targets, but rather she could patch together the prevailing sentiments that reflected back to her, as a bat's sonar returns to the user when it has struck something. She tasted apprehension, restlessness, and lust for money.

Not lust for blood, though. That was encouraging. The greed she had uncovered encouraged her: a quintessential Human emotion, easy to understand and respond to. Decidedly not alien in nature. Bounty hunters were predictable, so she wasn't in as much danger as she might have been. Still, it was no time to lower her guard.

Lyra pictured soothing waves radiating outward from her, calming a storm-tossed sea. *Peace. Weapons down. Not an enemy.* The recipients would feel, perhaps strongly, the overtones of the message, but not the specific words she used—unless they were psionic as well. She paid careful attention to her targets' response, and was gratified when the weapons now lowered. *Yes. Good. Correct.* Nothing wrong with reaffirming the proper decision.

After a moment, however, there came a spike of dissension. Someone had wriggled from under the blanket of pacifism, or perhaps never been enveloped by it in the first place. Lyra heard a sharp rebuke, with her ears and with no more refined instrument. Pressing inquiries gave way to heated challenges and verbose objections, and soon a tall silhouette came striding forward to the edge of the roof.

The figure vaulted down with an unnatural glide to land with nimble grace on the sidewalk. With the newcomer stooped to a kneeling posture to absorb the fall's impact, the first thing Lyra saw was the top of his head. On either side, shocks of pale blue hair splayed out in a reverse mohawk. Jagged points of hair tufted up and out in icy forests, and between them, Lyra's eyes traced the razor-straight scar vertically bifurcating the skull from front to back.

Brain surgery.

He straightened to his full height in the sun. The bounty hunter wore a punk-rock menagerie of black leather clothing, bedecked with silver studs, zippers, and rings. As he stood, flaps of leather folded themselves back into the recesses of his garments, and Lyra recalled the gliding motion that had carried him to the ground. Scowling magenta eyes arrested Lyra from beneath an impish brow laced with twin rows of pointed barbell piercings.

Lyra met his defiant gaze, redoubling her psionic intonations: *Peace. Submission—*

"You can save your energy," he chuckled. The bounty hunter had a strong Australian accent. "I can't hear a thing you're saying. See this?" Smiling, cocking his head, he traced a black-lacquered nail along the length of his scar. "Had my corpus callosum rebuilt awhile back. Does wonders for keeping the old touchy-feelies in check."

He advanced into the street, his smirk broadening over a square jaw. "I'd say you should try it yourself—but someone's already cracked your coconut and had a look inside, hey?"

Lyra could not stop her hand from reaching, almost of its own accord, to rub the shiny scar that encircled her own head, just above her temples. Her lengthening peals of feathery blonde hair now concealed, for the most part, the evidence of her psionic surgery—but on her forehead the mark would be forever visible.

The bounty hunter stopped at arm's length before her, grinning. "So we've got something in common," he purred. "And ain't you a dazzler. Almost makes me want to give up the two million caps and carry you off into the sunset. Have a happily-ever-after with just the two of us. What do you say?"

Lyra swallowed. They were offering two million capitals for her capture? It stood to reason that there was a price on her head, of course—she had helped to assassinate an Illuminatus, and the United Corporations Order still reeled from the blow. But it was an obscene amount of money. It suggested that the Greys, with their bottomless resources, harbored a bitter grievance against her for escaping from their clutches, and crashing their spaceship in the process.

And the bounty hunters were using nets and darts… because the Greys wanted Lyra captured alive. The thought of being returned to their alien devices and callous experiments yet again was more than she could bear. Perhaps the men lying in ambush here didn't understand the ramifications of turning her over to those cosmic outsiders; she was likely just a job, a paycheck, to them. She would not blame them for chasing an amount of money that would make anyone act crazy. She would not respond with lethal force…but she would not forget the danger they posed.

Think, Lyra, think. What were her options? She could fly away from the peril she faced, but at no faster than the speed of a running adult. If a marksman got her with a dart, she'd crash back to the pavement on her face. It was a risk she'd take if she had to, though. *For now, just keep this guy talking, and figure something out.*

"Are you a psionic?" she asked.

"Pssh," the hunter sighed. "Nah, I'm pretty much the opposite. A bionic who's immune to your little tricks."

The other hunters now crawled down from the rooftops to join their leader in the street. She surveyed their clothing and tactics, confirming her suspicions that these were not Protectorate men. The majority of them looked like bikers, in fact: she saw several bandanas and denim vests. The women had tall boots and wind-whipped hair. Fanning out in a loose circle, they kept their distance from Lyra while surrounding her. She and the punk-haired challenger stood facing each other in the center—but when she looked back to him after a moment's inspection of her surroundings, his hair was now lime-green instead of cool blue. Likewise, his eyes had changed from hot pink to lavender. More surgical alterations, then. The teasing smirk was wider than ever.

"Chromatic melanoctye supplementation," he said. "Because tattoos are so done."

Lyra tried an easy laugh, hoping it didn't sound nervous. "Now you're just showing off."

A sly wink. "Well, I'm still only flesh and blood—*mostly*. Maybe I ain't immune to *all* of your charms."

Lyra cringed inwardly, but tried not to show it on her face. What was this guy expecting from her that would eclipse a two-million-cap payday?

"Who did your surgeries?" she asked. That seemed like a safe question.

"A crackerjack bunch of cutters at an aug clinic in Flagstaff. Cost me mighty big bikkies, but I'm about to recoup all of it, and more."

"I don't doubt it. You must be the best hunter around. What's your name?"

"Name's Pavo. It's much pleasure, Lyra Vaughn—been wanting to meet you for a while now, love."

"Uh, thank you." Lyra looked around for an opportunity to bolt, but every eye was fixed on her. Weapons were still unholstered, and the crowd seemed to be rapt in attention.

"Well, that's enough yabberin'. Let's get on with it, hey?" Pavo produced a silver roll of duct tape. "Be a dear and hold your wrists out, there."

Lyra began to sweat. Talk had apparently gotten her as far as it was going to; whatever came next was going to be a gamble. At least Pavo had given her a vital clue.

He was immune to her powers, but he couldn't hear the instructions she gave to those who weren't.

Stop Pavo. Let me get away.

She agonized while not breaking eye contact with the kidnapping psycho, but to look again at the surrounding henchmen might make him suspect her plans. At first, nothing happened, and his voice sprouted an ugly edge.

"Come on, then," he insisted, shaking the tape. "I haven't got all—"

Then Pavo broke off, glancing away from her. In a flash he dropped the duct tape, going for his pistol.

Thok.

A dart streaked past Lyra and snapped against Pavo's throat. The hollow tip shattered against his toughened skin, though, and the drug-filled barrel fell harmlessly away.

Thok-thok-thok.

More tranquilizers pounded the bounty hunter. Most of the needles exploded on impact, but a few lodged in his skin. Pavo swept these away with one hand; with the other, he leveled a boxy black handgun at the perimeter group. Thunderous gunshots echoed through the valley as jets of flame burst from the barrel.

Ka-chunk.

A web wrapped Pavo in its smothering embrace, weighing him down, but he thrust the ropes aside with one arm, and kept firing. Darts stuck into him at odd angles; by now he had surely taken a dose that would knock out a rhino. Lyra backed away and crouched to gather her gun and traveling pack, inundating her mind with as much focus and energy as she could summon in the maelstrom of gunshots and screams.

Pavo's weapon emptied, and the slide locked back. He fumbled for another clip, struggling with the heavy net. His skin had taken on a rosy flush, too high-colored to be the result of exertion, adrenaline, and rage. He glanced the magazine against the bottom of the pistol, lacking the coordination to feed it into the well. In the instant before Lyra rocketed off the pavement and straight up into the air, Pavo turned his eyes to her. The lids were sluggish, but the twin golden orbs beneath them were fiery, predatory, intense: the danger-yellow shade of the eyes of a vicious beast that, due to being caged, was all the more wild within.

Chapter 5

Lyra triple-checked the wooden latch, although she doubted such a flimsy thing would stop her pursuer. She crept away from the front windows and turned, tossing her pack onto the bare wooden floor. There were no shades or shutters for the windows, and almost no furniture in this ancient painted-brick house.

Flight was exhausting, and, even for her well-conditioned mind, only sustainable for about the length of time that a strong athlete could run or climb before being worn out. It was useful for avoiding obstacles and covering some ground in a hurry, but was not a viable option for extended travel. She'd gone a few miles by soaring over the forest and exiting the canyon, and as her stamina had begun to flag, found a tiny cluster of derelict buildings in the crook of a modest stream. The hiding spot would have to do for now; it was unclear what means to find her were at Pavo's disposal, but she could not doubt that he would be after her as soon as he recovered.

Recovered from whatever it was that had happened in the street at Springdale. Lyra put her back to the wall and slid down to a sitting position, then dug in her pack for a pillow and a fruit-and-nut bar. What kind of superhuman nightmare was she dealing with? Needles shattered against his skin; powerful toxins slowed him down just enough to let her get away for a while.

And what had happened to his compatriots? Had she just gotten a dozen men and women killed during her escape? Yes, she had hardly been left with an alternative, but the bloodshed irked her. Ten years after the Great Harvest, when an alien invasion had ripped through the world's cities, one would think that men would put aside their differences and unite against a common enemy. She'd heard of species throughout the galaxy who at some point in their planetary history uncovered the truth that they were not alone: that other species and faster-than-light travel did indeed exist, along with galactic society, which was centered in the capital space station of Ios. After learning these truths, other species would embrace higher technology and learning, and take their place within a boundless new world of possibility.

Not so with the children of Terra, whose troubled planet had become more war-torn than ever in the wake of what would have been, for many other species, the dawn of a golden age. Was violence intrinsic to the heart of man? Could their struggles, instead, be traced to the manner in which this failed rebirth had been thrust upon them?

The chilling message of the Lacerta queen that she and Orion had encountered months ago resurfaced; in truth, it was never quite dormant. Lyra recalled the revelation of a common thread between the lizardmen's species and her own: in both cases, the enigmatic Greys had visited in the distant past to bestow dubious gifts of technology upon them. Then the demented benefactors had returned throughout history, cataloguing and fine-tuning their influences upon the development of each species. The Lacertas seemed to believe that the Greys had groomed them as a physically powerful—albeit stagnated and subjugated—breed of warriors. In the eyes of the Greys, however, the Lacertas' limited affinity for technology and language, their imbalance of brain and brawn, made the lizardmen of little real value in the final analysis. The implied assumption was that Humans were now the preferred stock for Grey servitude.

Lyra was unable to learn more than this, because the queen had been killed. The knowledge, incomplete as it was, cast all her experiences under a disturbing pall. She had been captured, given a partially-successful psionic surgery, escaped, and was now hunted again. It was as if the Greys were loath to admit defeat and simply cut their losses by killing her. One way or another, they seemed determined to make good on their investment.

She unrolled a cot onto the floorboards, and stretched out. Clouds assisted the sun's retreat behind the sandy-striped mountains, and the old house plunged into twilight. She was weary, but dared not sleep: Orion was in even more danger than she was. She would try again to contact him. She would put away the despair of past failures, and the fear of what they might mean, to reach him. She would make this attempt as fresh as every other time, full of hope and promise, utilizing her skills to their fullest.

Entrancement engulfed her almost at once in the stillness of the quiet room. Around her, the emptiness of the house blended to overlap a yawning void as she slipped between worlds. Dusty billows rose and stirred in a translucent fog. Through the clouds she drifted with her body in perfect placidity, using her mind alone to move and see.

The astral plane was a place of simple existence, and nothing more—consciousness in an unadulterated state. Other beings could be encountered here, and information exchanged, provided that the participants had the requisite level of self-awareness to use their minds in such a way. Nothing physical happened here; movement, or any other action, was a function of how focused the mind was. This affected everything from orientation, perception, and coordination to travel speed. A skilled psionic could find and communicate with beings great distances away—perhaps even on other planets, although Lyra had never attempted such a thing. A confused dreamer, on the other hand, might access this place—even by accident—and muddle around aimlessly. Such a person was more likely to be found and acted upon by others before his initiative was strengthened; thus the phenomenon of being "visited in dreams". Practice and meditation could strengthen a mentalist's skills—and for Lyra, whose mind was well-attuned, accessing and navigating the realm was a simple matter.

Ghostly shapes entered her periphery: sticklike figures with bulbous heads. She navigated away, leaving them behind. The Greys frequently patrolled this plane; the aliens' combination of physical frailty and psychic might led them to pursue certain of their inscrutable objectives here. A hapless traveler who let them get too close might have his mind violated, even forcefully occupied; many of the early stories in which people first encountered the Greys involved sleep, hypnosis, or meditation, when the Theta wavelength was active in their brains. Viewing the aliens as indistinct, approaching outlines meant that the beings had a sense of her and had begun to probe in her direction with their thoughts. By evading them before they got too close, Lyra was guarding her mind from making a connection with theirs. When she sensed, and reached, the person she sought, close proximity to them would signify a strong mental connection that would allow them to converse freely.

Lyra filled her concentration with thoughts of Orion. She pictured his youthful yet somehow worldly face, his glinting jade eyes and sandy hair. She strengthened the mental image with memories of his gravelly, synthetic voice, and the cybercomputer grafted into his left forearm—souvenirs of his horrendous abductions, a shared experience that served as an unshakeable bond between them. Her distinct image of the scavenger, and the memories and feelings she had for him, would facilitate an instinct that would lead her to him.

And there it was: a gentle tug, as if a compass in her brain pointed the way. Lyra turned in the direction of its guidance, and pressed forward at a brisk pace. She wanted to reach Orion while the signal was clear, but could not travel recklessly and attract unwanted attention. It was unclear how much distance Lyra needed to cover; her perception was that Orion was not close by, but he was still alive, and on this planet. Although her connection would only be perfect if he was sleeping (Orion was not a psionic himself and was unlikely to meditate), if he was awake he would still feel her presence in some manner. He would know that she was alive and searching for him.

The psionic girl traversed gulfs of emptiness, fixing her thoughts on the growing pull towards her goal. There was no scenery to gauge her progress, only the imprecise knowledge that she moved a great distance, from time to time avoiding the otherworldly beings and always seeking that ever-strengthening allure.

The magnetic invitation became strong indeed, and was unmistakably the friend that she sought. Just when she was certain that Orion's welcome shadow might coalesce from the ageless dust, a new and insistent presence crept toward her mind.

A strange and powerful being sought ingress. She hastened to guard her thoughts, stopping her quest in order to concentrate more perfectly on the nature of this thing that came, with tentative and imprecise forays, to approach her.

It was not Human—this she knew from the foreign nature of its thoughts, and from the fleeting glimpses she caught of a squat, lumpy figure that stalked her in the clouds. For her part, Lyra moved into the well-rehearsed opening moves of a mental skirmish: she must gather information from the mind of this being, without opening her own to it in the process.

Her opponent was skilled. Lyra tracked the presence through shrouds of perplexity, only to find at each attempt that the being had eluded her, never to be found at the place it seemed to be. In haste she would readjust her own position, lest she be drawn into a trap by some clever feint. Likewise Lyra doubled back upon her path, twisting her thoughts in serpentine trails, moving, weaving, peppering the other thing with a barrage of questions while simultaneously constructing, and adhering to, false beliefs about her own identity.

The stalemate continued, and all the time Lyra perceived Orion's presence just past the challenging creature, on the other side of its shifting and perseverant designs. Each time she feinted, attempting to dodge past her adversary and reach Orion, the inquisitive specter would readjust with acrobatic efficiency, contorting its unseen barrier to cut her off. Try as she might to press around, over or under the obstacle, it reformed to stymy her efforts, forcing her to nimbly retreat lest it enclose around her as well.

There was nothing to be done. It was a repeat of all the other times she had attempted to reach Orion: the same certainty of his mien, the same prodigious but unknown distance between them. The same sinister guardian interfering. The same deadlock between she and it. Lyra was left with a single option if she was not to continue this maddening waltz into eternity: she would have to confront the thing, and learn what she could about it without giving it the opportunity to access her mind at the same time.

She had considered how the deed might be done, while hoping that it would not be necessary. But the horrible reality of her position now faced her. She was hunted and alone, and Orion, while still alive, was similarly harried. If she did not find Orion now, they would never see each other again. She would employ her last resort; if it failed, it would simply hasten the end that would come if she did not act at all.

Lyra withdrew from the presence of the treacherous being, falling back to a distance well outside of her ability to sense it—or it, her. In the moments before the enemy vanished from her perimeter of awareness, she took note of its position. It sent out wandering tendrils into the gloom after her, feeling with its thoughts after the intruder that had tried and failed to breach its defenses. Lyra weaved like a veiled dancer as she departed, spinning gossamer sheets from the cloudy billows to hide her from the groping tentacles.

She backed away still further, leaving the crawling emissaries behind, and circled about in a wide berth. Lyra waited, and changed position again. Then again. Her thoughts longed to crackle with anticipation, the song of impending battle, but she quelled her emotions, smothering them beneath a veneer of placidity. She would not advance until the opportune moment, when her adversary had all but forgotten her. The risk lay in discerning its whereabouts in the very instant before she struck: there would be but one attempt, and failure would leave her vulnerable to a devastating counterattack. But she could not dwell on that outcome—to allow such a possibility to enter her thoughts was to guarantee its happening.

It was time. Lyra burst from her stasis like a granite statue animated by a lightning strike. She poured her essence into a mighty surge, streaking to her target. Everything blurred at the edges of her consciousness; there was only her and the speed of her thoughts. The other came into range, turning its thoughts to orient itself, but faster than a cobra's strike, she leveled a psionic spear—a lance made of her pure mental cunning—and thrust it into the ill-prepared stranger.

A screech of violated anger erupted from an otherworldly voice, and psychic energy blasted her with a painful, crippling shock. The force of the tempest threw her back as if she'd made contact with a live electrical wire—she skidded through the fog in agony for a few seconds before she could shake free of the sizzling pain and orient herself again. As soon as she had recovered, Lyra fled.

Escape was an imperative. She summoned wings of purpose-driven fancy to deliver her from the creature. For a time it pursued, although rattled by the shock it too had received, it lagged behind and then dropped away altogether to regain its composure and lick its wounds.

Lyra needed to do the same. Before returning to her physical body, she would put enough distance between them so as not to reveal her location on Earth to the enemy. The information she had gleaned burned in her mind like a lantern in the darkness.

It was Pyxis—this she had suspected, but now knew beyond any doubt. The commander of the Greys' flying saucer had survived the ship's crash, and had found Orion before she had. It was Pyxis who had overseen the abduction and exploitation of the young scavenger and herself. The knowledge that, by saving her, Orion had traded her freedom for his own tempted Lyra with a desperate rage.

But she would not give in to wanton emotion. Her mind was her greatest asset, and she would utilize it to the utmost. She had stolen a glimpse, however brief, into Pyxis's thoughts. She knew the whereabouts of the alien and, therefore, of Orion. It would be dangerous, of course, to confront it again, but Lyra was forewarned and forearmed.

She woke gasping for breath, but could not seem to draw enough air. Golden light ringed the window above her; it was morning. Her trance had lasted all through the night, much longer than she had anticipated. Finding and sparring with the alien leader had consumed hours. Blinking off the sluggish remnants of the night's odyssey, she tried to roll over—but her movement was restricted.

Lyra's gasp of horror was muffled by a tight strip of tape. Worse, powerbinders restricted her wrists and ankles. As her eyes widened in frantic silence, a crimson-haired countenance moved into view above her.

"Hello again, love," Pavo grinned.

Chapter 6

H arlow smoothed back his dark hair and straightened his tie before his reflection in the elevator doors slid apart. The top floor of UCO Headquarters, seventy-two stories above New Zaragosa, sparkled in the crisp morning sunlight.

Dr. Vivienne Tainer, the Secretary of Human Health and Well-Being, came forward to meet him as he stepped off the elevator. Over the last several weeks, Harlow had reported directly to Tainer, an accomplished epidemiologist, instead of going up the regular Protectorate chain of command. Harlow had difficulty in determining the executive's age: the short grey hair, slight frame, and conservative business suits suggested a woman in her sixth decade, but Tainer wore no glasses and exhibited a liveliness which led Harlow to wonder at the various benefits of the rejuvenation clinics that the woman employed.

"Punctual as always, Detective," she said, strolling ahead of him into the conference room. A group of Protectorate officers retreated from the door to allow their ingress, and remained in the lobby. Already present within was Findley van de Kamp, Supervising Director of the UCO. The fastidiously dressed executive, seated at the head of the large satin-brushed metal table, nodded at Harlow before turning his intense gaze back to the banks of floor-to-ceiling windows.

The city sprawled beneath them, and an immense flying saucer brooded atop it like the crown of a contemplative monarch. This

49

imposing craft easily dwarfed the sleek saucer Harlow remembered from some months ago. That had been a *Scout*-class saucer, he recalled; this *Principal*-class ship would practically engulf the entirety of the spaceport that had been built for it. Any larger, and the vessel would be a capital ship: a floating country, unable to enter atmosphere.

Today, the craft appeared over the city for the first time; tens of thousands of people were surely awestruck at this moment. The mammoth saucer revolved like a carousel. The purposeful whirl invited Harlow's eye, and for a time he stood mesmerized along with Tainer and van de Kamp, the three of them silent as they scrutinized the otherworldly sentinel. Attentive inspection revealed slight departures in the familiar design: antennae bristled from the upper hemisphere at irregular points, and Harlow discerned certain grooves in the outer circumference that, while appearing to be minute ridges at this distance, must have been titanic gulfs carved into the weird craft's inscrutable surface. Along the lower hemisphere of the great disc, strange lights pulsed in unearthly rhythms, summoning colors that he could not quite define.

Footfalls behind Harlow broke the spell. He turned away from the alien ship as Millard Strughold, the white-haired Regent, entered the conference room.

"Good morning, Regent," van de Kamp said.

"Indeed it is." A beaming smile spread apart the fleshy flaps of the magistrate's face. "A fine morning, my friends, as we prepare for this momentous occasion."

Harlow was at once relieved and perturbed by Strughold's good humor. Of course, it reassured him to find that the mood among the UCO's elite was sunny: Harlow was here to report on his progress in finding Vulpecula—and there was lamentably *little* progress. It wouldn't do to give a lackluster narrative to an already dour room.

However, the buoyancy in the room could well be a veneer, a

preparation for an imminent performance. Strughold, verbose as he was, would not consider it a 'momentous occasion' to listen to a Protectorate debriefing. It was as if some other high-ranking visitor were expected—and in a flash, Harlow knew who it would be.

The sky darkened as the alien ship moved over the morning sun. The conference room seemed to fill with a serene hum, a cadence somewhere just outside of Harlow's senses. A gentle distortion thickened the air; he had the sensation of moving under water. He blinked once, slowly, to clear his vision, and the sensation vanished. Four diminutive figures now stood at the room's entrance.

Three of the Greys were identical: barely more than a meter tall, with unblemished, ashen skin. Inky eyes, absent of a pupil or a glint of light, brimmed with secret knowledge. They remained at the door, near the Protectorate men. The fourth alien, while taller and heavier than its brethren, was yet small in comparison to the Humans. Its head, though, was massive for its size, and divided into two great lobes with ridges of oyster-pearly skin. A satin cloak of scarlet and sunflower dragged the carpet behind it when it took three short paces forward, approaching the table.

A hush settled upon the assembled group. Harlow flicked his eyes to his superiors, reading their body language for clues as to proper etiquette; among Humans, it could be considered odd to remain standing with a table and chairs nearby, and in the presence of a considerably shorter being. But the alien would not have the same social customs, and Harlow could only wait to follow someone else's lead. Was it not a breach of etiquette, failing to inform one that he was about to meet an alien dignitary face to face? Perhaps this was an ambush; Harlow, having failed to achieve satisfactory results, was about to be thrown to the wolves.

He hurried to assess the room. It was nearly a minute now, and no one had spoken. Vivienne Tainer, blank-faced, stood behind a chair;

Strughold clasped his hands, still grinning. And van de Kamp…Harlow studied the docile half-smile on the Director's face. The alien and the executive's eyes locked, as if the pair was unaware of the others in the room. Minute changes in expression flickered on van de Kamp's features periodically, but always the meek little smile remained.

So that was it: a psychic conversation between van de Kamp and the alien, while the rest of the room waited in silence. Harlow didn't know the UCO Director well enough to suppose that the man was a psionic, but the Greys would certainly prefer their Human ambassadors to have that capability. Rumor had it that the aliens disliked using physical speech, and communicated mentally whenever possible.

The large-brained creature now turned to survey the others in the conference room. Glistening black eyes moved over each of the Humans, twin inky pools with a convex reflective surface that distorted Harlow's image. He thought of a black mirror with some anamorphic doppelganger lurking within. Its gaze lingered on him, and Harlow fought to control the sudden flush to his cheeks. He would not reveal his discomfort, and thereby insult this alien luminary. He would not give place to the disturbing miasma that threatened to cloak him, and forfeit his place among the worthy. Finally the unsettling stare moved on, and Harlow quashed the welcome relief as well: to betray that emotion would be equally unacceptable.

The alien's thin mouth twitched twice, and then opened. Its wheezing croaks formed words in a timbre that was ragged with disuse, and with the echoing hollowness of stones being dropped into a pit.

"I convey my appreciation for this meeting," it said. "I am called Eridanus, commander of the ship *Harvester*, and plenipotentiary of the Greys of Ios, who send greetings to the species of Terrans."

Harlow took a quiet breath. Ah-RID-ah-nus, it had called itself. The extraterrestrial's speech carried the awkwardness of unfamiliar custom, but the gravitas was easily grasped. The status of this being

52

could not be overstated. What would it be like to speak on behalf of an entire species? Although his eyes did not seem to want to leave the figure of Eridanus, Harlow found himself looking almost unconsciously at van de Kamp.

"You honor us, Your Excellency," the Director said. "You have among you those notable persons who enjoy my full confidence, and who might be of particular service to you. Please consider us at your disposal."

The Detective raced to sort his thoughts. Far from an ambush, this meeting was a vote of confidence so weighty that it bordered on terrifying.

Eridanus raised a spindly arm, indicating the conference table. The Humans drew out their chairs and seated themselves. Standing before the windows with the city skyline at its back, the alien spoke.

"There was some debate, after the recent events at New Zaragosa, as to whether a continued interest in Humanity would prove worthwhile. The loss of a ship, its commander, and an Illuminatus brought us great displeasure—especially in view of the ingratitude displayed toward us by certain members of the Terran species. An open rebellion involving a rogue UCO scientist, and some artificially-engineered panacea used to bolster this treachery."

It wheezed softly before continuing.

"However, we are heavily vested in Terra. I cannot allow the effort and resources we have spent thus far to be wasted. We *will* see a return on this investment. And to that end, I will now hear what Humanity has done to redeem itself."

So much for proper etiquette, Harlow thought. The room had grown tense, but van de Kamp transitioned smoothly.

"The capable men and women at the UCO have been working tirelessly to put this unpleasantness behind us," the Director cooed. "Dr. Tainer, will you tell us what you've learned about the compound we've recovered?"

The epidemiologist stood and addressed the room. "The attack at the spaceport, which was so bravely aborted by Detective Harlow, left us in possession of the intended weapon: a type of synthetic virus, which we believe was developed in secret by a former UCO scientist, Dr. Noreen Vulpecula. My team at Health and Human Well-Being is currently analyzing the virus, and here is what we know so far.

"There may be some misconceptions associated with the term 'virus'. A virus is not truly alive—it is merely a package of genetic material that has the ability to do only one thing. This particular microbe was engineered to be highly infectious, but not necessarily detrimental to its host. So while an infected individual might display abnormalities after being exposed to the virus, we don't yet know enough about it to properly call this event a 'disease'. In fact, the intended purpose of the microbe, as envisioned by Vulpecula, is to transform ordinary men and women into heroes capable of great feats—and so, she calls this virus the 'Perseus Agent.'"

Tainer inserted a chip into a slot on the side of the conference table, activating a holostacker in the table's center. A three-dimensional representation of a spiky-bristled sphere revolved in midair like an unwholesome planet.

"Once the virus has entered the body of a host organism, it targets, and attaches itself to, specific cells. Many viruses are selective about what they infect: the spikes that you see here, called 'antigens', perform the task of matching the virus up with the type of cells it is looking for—cells that are equipped to reproduce the virus.

"Viruses are quite effective at finding their targets. The antigens read the protein coding of different cells, and if there is a match, the virus is able to attach itself to the host cell's membrane like two puzzle pieces fitting together. This is why a virus might only affect certain organisms—even if two life forms are closely related, there is enough of a distinction in their genetic coding to make a difference to the microbe's antigens.

"However, some factors—for example, corrupted or damaged DNA—can lead to cross-species contamination. You may have heard of 'swine' or 'avian' flu: these diseases resulted from such an event. It's theorized that the HIV and COVID-19 epidemics began in a similar fashion. And this highlights an important fact: the effects of such viruses are infectious, and difficult to combat due to their inherent adaptability."

Harlow sat up straighter. The doctor was building to something, and everyone in the room sensed that Tainer was about to share her revelation.

"I say all of that in order to say this," Tainer continued. "The Perseus Agent is an exemplary model of cross-species reconfiguration. It takes its genetic structure from the stem cells of the Greys. The protein coding is so adroit that the virus fools the host cell into physically *pulling it inside* the cell membrane."

As she spoke, the holostacker enacted a representation. A larger, oval-shaped cell encountered the bristling sphere, and absorbed it. Inside the host cell, the virus replicated.

"From there, the microbe has direct access to the cell's own repro-duction equipment. The Agent incorporates its own genes into the host cell's DNA, which is used to produce more viruses. And unlike many other microbes, which simply copy themselves repeatedly until the host cell fills up and ruptures, these viruses divide from the cell without harming it."

Harlow glanced away from the holostacker's reenactment to measure the room. Eridanus, mute, unfathomable. Van de Kamp, a well-practiced poker face. Strughold, however, knit his brows and squinted.

"How does a person's immune system respond to this virus?" the magistrate asked.

"It doesn't even recognize that there's a problem," Tainer replied. "The corrupted DNA doesn't appear to be damaged; in fact, the added ligands are accepted as an improved version of the original genetic structure."

"*Improved?*" Strughold asked with incredulity.

"Yes, Regent. You see, the cells that the virus specifically targets are myoblasts and osteoblasts: the body's factories for producing muscle and bone. After infection, each one of these transformed cells seeks out others with the new DNA in order to form a group and synthesize myocytes and osteocytes at an increased, and more efficient, capacity.

"There is, however, a downside to this process. All of that muscle tissue burns through energy awfully fast, putting an increased demand on the subject's metabolic rate. If the subject's caloric intake can't keep up with the body's demands, organ damage is inevitable."

Tainer now looked directly at Eridanus. "As I mentioned, the primary vehicle for the virus's transmission is based on the cellular structure of the Greys, due to the similarities in certain protein compounds shared between Greys and Humans. However, Grey physiology differs from ours in one very important respect: muscle mass.

"Grey anatomy clearly centers around a prodigious brain. The vast majority of the body's energy goes to meeting the demands of the brain and its processes—very little is needed for other purposes. For example, Greys need minimal effort for digestion: their 'food' is a sort of vitamin-rich soup, akin to the fluid used in Human intravenous treatment. If you were to transpose this metabolic action with the body of a Human being, soon the demands become too great."

Eridanus scowled openly, and Harlow wondered whether the alien felt greater displeasure at the details of the virus—or at the exposition of his species's physiology.

"And what happens then?" Harlow asked, wishing to move the conversation along.

Tainer's face was grim. "We performed an autopsy on the operative from the spaceport attack. Detective Harlow, at that time you were under the belief that the attacker killed himself, probably with a cyanide capsule, rather than surrender—a logical assumption, but incorrect: there were no toxins in his body.

"Prior to his demise, the attacker's heart rate soared, and his blood oxygen level dropped. His metabolism couldn't keep up with the activity of his body...in short, he succumbed to extreme overexertion."

Again Harlow thought of those final moments, looking into the wild eyes that had glazed and faded, as if a plug had been pulled. Could such a thing truly become an epidemic? Human lives flaring in brilliance and then snuffing out, like an overloaded light bulb going dark after a sudden blinding flash?

"Where are we in developing a vaccine, doctor?" van de Kamp spoke up.

Tainer shook her head. "Preliminary stages, I'm afraid. Traditional inoculations work by equipping the immune system with the tools it needs to fight off the infection: arming it with more effective weaponry, you might say. However, in this instance, as I mentioned, the autoimmune system doesn't even realize it's under attack in the first place. Combating this virus means we'll have to take an entirely different approach, and there's always the possibility that there simply is no viable antidote. We may instead need to focus our energies into preventing the spread of the infection, and accepting that nothing can be done for those in whom it has already taken hold."

Strughold leaned forward, interlacing his fingers. "Doctor, am I hearing you say that this disease is rampant and incurable? How can Vulpecula have succeeded in engineering such a thing right under our noses?"

"Vulpecula was among our brightest scientists, and she had access to a great deal of resources, I'm afraid. She'd done extensive work with nanobiotic transplantation, and knew her way around the obstacles associated with it. In fact, I believe her work in overcoming transplant rejection lent her some expertise in manipulating the immune system's response to this virus.

"However," Tainer drew the word out, and Harlow sensed reluctance at what was coming. The epidemiologist now spoke slowly, choosing her words with care. "We know of an even more brilliant group, with more experience in transplantation."

Eridanus' scowl deepened, but the doctor forged ahead gingerly. "Perhaps the Grey scientists could help analyze and combat the Perseus Agent," she said. "The answer to this plague may not be an autoimmune boost—instead, I'm interested in bringing in outside help, both literally and figuratively."

Tainer now spoke directly to the alien leader. "Rather than developing a traditional vaccine, I propose the use of specialized nanobiotics. If these microscopic surgical robots could be programmed to hunt down and destroy the Agent and its affected cells from within the patient's body, the tide could be turned quickly. We haven't yet perfected the technology for such a thing here on Terra—but perhaps your Excellency's arrival is fortuitous. With the resources of the *Harvester*—"

"An infectious disease will not be brought on board my ship," the stony voice cut in.

Eyes downcast, Tainer bowed her head. "Yes, your Excellency. My apologies—I didn't mean to make presumptions upon you."

At a gesture from Eridanus, Tainer seated herself quietly. The alien remained standing, facing the large window bay. The mesmerizing ship revolved like the inexorable hands of a clock, counting down to some predetermined reckoning.

"I will not risk transmitting this contagion across the galaxy due to the carelessness of your species," the monarch said. "It originated here, and will be dealt with here. And should this situation grow beyond your control, Terra will be quarantined, and if necessary, destroyed."

Chapter 7

A stunned silence held the assembly captive. Even Strughold, Harlow noted, seemed to be searching for his tongue. At the head of the table, Eridanus continued in a flat tone.

"I say this not to threaten or estrange you. These drastic measures would bring us great dissatisfaction, we who have spent thousands of years cultivating an investment in the people of Terra. However, the facts of the present situation cannot be denied: you are confronted with a catastrophe of your own making. The Greys have displayed great benevolence to you, but we are not a guardian angel to effect your salvation at every turn.

"Your deliverance, then, rests in your own hands. I would advise you to strike at the root of this problem: your turncoat scientist. Find this rogue doctor, and compel her to undo what she has done. If there is any assistance to be offered by the Greys, it will come when she has been apprehended."

Harlow's mouth went dry, and he hardly dared to breathe. Even looking around the room seemed too risky: the others would be searching for someone to pin the blame on. He wished he were invisible—and knew what was coming next.

"Your Excellency," van de Kamp's voice was soothing and placid. "Your concerns are certainly understandable, and we appreciate your patience thus far."

Understandable? Harlow thought. *We're talking about a plague that can't be stopped. We're talking about destroying the entire planet. Three billion lives...*

"I don't believe an extreme response from the Greys will be required," van de Kamp continued. "It's our top priority to bring Vulpecula to justice, and mitigate the damage she's done. Along those lines, we've been looking forward to a progress report from our Protectorate liaison. Detective First Class Harlow knows the doctor better than anyone we have, and has been working tirelessly to effect her capture." The Director gestured with an open palm. "Detective, the floor is yours."

Harlow struggled to rise from his seat, fighting what felt like the gravity of a skyrocketing fighter jet. His palms were slick. Bland smiles on Human faces, and an expectant glower on a non-Human one, regarded him. Was the fate of the planet in Harlow's own hands at this moment? It defied reason. By speaking carelessly, even by giving the impression of weakness or incompetence, would he indeed doom the entirety of his species? How could he deliver the world from this being's clutches? Only by delivering another fanatic into that wiry, unforgiving hand.

Harlow cleared his throat. "Distinguished leaders, the topic before us now is the whereabouts of Doctor Noreen Vulpecula.

"Many of the people who could have, at one time, helped us to deduce this information are now dead—notably, the entire team that assisted in her pioneer surgical work, and in engineering what was to eventually become the Perseus Agent. We have only one solid lead: Vulpecula's closest associate, Martín Auriga.

"We are all familiar with Mr. Auriga, due in part to the high-profile nature of his crimes, and due to Regent Strughold's entirely justifiable response to them. Auriga's execution date swiftly approaches.

"It is my position, after interviewing the condemned man, that

61

although it has not happened yet, Auriga expects that Dr. Vulpecula will attempt to contact him soon—in fact, that she is overdue for such an attempt."

Van de Kamp and Tainer were nodding, already making the step ahead to where Harlow was leading; Strughold's jowls wobbled as his mouth sagged open.

"How's that possible?" the Regent asked. "Is there an informant somewhere? One of the guards, delivering messages?"

"That could be," Harlow said, "but it's not particularly important, or even a bad thing. It presents us with an opportunity.

"By feeding information to Auriga, Vulpecula would show that he hasn't outlived his usefulness to her. Why go to the trouble of forwarding instructions, progress reports, or anything else to a man who will be dead in less than three weeks?"

"Perhaps she just wants to say goodbye," Tainer said.

"Vulpecula is notoriously unemotional," Harlow replied. "Besides, Death Row inmates are still allowed to receive mail—it's heavily screened, of course, but the doctor could have sent him a simple farewell, or had someone do it on her behalf, as long as adequate precautions were taken to conceal the origin of the message. It's a bigger risk to communicate with a prisoner in secret, which is what Auriga is expecting. Would she take such a chance, and go to that kind of trouble, if there were nothing to be gained from it?"

Van de Kamp wore an eager smile. "He expects her to break him out of prison—what else could it be?"

Harlow made a concessive gesture. "That's the most likely scenario. Before his capture, Auriga was instrumental in the doctor's plans—a soldier *and* a developmental assistant. That kind of combination won't be easy for her to replace...and by rescuing him, Vulpecula would reap the added benefit of such a demonstration to her acolytes: showing them that she rewards loyalty, and does not forget her disciples."

"Not to mention making us look foolish in the process," Strughold added firmly. "This escape *cannot* happen. Auriga is the UCO's most infamous prisoner in years. His execution is symbolic as well as strategic."

"Not to worry, Regent," van de Kamp said. "The Detective is well aware of the stakes here. He understands that failure is not an option."

"Yes, Director," Harlow said. "The attempt will be unsuccessful, and will supply us with the information we need to track down Vulpecula."

"Why wait a moment longer?" Strughold asked. "If the prisoner has some knowledge of the doctor's location, just get it from him now."

"I can certainly appreciate that sentiment," Harlow said, choosing his words. "But extracting information from someone against their will is a complicated and unreliable process.

"Let's say that we take the most straightforward route, and place Mr. Auriga under duress," Harlow said, spreading his hands. "Thankfully, we can bypass the moral imperatives that used to interfere with tactics of this sort—he's a condemned man with no rights whatsoever, and we can do as we please with him. But if you use these 'enhanced interrogation' techniques"—here a mirthless chuckle circled the room—"how do you know that what he says is the truth? He could just be telling you what you want to hear so that the torture will stop."

"What about extrasensory measures?" asked van de Kamp. "I believe we still have access to some powerful psionic agents with the O3."

Van de Kamp was referring to the Office of Occult Occurrences, a branch of galactic law enforcement responsible for investigating crimes that involved supernatural elements. As fledgling members of interplanetary society, it would be a big favor for the Humans to call in, while simultaneously acknowledging that the people of Terra couldn't solve their own problems—but it seemed that the Director wisely wished to avoid leaning upon the Greys after the dissatisfaction shown by Eridanus only moments before.

"I'm grateful that you'd consider using that kind of clout for my purposes, Director," Harlow said. "At the end of the day, though, manipulating someone's brain is never without risk. The person's mind could respond to such an invasive measure by simply forgetting the information that we want to extract. Auriga is sly, and his mind is strong; it will have to be trickery."

Strughold nodded now. Harlow allowed himself a small sigh; the room was in agreement with him, and he wasn't being grilled over his methods, or accused of incompetence. The UCO brass was accepting him. Eridanus, standing against the wall, seemed to be hardly listening, but those glistening onyx eyes recorded Harlow's every move.

Unsettled, the Detective tried to pull himself back on track. As he outlined his ideas and options—feeding false information to prison guards, engineering a bogus "transfer" that would lure Vulpecula's rescue attempt into the open, and so on—the alien's words echoed in his mind.

Beyond your control...Quarantined...Destroyed...

After the meeting, Tainer shook his hand, and hurried off. As she made a single backward glance at the room, the elevator doors swallowed her. Van de Kamp approached and squeezed Harlow's shoulder, leaning in with a low voice.

"Excellent work, Detective. I know you're working as hard as you can on this, and the results will be immediate and satisfactory."

Harlow tried to smile. "Yes, thank you, Director. It may take a while to earn the prisoner's trust and recover the information I need, but I assure you that every ounce of progress will be shared with you immediately."

Van de Kamp offered a handsome grin. "Yes, indeed. Trust is at the heart of this matter, isn't it? We all trust you here, Detective, and I'm certain that Mr. Auriga will as well."

Behind the Director, the alien leader now approached Strughold.

The hollow voice reached Harlow's ears with difficulty, but rasping phrases filtered through: "...pleased with your outlook...an exemplary dignitary..."

Van de Kamp was still speaking to him. "...well aware of this operation's importance. I want you to know that any assistance or resources I can offer you..."

"...my guest aboard the *Harvester*..."

Sweating, Harlow thanked the Director and excused himself. Stumbling past the three Greys who had escorted Eridanus, he punched the elevator button feverishly with his thumb. As he waited for the car, the thickening of the air began again. The sluggish underwater sensation returned to the room. The sonorous pulse filled him with nausea.

Inside the elevator, the mirrored doors slid together, and he glimpsed his disheveled reflection. He made it to the underground parking garage before vomiting into a trash can.

***

"You wore a tie today, Daddy?"

Carina climbed on his lap, pushing him deeper into the leather sofa. He steadied the girl with an arm around her shoulders; her fingers started at the loosened silk knot and traced the zigzag pattern down. He'd washed his face and removed his jacket, but hadn't found the energy to change into casual clothes.

"Yes, sweetie," Harlow said. "Daddy wore a tie."

She played with the silk, rolling and unfurling it like a flag. "You saw the good guys today."

He tightened the barrette that was falling from her dark hair, and kissed her forehead. "What, honey?"

"When you see the bad guys, you wear black and carry a gun. When you see the good guys, you wear a tie."

"You're a smart girl, you know that?" Harlow chuckled. "How are

65

your studies going?"

The girl hopped down from the couch and crossed the living room to retrieve a tablet from its neat lacquered shelf. The display powered into tones of purple and blue as she offered it to Harlow with a gap-toothed grin.

He scanned the table headed "*APTITUDE RESULTS HARLOW, CARINA*": *Mathematics, Satisfactory. History, Exemplary. Language Arts, Satisfactory. Social Studies, Exemplary. Technological Skills, Exemplary.*

"Fantastic, Carina! I think you're going to be getting that party we talked about."

The girl clapped her hands. "I'm going to make a guest list, and make my own invitations!"

Harlow kept scrolling: *Physical Aptitude, Satisfactory. Behavior and Discipline, Exemplary. Attention and Motivation, Exemplary.*

How did I get so lucky? He thought. *What a wonderful daughter. Now if I can just figure out how to make her stay seven years old forever, where she always loves Daddy...*

Carina waltzed around the room, circling back to the sofa. This time, instead of climbing into Harlow's lap, she seated herself beside him. As she turned to the bay windows, a hovercar hummed past, streaking between skyscrapers in the setting sun.

"Daddy, are we rich?" the girl asked.

Harlow smiled, and pulled her close. "What makes us rich is that we have each other, and your Mommy. You can be rich without having a lot of money."

She returned the hug, but he sensed that she was still thinking. "But we have money too, right?" she pressed.

Another car zipped past the window.

"You don't have to worry about money, sweetheart. We're fortunate. We own this part of the building. Our home is what's called a condominium suite. Your mother and I have good jobs working for the UCO, and we make money. That's not something that little girls need to be concerned with."

Carina smiled. "Fortunate," she repeated. "Then the Greys must be *really* fortunate."

Harlow frowned. "Why is that?"

"Because we own part of a building," she said, "But they own the whole entire *planet!*" She swept her arms as wide as she could. "They must be really, *really* rich!"

Harlow swallowed, his face flushing. "What? That's not true, honey. The Greys don't own the whole planet. Nobody does."

Carina shook her head. "That's not what Circinus says," she insisted. "It says they own the whole planet."

Harlow took up the tablet again, and pressed a key. *INSTRUCTOR*, the heading read. *CIRCINUS*. A solemn-faced Grey with a narrow, lipless mouth stared mutely from the screen. Children of lesser ability were taught by holostacker training modules; the more gifted received instruction from the Greys in person. It was a source of pride among parents in New Zaragosa, but now, for some reason, the idea gave him chills.

He powered the tablet off, and gave it to her to return to its place on the shelf. "It's time to wash up," he said. "I'll read you a story before bed."

∗∗∗

The *Harvester's* massive silhouette choked the moon's ghostly light. The alien ship displayed only meager illumination at night, but it could be readily seen throughout the city nonetheless. Harlow didn't need to turn towards the window to feel its oppressive, mammoth presence.

He dug through the kitchen cabinets, and found an old bottle of bourbon. Liquor, another hallmark of the privileged in the Great Cities...especially if it was any good. Rotating the bottle, he tried to remember where and when he'd gotten it. A gift, probably, for doing his job well. That was the reason for most of his possessions, and the home they were kept in.

He sat in the dark and sipped the whisky. He had to find Vulpecula—finding her was his purpose. His life would be in stasis, a self-imposed purgatory, until he did. In the silence of his home, Dr. Tainer's words rang around him.

Viruses are quite effective at finding their targets.

Harlow felt the scintillating saucer alongside the windows, and shuddered.

Viruses are not truly alive. They exist only to do one thing.

The glass was empty, and his mind was full. He reached for the bottle again.

If you're filled up with a virus, you're being taken over on the inside. And are you really alive?

Chapter 8

With her hands pinned behind her, each bump in the road jostled Lyra so that she banged against the vehicle's frame, bruising her shoulders and arms. Her feet, pinioned as well, were hard to brace against the inside of the rattling machine's cabin. Pavo's transportation, a sort of oversized dune buggy, was built for speed and utility, and not comfort. The same could be said of his operation of it. She'd have feared flying out of the seat altogether if not for the single lap belt cinched painfully tight at her hips.

Lyra's mouth was still taped, but she could see, at least; so she gathered what she could from the lurching glimpses of her surroundings. Tall spruce trees reached skyward, and the daylight was strong and healthy. They bounced along, probably on a dirt road, and she saw none of the old telephone poles that guided the way to long-dead settlements.

Lyra fought to sit up straighter, twisting her body for a brief view of the ground. It was flat, and carpeted with dry brown needles. Pavo looked over at her, and she relaxed back into the seat quietly.

Exhaustion, pain, and hunger hobbled her just as surely as the powerbinders, and the bruising jolts of the vehicle battered her focus. Her psionic powers would be weak, if she could call them forth at all: manipulating small objects, perhaps, but nothing approaching her full potential. Had she been well fed and rested, it would be a simple matter of disabling the engine, breaking her bonds, and dealing with her captor directly. Given these circumstances, though, she'd have to work a bit harder for her freedom.

Gingerly, she tested her concentration. The grating rasp of the buggy raked her nerves, another bump bashed her elbow against the metal frame, and she couldn't slip into the zone of effortless manipulation. *Don't reach for it,* she thought. *Don't force it. Just let the power line up with your thoughts...*

After a few moments, the jostling ride faded into the background of her consciousness, and a gentle tug appeared at one corner of the tape that covered her mouth.

Yes.

She worked at the tight silver strip with her mind, and pulled it partway free on the side facing away from Pavo. She turned her face to the right, inching up in the seat to peek out at the landscape once more. Now the shoulder of the road sloped away into an embankment. A couple of dozen meters away, a shallow stream parted the copses of spruce and fir. The water ran parallel to the road, but seemed to be drawing nearer by degrees as they drove. Lyra strained her neck to see ahead, looking for a bridge—

Pavo nudged her roughly. "Settle down there. We've still got a ways to go."

Chagrined, she sank down again. *Patience. Let him get comfortable and forget about you.* The buggy rumbled on. She kept her focus sharp by teasing the strip of tape, peeling it incrementally from her cheek. The uneven road seemed to incline; she could see less of the treetops. She held her breath, hoping she was alive ten seconds from now, hoping what she was about to do wouldn't break her neck.

The tires bounced, and the road's surface changed abruptly. The wheels roared over a hollow emptiness; they were on a bridge.

Now.

She ripped the tape from her mouth; it flew through the air and plastered itself across Pavo's eyes. Gasping, he clawed at the blindfold with one hand and she used her mind to wrench the wheel out of his grasp with all her might. The buggy careened to the right, lifting onto two wheels, and smashed into the flimsy guardrail. The combination of speed and imbalance flipped the vehicle, and they sailed over the side.

The world went topsy-turvy, and Lyra tucked her head and shoulders down, curling into a fetal position as they hurtled through the air, still spinning. The crash rattled her bones; she banged her head and bit her tongue as icy water sloshed up, drenching her. Beside her, Pavo shrieked with fury and, she hoped, pain. Still using telekinesis, she fumbled at the safety harness for a few seconds before the button depressed and the seat belt whipped back from her lap. Immediately gravity took hold and she splashed against the vehicle's passenger door. The water wasn't deep, but with her hands and ankles bound, she could only wriggle like a worm to keep her head clear of the surface.

The shock of the numbing water was already setting in, sapping her muscles. She jackknifed her body, hammering the powerbinders on her feet against the steel roll cage. She cracked the bulky anklets again and again, screaming in hoarse gasps with the effort. On the fifth impact, a fracture appeared in the restraint's housing; another kick widened the fissure, and she thrust her legs back into the frigid water, flooding the device.

A drop of blood spattered on her blouse, and she stared at it in alarm. Could it be hers? She didn't know where she was bleeding from. Lyra looked around: the car was on its side; she lay in the passenger seat, and Pavo, still belted into the driver's side, hung suspended above her. Another crimson drop fell, mixing into a ruddy dilution on her soaking shirt. At first he seemed to be unconscious, but then he turned his face to the side. As she watched, the forked tufts of hair shifted

71

from lime-green to midnight-blue, and his searching right hand rose to grasp the edge of the tape over his eyes.

He tore the adhesive strip off, taking one of his eyebrow piercings with it. Blood dripped freely from the torn skin, and his eyes, now coal-black, fixed on her. His lips curled back in a groan.

"Oh, that wasn't nice at all," he snarled.

The pressure on Lyra's ankles snapped as the submerged binders shorted out, and her legs were free. The cold had stolen her dexterity, though, and she scrambled clumsily, banging against the roll cage instead of crawling under it to exit the vehicle. Her hands, still twisted behind her back, were numb, and she flopped about to get a better position and fit through the bars. Above her, Pavo was sawing through his jammed seatbelt with a long, wickedly serrated pocketknife.

Lyra plunged into the water, ducking under the bar and kicking her way out into the stream. Once outside the vehicle, she was able to get her feet under her and stumble toward the shore. Dragging herself onto the bank, she sagged wearily; even the sound of her pursuer tumbling free and hitting the water with a splash failed to rouse energy from her drained body.

Panting for breath, she attempted to zero her mind and regain focus, but it was futile. Flight, or other martial applications of her talent, was out of the question. She could hardly remain on her feet. She sank to one knee, and stole a few moments of relief, trying to quell her pounding heart. Behind her, Pavo sloshed through the brook. She stood and turned to him, backing away as he waded toward her.

A glint summoned her eye: a small key on a chain around his neck—the kind that would unlock a set of powerbinders. She fixed on it, screaming silently with the last ounces of her will. The key twitched. She called for the key, summoned it, drew it to her with desperate abandon. It lifted from Pavo's chest, pointing in her direction; instinctively his hand went to clench it but it shot free, breaking the chain, streaking right to Lyra like an arrow. She swiveled around, lining up the cuffs, and it plugged into the lock and twisted. The powerbinders clacked loudly and fell from her wrists.

Pavo gained the shoreline, limping, baring gritted teeth. Lyra was only a few steps ahead of him. She spun, and fled into the forest.

***

She staggered through a maze of towering trees, while Pavo trudged heavily after her. She listened to his uneven steps, wondering why he hadn't intercepted her yet. She'd seen him favoring one leg.

"You're only making this harder on yourself," he called. "Where'd'ya think you're going, anyhow?"

It was true; here she was leading them both into the middle of nowhere, with no supplies and fighting exhaustion. The ill-fated attempt on Josiah Corvus's life had taught her that she, like all psionics, was prone to blacking out from too much exertion. Dizziness slowed her thoughts: how far were they from the crashed buggy? She no longer saw the brook; had she been heading parallel to the road, or away from it?

How much longer could she keep this up before Pavo caught up with her?

"Let's talk this out," she yelled back to him. "We can sit down and talk about this."

"Talk about what?" came the answer.

"About the fact that we're at an impasse. I can't get away, but you can't make me come with you."

She collapsed onto a wide log, panting. After a few moments, Pavo came into view, the boxy black pistol in his right hand.

"Oh, I can make you," he said.

"Put that away," she said, keeping the quaver from her voice. "You can't shoot me, and you know it."

He debated briefly, and then holstered the weapon. As he walked to the fallen tree, his limp was quite pronounced.

"How badly did you get hurt in the crash?" she asked.

He sat a few feet away from her. "Didn't happen in the crash. Leg was pinned and I had to give the old ankle a fair twist to get her out of there."

Lyra looked away, stung by elation that was wrapped in shame. *So maybe I can get away from him after all. But it's my fault that he's hurt, and stuck in the forest...*

"You shouldn't be walking on it," she said. "I'll find you a big branch to use as a crutch, or—"

"Nae," he said. "She'll be right."

"Are you sure? Do your bionics heal you faster?"

"What are you, my nan?" he chuckled. "I said she'll be right."

"Oh. Okay." Silence for a beat, and Lyra leaned forward, elbows on her knees. Her concern for him faded into apprehension.

So he's not injured, and will be in fighting shape pretty soon. And so will I, if I can rest. How long will it be—ten minutes? Five? Can I be ready that fast?

"Well, you were deadset about one bit," he said, stretching his legs out. "I can't pack you all the way to the bleedin' back of Bourke against your will, now can I?"

"Where's—"

"It's an expression, love. Now, even if my Ute ain't punched the big ticket, which I assume it has—"

"What's a 'yoot'?" she asked.

"Utility vehicle—stop interrupting. Even if it ain't cactus, what's a fella to do? I haul you back there and sort it out, and get on the road only to have you cause another crash inside of two clicks." He shook his head. "It won't do."

"In that case, we'll just go our separate ways," Lyra said. "It's been nice knowing you."

"Oh, no you don't," Pavo answered. "You can't gimme the flick that easy."

She raised an eyebrow at him.

"It means get rid of me," he said.

Lyra chuckled. "Oh, good. I thought I was going to have to slap you."

Pavo guffawed. "What, did you think I was askin' if you wanted to have a naughty?" He looked around. "Although it is just the pair of us here, and I wouldn't mind—"

She slapped him then, right across his square jaw.

"Okay, just foolin' with you. Take her easy," he said. "Might as well be mates if we're to be stuck out here in the walkabout, ain't we?"

"You're not mad at me for crashing your Ute?" she asked, then wished she hadn't reminded him.

"Nah," Pavo said. "I mean, I ain't *glad* you done it, but..." he tapped the scar on top of his head. "Remember?"

Lyra's thoughts whirled. "You mean you can't feel *any* emotion? That's what the surgery was for?"

"That's putting it a bit too simply," he said. "The corpus callosum is a conduit between the two halves of the brain. You have an emotional, artistic side and a logical, reasoning side, and information goes back and forth to help you process objects, situations, what have you."

"And for most people, those worlds are at least somewhat intertwined," she supplied. "You use your left brain to write words on a piece of paper—a utilitarian task, to convey information—and your right brain to try and make your penmanship look attractive: an artistic task, to evoke a certain emotion."

"Right. But what if you could be more selective about the information that's being shared between the two sides?" he said. "You could make decisions faster, more pragmatically, without getting bogged down by emotions."

Lyra's mouth was dry. "Like the need to twist your own ankle to get out of a wrecked vehicle, or ripping one of your piercings out so you can get your eyesight back."

Offering your friendship to someone you just kidnapped a couple of hours ago. Slaughtering an entire team of bounty hunters you were working with a couple of minutes ago.

"No use in mucking around, hey?" he answered. "What's the use of hanging about in a walloped Ute, with the bloody lights out?"

"But you're not a total robot," she said. "You have emotions. I've seen you laugh."

"Aye. It was a rebuild, not a lobotomy, love. The circuitry responds to adrenaline, and inhibits unwanted hormones from reaching the cingulate gyrus. The point is to make you perform better in high-stress environments, not to suck all the fun out of life.

"Going back to the stuck ankle: there's an obvious solution. Just give the old leg a heave and get her out of there. You still feel the pain, but you have a different reaction to it. It'll hurt, but what of it? It ain't the pain itself that draws most people up short; it's the emotional part, the anticipation. Knowing that it's going to hurt is worse than the actual pain."

"Or the knowledge that you've damaged your own body, when taking care of it is your number-one priority, biologically speaking," Lyra said, nodding. "I once saw a kid trip on a broken sidewalk and skin his knees. He got up and kept going—didn't say anything about it, until a minute later when he saw a little trickle of blood where he'd gotten scraped. Then he screamed like a banshee."

"Aye," Pavo said. "An emotional response to pain—what bloody good does that do you? I've shut it off; now I'm the better for it."

Lyra pulled off a soaking boot and shook the rocks out of it. The conversation was beginning to remind her of another one she'd had months ago, in a whistling firelit shanty on the Texas desert plains. She and Orion had discussed the surprising benefits of their unwanted

76

surgeries, and she had implored Orion, who had begun to feel like a machine, to resist the temptation to act like one.

How odd, the lengths to which people would go to avoid a change of perspective. For Lyra, empathy was second-nature; and here she was talking to someone who'd paid good money to have his skull sawed open so that he could circumvent his emotions. Pavo had, in effect, made a lifelong commitment to his current mindset. He'd never be able to change his mind about something—to "sleep on it" and see how he felt later. He'd never grow to understand a person or a problem from a different point of view. He'd never be able to fall in love.

The point is not to suck all the fun out of life, he'd said.

But for Lyra, understanding others—their motivations, their likely responses—was part and parcel to her survival. In fact, she was doing it now: analyzing Pavo, striving to understand his worldview, so she could predict his actions and be prepared for them.

"What would you have done with the money?" she asked him. "You wanted the two million capitals for capturing me, but you can't want money for its own sake. There has to be something concrete that you wanted it for."

"What do you think I wanted it for?" he laughed. "I could buy a house bigger than Queensland Number One and put me bleedin' feet up for a good while."

"Having that much money wouldn't guarantee your survival," she said. "I think it would put a target on your back. You'd be at risk of everyone you met stabbing you in the back."

"I'm already at risk of that, love," he said. "But this way at least I'd be popping bottles in the meantime. And I'd have a few large units paid to look after me, you see."

"What, you want to live like Pablo Escobar? Look over your shoulder all the time, and end up getting shot in your swimming pool?"

"Gatsby, love."

"What?" she said.

"That was Gatsby as got capped in his bathers. Escobar did for himself on a rooftop when the fuzz got too close," Pavo said.

"Still, you know what I mean. Money creates as many problems as it solves."

He stretched his leg out, rotating the ankle in slow circles. It seemed to be on the mend. "Hang it up if you ain't right again. If I had all the tea in China, it wouldn't do me no good in a sitch like this here, now would it? About as useful as an ashtray on a motorbike. Would be better to have a mate to help out."

Pavo rose from the log, testing his ankle. After a few cautious steps, he nodded, smiling. The limp was already less pronounced.

"Caught your breath, then?" Pavo said. "I figure we might head back to the Ute, see where we stand. If she won't manage, I've got a tent and some other trappings as would be good to have out here."

It was astonishing, the quickness with which he apprised his situation and adapted. He'd done a complete reversal, and emotion had had absolutely nothing to do with it. Lyra reminded herself that the mercurial bounty hunter would revert back to his original nature just as quickly when the circumstances changed. And she wouldn't have the advantage of reading his mental state and being forewarned. He'd partner up with her as long as it made sense to him, and then at the drop of a hat—

Lyra wrinkled her nose. "When was the last time you had a bath?"

Pavo's face scrunched in distaste. "I smell it too. Ain't me."

Rotting flesh and offal mingled with an earthy stench, threatening to gag her. She stiffened, and searched their surroundings with wide eyes. Not far away, a tree trunk split with a *crack* like a gunshot. A massive force wrenched another trunk out of the ground; as it toppled, she caught a glimpse of something shapeless and greenish-gray through the cascade of falling needles. Something huge.

"Thrasher! *Run!*" she screamed.

Pavo took off at lightning speed, his ankle injury having almost vanished. Lyra bolted after him, heading for the wrecked vehicle in the creek. The behemoth thundered behind them, smashing a hapless path through the forest. Needles and sticks pelted her back, and she pumped her legs until they burned. Ahead of her, the magenta-tufted head bobbed and dodged; Pavo sprang into the air, kicked off a tree trunk, and slid over a mossy rock. She leaped over a crevasse, reached for an overhanging limb, and swung for the opposite bank. They were running downhill now, and debris from the pursuing destruction tumbled after them. The awful colossus growled, a guttural roar that accompanied the thunderous havoc it was unleashing.

Her feet splashed through frigid water. The creek's rocks were slick, and she skidded, wheeling her arms to keep balance. Pavo was digging something out of the half-submerged buggy. He heaved it at her: a dripping-wet backpack. She caught it as she flew past him. *Weapons?* She didn't have time to stop and root through the bag—had to keep running. She flung it over one shoulder, gasping for breath. The monster was right behind them. Pavo rocketed alongside her; ahead, the trees were clearing away, and she saw the sky, and vast open space. A cliff.

Lyra skidded to a frantic stop at the edge, but Pavo tore out of the forest line and jumped into the abyss, spreading his arms wide in the empty air. She did not look back, and leapt from the cliff after him.

Chapter 9

The wind whistled a death knell to her as she plummeted. It tore at her face and clothes, battering her wet garments with a chill that took her breath away. Ahead of her in the emptiness, Pavo stretched his body out in cruciform fashion, exposing the leather flaps folded neatly into his garments. Using the makeshift wingsuit, he stabilized his fall into a steady glide. Lyra fell past him; the trees were still rushing up to meet her.

Focus. Clear your mind, she thought. Exhausted and with the added weight of the soaked backpack, she couldn't center her thoughts on the life-saving act of levitation. Her apprehension spiraled into panic, and she choked back a scream. A tree branch smacked her, raking her face with scratches and bloodying her nose. That was a wake-up call: at the height of the treetops, she had only a couple of seconds before hitting the ground. She let the backpack fall, and forced every scrap of effort she had into the concentration she needed. *Do or die.*

Her descent slowed, as though she had dove into water, and she landed hard on the forest floor, rolling to transfer the shock into the ground. It felt like jumping out of a second-story window instead of off the edge of a ravine, but the impact was still enough to rattle her. Dazed, she lay near the base of the fir tree and tested her nose. It was sore but not broken, the same as the rest of her body. A hundred yards farther ahead, Pavo alighted neatly on the soft ground. He came jogging back to her, the studs and rings clinking on his punk-rock clothes.

"How'd you fare?" he asked when within speaking distance.

Lyra jumped to her feet, her face burning. The close shave had reinvigorated her, as did a rarely-felt emotion: rage. She pushed out with a wave of unseen force, plucking Pavo from the ground and slamming his back against a tree trunk. The tree shook with the collision, and he gasped as the wind was knocked out of him.

"I'm fine, no thanks to you," she fumed, marching up to where he was pinned against the tree. "Don't ever pull a stunt like that with me again. You throw me a heavy backpack and watch me sink like a rock, while you glide away nice and easy?"

"Couldn't tote the bag and break my fall at the same time," he said, his face contorted. "You were more apt than me, and no time to argue. Just the most logical decision, made quickly—like we talked about."

Lyra stabbed a finger at him. "Keep it up, and I'll decide the most logical decision is to feed you to that thing back there."

A sharp point jabbed her in the side. Pavo had slid a blade out from some place of concealment, and nestled it between her ribs.

"Careful, love," he said. "If I ain't collecting that reward money on you, means I ain't gotta have you in mint condition, hey?"

She backed away, releasing her hold and dumping him to the ground. Pavo took his time getting up, dusting his clothes off with a smirk. The knife vanished back into his jacket.

"Despite what you might think," he said, "I ain't keen on busting it up with you. If you're bound to go all aggro on someone, save it for when we take on that big ugly mate."

"The Thrasher?" she asked. "You can't be serious. We're not going to fight that thing."

"Think I want to do it for sport?" Pavo said. "I'd like to duck it, but this has to be done."

"Now who's being logical?" she said. "We just got away from it. Why risk our lives to go head-to-head with something that ought to be on the receiving end of a tactical air strike?"

"It might sneak up on us while we're sleeping."

"We're not going to be sleeping together," she said. Then, realizing what she'd said before his impish grin could return, she added, "Take that any way you want to. One will keep watch while the other sleeps."

Instead of smirking, though, he fixed her with a solemn look. "If I said I wanted to kill it because I don't like it, that would be reason enough for most people."

"But there's a reason why you don't like it," she countered. "Must be a good one."

"You know how those bloody things come about, right? One of those Lizzie larvae don't find something big to snicker onto when it's a pup, and it just mucks about eating rubbish and carrion, and growing into a proper fat nightmare."

"Yeah, they're getting more common now because the Human population is half of what it was ten years ago, and the parasite hatchlings aren't finding suitable hosts," she said.

"Bloody oath. Well, let me tell you, lass, they keep growing and growing. That one we saw ain't within cooee of how big they can actually get."

Lyra shuddered. "That one was almost as big as an elephant. How much worse could they possibly get? The size of a whale?"

Pavo's face was grim as he shook his head. "Nae," he said. "The really big ones are like shopping malls."

"No way. That has to be an exaggeration," she said, but the set of his mouth told her it wasn't. Still searching his face, she asked softly, "Have you seen them that big?"

"Brisbane," he said. "Back when there was such a thing."

"*That's* what happened? It was awhile after the Great Harvest. I heard it was an earthquake."

Pavo shook his head. "Precious few earthquakes down under. It's one big tectonic plate—no fault lines in it. There was mining all over Oz—Australia, you know—diamonds, coal, minerals, and all that... until they came."

"Until the Lacertas came from the mines?"

"Aye, riding on them gargantuan horrors like bloody battleships. There ain't much in the way of cities in the Aussie interior—the whole population's spread along the coast. So the disgusting buggers only knocked about, eating whatever odds and ends they found in the walkabout; they didn't find enough Humans to have a good set of the scaly-skins like everywhere else on Earth."

"And when they finally spread out to the coast, they were colossal in size, but still in their larval state," Lyra said, imagining it. "How did you respond—tanks, missiles, bombers?"

"Aye, but all that battered the city just as bad as the monsters did," Pavo said. "Place looked like ten Godzillas on a rampage. *I* responded by skipping out for New Caledonia."

An unearthly bellow made them both jump. The abomination was lowing with a guttural gargling roar, and Lyra's chest buzzed with the sonic vibration. It sounded closer than she'd expected.

"So you ran then; why not now? You have to atone for your past cowardice?" The words came out sharper than she'd intended, but fear had rushed them from her lips. Somewhere behind them, rocks crashed to the ground as the abomination somehow made its way down the bluff. She envisioned writhing, rotting appendages clinging to the cliffside, the monstrous thing undulating down the escarpment's face like a grotesque wall-walking child's toy. Running still seemed like the only reasonable thing to do.

Pavo's eyes, twin silvery pools, were distant, and she thought of his mercurial nature. "Fight or flight" wasn't just instinct with him, but a matter of literal purpose. He whispered something that she didn't catch.

"What did you say?" she asked, moving closer. The bellow sounded again.

"I said, what if I could change it this time?" he said, looking past her. "What if I could stop it now, before another city fell? Before more people had to die? What if this was the moment the whole world changed?"

"We don't have the tools," she said. "The weapons, the preparation, the backup."

"Nae," he said. "It should only take one bullet."

***

As soon as you think something, your whole world changes.

Anyone can change the world with a thought.

I'm just not afraid to make it happen.

Well, in truth, she *was* afraid, but she wouldn't allow herself to admit it. Backing steadily through the forest, shifting in and out of shadow, Lyra suppressed a flinch with every fir that came crashing down. The Thrasher was right on her trail, muscling its way through the timber, flattening a path straight to her doom. She kept her eyes on the collapsing treetops, using them to gauge how far away the pursuer was. Her adrenaline was spiking, and that would help to fuel the power she'd need, but she'd only have enough strength to do this at just the right moment.

Pavo, you cross-wired lunatic, you'd better be right about this.

The sickly greenish-gray flesh came into view, and the Thrasher gave its gargling roar again. She steeled her nerves, backing away, maintaining her pace, breaking line of sight only to glance behind her occasionally and ensure she didn't go sprawling over a rock or root. She could see the thing plainly now: tentacles flailing, eyes rolling, mouths gaping. It was a horrifying impossibility, a thing that

84

shouldn't exist. Now she understood Pavo's resolution to destroy it, and simultaneously wanted to flee more than ever.

A tree trunk snapped in half with the sound of a whip cracking, and the top of the massive beam toppled towards her. Time to act. She mentally pushed against it with even force, letting gravity control it as it fell but redirecting it back along another path. The giant trunk tumbled onto the Thrasher, clubbing it across the back, staggering it for a moment. A shriek of wild pain erupted from a host of hideous mouths, and it reared up on three misshapen appendages. It lashed the air with its tentacles in fury, and stomped back to the ground with a shock that caused the earth to quake.

The beast rushed forward, and she scrambled backward. Another great fir toppled, and she guided it into the monster's path. This one smacked it in what might have been the face and chest, if such anatomy could have been applied. Splintered tree limbs gouged its viscous flesh, and it roared louder. When it charged at Lyra, the broken tree caught horizontally between two others, clotheslining it across a makeshift barrier. The Thrasher strained against the jagged barricade, trying to break it in half a second time. Sharp slivers of wood ground into its wounds, and black blood bubbled.

Breathless, Lyra stumbled away from the pinioned horror. Some of the branches had locked into the forks of the standing trees, and the broken stubs of missing boughs jabbed deep into ragged wounds. It pushed forward and screamed in agony; it tried to backpedal and couldn't extricate itself.

A swift shadow blotted the sun as it sailed over Lyra, and then an immense boulder collided with the Thrasher. The dull *thud* of its bruising impact made her gasp, and the monster was stunned into silence for an instant before redoubling its furious howls. It slapped feebly against the tree with weakening tentacles. Lyra clapped her hands over her ears and looked back to see Pavo lifting an even bigger rock over his head—this one, as big as he was, might have weighed 600 kilograms. Until this moment, she hadn't guessed that his bionic implants could have made such a thing possible. His own primal roar as he flung it through the air was unearthly and alien in its own right. In that moment, she feared Pavo as much as she feared any nameless abomination in the world.

The boulder met its mark with bone-shattering force. The battered Thrasher sagged against its wooden prison with a groan like a wearied sigh. Oily blood pooled into furrows carved in the ground.

Pavo's chest swelled with deep breaths as he strode up to the fallen beast. Many of its eyes were either closed or glassy and listless, but one still moved in its socket, focusing on its executioner with resignation. He stood over it, unholstered the Glock, and fired one shot through its eye. The Thrasher convulsed a final time, and went limp.

***

"Axle's cracked," Pavo said. "She won't manage."

Lyra was kneeling upstream from the wrecked Ute, filling canteens. "Great," she muttered. "Just great." They'd hiked for two hours back up the embankment for nothing, then. Or only for a couple buckets of water. It would be dark soon; no transportation, and they would have to camp in the forest. This was a troubling enough prospect, but what brought her more unease was the memory of Pavo's rage as he'd hefted that boulder. Seeing—even physically *feeling*, thanks to her psionic empathy—such unbridled rage from a dispassionate individual like Pavo had unsettled her. It was akin to seeing the expression change on an inanimate statue's face.

She'd seen killing in anger before, of course. She'd even had to kill for her own survival, as distasteful as she found it. Her prior companions had been sufficiently cold-blooded: Auriga, a mercenary and ruthless survivalist; and Orion, who was literally half machine. Still, she had known them both, had seen into their minds and known that they

86

fought, not because they hated what was in front of them, but because they loved what was behind them.

Within Pavo, however, she sensed only a void. Whether it had been defending himself from the other bounty hunters who had turned against him, or dispatching a beast that could grow to threaten millions of Human lives…he ended lives with the detachment of a god who was killing insects. She wondered if his own life meant anything to him, either.

When she stood, he was already hanging a hammock between two trees. "Why not be a mate and get us a good little blaze going?"

Dry brush was plentiful, and in a few minutes she'd gathered a pile and encircled it with rocks from the creek. Fortunately, the matches in the knapsack were the waterproof variety. As the blaze snapped and whispered, she studied his handiwork: the hammock looked comfortable, but not very large. She groaned inwardly, expecting that he'd want to share it.

Smiling, Pavo fetched a large bag from the back of the wrecked vehicle. As he hammered tent pegs into the ground, he motioned to the hanging bed. "I'll be just right in that piece. Be done with your digs in just a bit."

Surprised and amused, Lyra dug through the other trappings from the Ute's open cargo space. Several parcels had been scattered around the vehicle: boxes, backpacks, canvas bags. Some were soaked or had even floated a little ways down the creek; others rested on the banks, or were still wedged into the storage compartment. She tore open a cardboard box, and found a waterlogged wool blanket. No good. A portable cloth cooler held two smashed loaves of bread and some salvageable lunch meat. In other parcels, she found ammunition, a first aid kit, a large umbrella, plenty of warm clothing, two mason jars of moonshine, and lots of assorted foodstuffs.

And there were still many unopened packages. In the barter-driven economy of the outlanders, Pavo was a very rich man. She stole a quizzical glance at him, but Pavo's back was turned while he unrolled a small tent and put it up.

She heated cornbread and bacon, and opened a plastic jug of lemonade. The simple dinner felt divine, as did the chance to be off her aching feet for the night. She couldn't rest easy yet, though.

"Just so you know," she told him, "last night I was in a deep trance, and that's the only reason you got me by surprise. If you even think about trying to handcuff me again, I'll know about it, and that twisted ankle will be a pleasant memory by comparison."

"Would you really know about it, though?" he said, baiting her.

She turned back to the fire, chewing thoughtfully. No, she had to admit to herself that Pavo's thoughts were sealed from her. She could only guess at his motivations using conventional interpersonal skills, and those seemed largely ineffective against someone with his caprice. She realized how much she disliked being thrown for a loop, even if it was the gentlemanly gesture of offering her a tent that had done it.

That infuriating smirk—she wanted to slap him again. Instead, she blurted out something else completely, surprising herself.

"Even though I'm the psionic, it seems like *you're* the one reading *my* mind," she said.

"I'll bet that pisses you off nice and proper, then."

"When I'm pissed off," she said, "*you'll* know about it."

Pavo gestured at her with his chin. "That's exactly why I had to give you the bracelets, love. You pose a much greater danger to me than I to you."

"And don't you forget it."

"Very well, hands off. True blue," Pavo said, raising his palms outward. "Turns out I shouldn't have trussed you up in the first place, seeing as how we'll be traveling together now without the need for it. In my defense, though, I'm used to working with blokes who won't do what I ask."

She glowered at him, unconsciously rubbing her wrists. "We're only together for as far as it takes to get some transportation and get me back to what I was doing before I met you."

"And what was that, if I might ask?"

She didn't respond at first. The answer to that question seemed many miles away, guarded by an unseen yet familiar enemy. She didn't want to talk about Orion with him.

"Keeping a promise," was finally all she said, and vague though it was, this answer seemed to be good enough for him. Moments passed; so did the bitter edge from her heart.

"All right. So we need transportation. How are we going to get it?" she asked.

"We're most of the way to Flagstaff," he said between bites. "Should be only a day or two to finish the job."

"You were taking me to Flagstaff?" she said, her astonishment deepening. "That's an outlander stronghold—the UCO doesn't have a presence there. How were you going to turn me in?"

Pavo laughed. "I never said anything about turning you in. I said I wanted to collect the reward money." A sly wink. "One don't necessarily have to involve the other."

He wolfed down a few more bites, and climbed into the hammock. "Speaking of turning in—I'll see you come the morning, if you're still about."

In moments, he was sleeping peacefully. Lyra studied his shadowed form for a few moments, and chuckled to herself in the firelight.

Chapter 10

The walls of Flagstaff reached taller than the Thrasher they had slain. Atop the imposing brick structure, sentries and sharpshooters hefted burly-looking rifles, or stood vigilant at mounted gun emplacements. The enormous barrels of the large-caliber weapons looked more than capable of reducing an advancing Lacerta horde to pulp...or even bringing down low-flying aircraft. Seeing this arsenal for the first time, Lyra no longer wondered at Flagstaff's autonomy.

A platoon of desert-clad outlanders stood mute and immobile behind the heavy steel bars of a massive portcullis. Lyra could gain nothing from their faces: obscured by large sun-cutting goggles and cloth face shields, each soldier's countenance was as impassive as those of the emotionless Greys. She delved deeper, seeking their underlying emotions, and tasted resolution, pride and duty—but these were muted. Surely these men and women were hardened, trained soldiers, but what Lyra sensed was not simply the suppression of emotion. It was as if the feelings they might have harbored were now sun-bleached and dried, like desert bones.

Pavo held a whispered exchange with one of the outlanders, a woman who was barely distinguishable from her fellows. Scrutinizing her, Lyra detected very little to signify her status—perhaps a different pattern in the camouflage of her face cloth. She expected to see some sort of bribe change hands, but the outlander soon unlocked the gate and beckoned them inside. As the bars left their housing, a piercing klaxon sounded. The siren only died when the gate slammed home again.

Lyra hid her consternation until she and Pavo were well down the Thoroughfare, away from the main gate. "Why do I feel like we just walked into a giant prison?"

"No wuckas," Pavo said, apparently meaning the odd phrase to dismiss her concerns. "It's just to keep the blokes safe in here. They couldn't give a rip who goes out, just who comes in."

"All right..."

"We'll want to borrow some wheels," he said, leading her to a small depot where rows of dusty solar-powered two-wheeled transporters waited like soldiers at attention.

"And by 'borrow' you mean you're not going to pay for them," she prompted.

"I have certain privileges around here," he answered, snagging two numbered keys from the attendant's podium. The attendant didn't react at all. "Think of it as...diplomatic immunity."

"Yeah, you're a true dignitary if I ever saw one."

"You coming or not?" he said, stepping onto one of the vehicles. "Try and keep up."

She twisted the key in its slot, and the self-balancing board vibrated beneath the soles of her feet. Pavo zipped out into the street, and she twisted the handles to maneuver after him. The vehicle was snappy and responsive, and in no time she felt acclimated to its controls. Pavo weaved in and out of pedestrian traffic, and flew past horse-drawn carts and carriages. Lyra stayed right on his tail, relishing the wind that tousled her hair and filled her lungs with exhilarating breath.

Orion would love this, she thought, and immediately felt a pang of guilt that he was not there. She set her mouth and lowered her brows.

Well, I'm doing what I need to do to get him back.

Pavo cut across the opposing lane and into an alley. She followed, cutting off a carriage and causing the horse to rear up on its hind legs. Then the buildings blotted out the sun in the narrow passage and Pavo pushed his speed even farther, leaning forward atop the controls like the captain of a ship driving right into a storm. They snaked a twisting course between garbage bins, broken pallets, piles of trash.

After whipping their scooters through a couple of detours, they hit a straightaway. The brick walls of the alley blurred as they raced along. Pavo angled toward the left, where an incline rose: gently at first, and then more noticeably. They were climbing a ramp. The edge loomed ahead, and she saw only piles of bricks and boards, laced with sparkling broken glass. She would have faltered, but Pavo shot right into the precipice—and remembering the forest cliff's edge, she gunned the throttle.

The freedom of weightlessness battled with her fear, and ahead of her, the arc of Pavo's flight carried him over a low brick wall and down to an alcove that was free from debris. The makeshift landing pad couldn't be seen from the alley over the piles of rubble. She set her wheels down, skidding for a few feet; the momentum and close quarters caused her to dismount with one hand braced against the brick wall. Nearby was a steel door with a camera over it, looking like the entrance to a subterranean vault.

"What is this place?"

"It's the cutter shop where I had my upgrades done."

"You had *brain surgery* in a back alley?" she asked, incredulous.

"Yeah, so what? Better than having it in a bloody flying saucer." He banged on the metal door with his fist.

Touché. She waited for the angry buzz and the loud *clack* of the door. It creaked outward towards them, exposing a white-lit interior that dazzled her after the dank of the alley. Shielding her eyes, she followed

Pavo through a powerful wall of chilled air, and the door closed again behind her.

They were in a tiny antechamber. Using a stalk mike, a surgical-clad attendant addressed them from the other side of a heavy plexiglass double barrier.

"Sterile environment," the woman said in a somber tone. "No jewelry, weapons, metal objects."

"Aye, I know the drill, mate." Pavo was filling a small locker with assorted guns and knives.

"No metal on your clothing, either," she clarified, eyeing the ringed and studded assortment of Pavo's wardrobe.

"I said I got it, you old bird. I've been here before." Pavo shrugged his jacket off, loosened his belt, and kicked off his boots. The subtractions left him in a black crew-cut shirt and a loose-fitting patchwork pair of breeches. A few of his toes peeked out from the holes in his socks, and Lyra almost cackled at the sight.

"Your piercings, too," the woman pressed.

"Yeah, yeah." Pavo looked pointedly at Lyra while removing the barbells. "I got one less of these, now."

As she pulled off her boots, pebbles tumbled onto the tile floor. She placed the boots and her jewelry in the locker adjacent to Pavo's, and turned to the plexiglass portal, but the attendant stopped her. "Your bra," she said, pointing to the visible straps outside Lyra's tank top.

"Excuse me?"

"Women's undergarments have an underwire and a metal clasp. Our electromagnetic equipment requires a completely metal-free environment."

Lyra folded her arms, ignoring Pavo who was lewdly raising a scarred eyebrow. "I'm not taking that off here."

"I can get you a robe," the attendant said without hospitality.

Lyra glared, but no better option seemed to be forthcoming. She'd come all the way here; it would be ridiculous to turn back at the threshold.

"Fine," she said, sighing. The attendant placed a heavy white robe in a connecting tray and shoved it through to her. Lyra shrugged it on over her tank top, turned away to make the requisite adjustments, and tossed the offending undergarment into the locker. Tying the robe with its cloth belt, she was reluctantly impressed by its comfort. Like something the richer vassals would wear at a spa.

She turned around, expecting to see Pavo leering at her, but he'd chastely turned to face the wall. It was the attendant who was watching her like a hawk. "Step into the decon chamber," the woman said. "We need to remove any microparticles for the protection of our equipment."

"Microparticles?"

"Dust, debris, the outer layer of dead skin cells. It won't hurt," the attendant said in a bored voice.

Lyra stepped forward, and the first plexiglass barrier slid closed behind her. The confined space was like being in a shower, with people looking at her from both sides. A spontaneous gust of wind, so strong she nearly toppled against the wall, blasted her. It ruffled her clothes and hair, stirring her with a 360-degree tempest. After perhaps twenty seconds, the wind abruptly died and the forward barrier regressed. Disheveled, she joined the blasé woman on the other side.

Pavo followed suit, his reverse mohawk doubly tufted after the indoor tornado. He ran his black-lacquered fingertips through his hair, making it worse. Lyra stifled a grin, and turned to the doorway indicated by their unflappable host. She was glad to be leaving this woman behind, with her searching eyes and monotone demands.

The facility's interior, pristine and businesslike, pressed upon her. Unbidden, unwanted memories of her captivity and surgery whirled in her mind, buffeting her like gusts of wind that did not belong indoors…and all at once, she knew where she was. The surreal experience heightened; as she moved down the corridor, hospital-white and astringent, there were no diminutive, shambling silhouettes watching her with inky almond-shaped eyes. Instead, an outsider of a different type was waiting.

At the end of the hall, standing before a set of double doors, a solitary figure stood. Lyra's gaze flitted over the white lab coat and the knee-length black dress underneath it. The severe, attractive woman with the burgundy lips and dark, ageless eyes strode forward two paces, offering her hand.

"Welcome, Lyra," she said. "I believe you know who I am."

Lyra swallowed hard. "Yes, I do," she answered. "You're Dr. Vulpecula."

***

"I hope my associate wasn't too indelicate in his treatment of you," Vulpecula began, leading them into an adjacent hallway. "Pavo's abilities promised results, even if they come with their share of drawbacks."

"What's that supposed to mean?" the bounty hunter muttered as they walked.

"I don't understand," Lyra said. "*You* hired Pavo to bring me to you?"

"That's right," the doctor said, flicking the lights on in a small office. Vulpecula seated herself behind a boxy wooden desk, and indicated two plastic chairs for her guests. Lyra didn't feel like sitting down, playing at this twisted game of hospitality—*coffee or tea, make yourselves at home*—but her head still swam, struggling to cope with the knowledge of where she was and who she was with. She eased into a chair, breathing slowly.

"Speaking of that," Pavo offered from the doorway, "I believe this makes it payday, if you don't mind. Services rendered, and all that."

Two million caps. Put me bleedin' feet up.

He'd never mentioned the UCO at all—she'd just assumed that was where the bounty had come from. Now she was sitting across from the most notorious fugitive of them all: the rogue scientist who had engineered an unthinkable pathogen, and was working to unleash it on the already desperate survivors of this ragged, wretched world.

Was she imprisoned in this facility? What could the doctor want with Lyra? No metal, no weapons...they'd ingeniously disarmed her—that is, convinced her to disarm herself—but Lyra didn't depend on guns and knives to defend herself. *Joke's on them. I'm not disarmed at all.* But would her psionic powers work against the doctor, though? Vulpecula was famously superhuman. Never having met her, Lyra's information was entirely secondhand, but stories abounded among the outlanders that she was faster than a striking snake. Stronger than an ox. Bulletproof. Bladeproof. Immortal.

"Yes, first things first," Vulpecula said. She unlocked a desk drawer, and stacked twenty capchits in neat rows before her. Each was roughly the size and shape of an eyeshadow palette. "Just so you know," she told Pavo, "I've scrubbed the backlogs on these chits, so they don't show as coming from me or my aug clinic. But they're still going to raise an eyebrow in your direction if they're looked at too closely. Don't do anything stupid, like depositing them into Old Texas Union, until you've further laundered them yourself first."

Pavo scooped the little appurtenances into his pockets. "Never thought I'd look forward to laundry day so much," he said, grinning at his joke.

"Well, there's more where that came from, if you'd care to stick around," the doctor said.

Lyra sat there, mute and in disbelief. How had she walked into a trap like this? Were these two accomplices buying and selling her like property, and doing so right in front of her?

"What am I doing here?" she finally asked.

Vulpecula turned to her, hands clasped on the desk—Lyra supposed in an attempt to appear nonthreatening, even placating, but the gentle smile on those burgundy lips only set her more ill at ease.

"I was hoping you'd help me with a pressing issue," Vulpecula said. "Something that I think would benefit us both a great deal."

"And what might that be?" Lyra had found her voice at last. "Disseminating a deadly virus upon the general population? Assisting in experimental surgeries that would make the Greys envious?"

Vulpecula sighed, and leaned back in her chair. "I never paid much attention to the smear campaigns against me. In truth, the things they say about me on the news never bothered me at all—and not just because they're more than half true. But in a situation like this, I'm afraid my bad press finally catches up with me."

"Okay, so you're going to try and convince me that you're the good guy. Spare me."

"No, I'm telling you that there *is* no 'good guy'. It's not that simple."

"So make it simple."

Vulpecula pushed her chair back and rose. "Very well. That will be easier to do if you'll follow me."

As they walked, Lyra was loath to match pace with the woman, and yet didn't want to be left behind. Vulpecula's thoughts were nowhere near as inscrutable as her lackey's; in fact, waves of determination mingled with impatience rose from her. Psionically speaking, the woman reeked like a skunk. What bothered Lyra was the utter lack of duplicitousness she found in the fugitive scientist; it was painfully easy to tell that Vulpecula wasn't lying. Her surety was that of a zealot.

People with this level of ferocity—of *fanaticism*—rarely led long lives. No wonder they said Vulpecula was immortal. And Pavo was uncharacteristically quiet in the presence of his boss; it underscored Lyra's difficulty in finding her own tongue. She remembered the unresponsive hoverboard attendant, the noncommittal gate sentry, the blasé woman at the entry port of this augmentation clinic.

Was everyone in Flagstaff under Vulpecula's thrall? Had Lyra weaved her way into the dark heart of this nest for a secret audience with its queen bee?

Vulpecula paused before a set of double doors. "I should warn you, what you're going to see might be disturbing—especially given your prior experiences with the Greys. I must ask you to suspend judgment until I can supply the proper context, though."

Lyra wiped sweat from her brow, although the facility's air-conditioning was still prominent. Vulpecula hardly needed to spell it out for her; she was about to walk into a chamber of horrors that rivaled the laboratories of the alien spacecraft where she had been imprisoned. The inner sanctum of a fiend, perhaps conducting Nazi-era Human experiments in the blasphemous name of Human advancement. Again she was tempted to turn back, but where would she go? The knowledge she gained here might save her life one day soon. Hers, or Orion's. Lyra couldn't turn her back on that possibility just because of how distasteful she found its delivery.

The next room was a trapezoid-shaped viewing bay, with large windows facing a morgue. Despite Lyra's attempt to steel herself, she could not suppress a shocked gasp: the corpse stretched out upon the table was ashen-skinned and bald, and for a split second her mind supplied the awful image of a spindly, hairless Grey alien. When her reflexive shudder passed, however, she took a closer look: the body was that of a teenage boy, his skin shabby and dismal in death. His head had been shaved, and a dark scar wound its way in a perfect circle around his skull just above the temples: the emblem that Lyra shared, unmistakable evidence of the aliens' cranial surgery methods.

White-coated doctors ministered to the body, which was cut open at skull and thorax in a businesslike but gruesome display. She was witnessing an autopsy. The doctors took tissue samples, employed strange measuring devices, and murmured to one another about their findings.

"He was already a dead man walking when we found him," Vulpecula said. "They dropped him out in the desert after a botched surgery. His psionic capabilities were off the charts, but cognitive function was practically that of an earthworm. Like a lobotomy patient who could disintegrate an entire city block, and not even realize it."

Lyra turned away from the window, weeping.

Using a stalk mike, the doctor addressed her team on the other side of the glass. "Preliminary findings, gentlemen?"

One of the attendants turned to answer, his surgical mask billowing as he spoke. "I'd like to avoid confirmation bias, doctor, but so far your assertions appear to be entirely correct. The subject displays organ damage consistent with metabolic acidosis. Heavy presence of lysate centered in the brain, most likely attributed to osmotic lysis."

"Hypervolemia? Reduced tissue perfusion?" Vulpecula asked.

"Yes to both," came the answer. Vulpecula clicked the mike off.

With difficulty, Lyra composed herself. Beside her, Pavo wore an intense frown. "How about having that in English, mate?" he asked. "What happened to the guy?"

Vulpecula folded her arms. "The same thing that's going to happen to Lyra and Orion."

***

"During my time with the UCO, the things I learned about the Greys' approach to surgery led me to a frightening conclusion," Vulpecula said. "I came to believe that the goal of their surgical experiments is to perfect a formula to raise an army of shock troops: powerful warriors that require little training and upkeep, and can therefore be cultivated—and replaced—at a rapid pace. Shock troops are easily indoctrinated, aggressive, and expendable. They can be thrown at a problem in great numbers, making them suitable for tactics that more valuable resources shouldn't be wasted upon."

"Like missions that only require a one-way ticket." This from Pavo.

"Yeah, like assaulting a heavily-defended objective. Invading a planet? Is that what they want with us, after all this?" Lyra fought to keep her nausea under control.

"Possibly, although the Greys didn't use those tactics to subjugate Terra," the doctor said. "From what we know of them, it's simply not their *modus operandi* to invade and conquer planets outright...although we must accept that there's quite a bit we *don't* know about them."

"I'm thinking that if we found the answers to these questions, we'd wish we hadn't," Pavo said. "Who cares *why* they do what they do? Let's just get them stopped."

"I can appreciate that," said Vulpecula. "Although Sun Tzu would disagree."

"Well, Sun Tzu ain't the one in hot water here. He ain't got a care in the world."

"Speaking of that, I thought you wanted to get paid and retire, Pavo," Lyra chided.

"I doubt that I can," he answered. "Not much point in relaxing if they're likely to pluck you out of your deck chair and put you on the forward lines, is there?"

"That's true," Vulpecula said. "You'd make an excellent soldier, and the Greys know it."

The bounty hunter turned gentle cerulean eyes on Lyra. "Besides, if the clock's counting down on you, I'd rather deal with that than go on vacation anyway."

"Thank you," she whispered.

"I'm afraid Pavo's right. The Greys don't care about the long-term well-being of their subjects," Vulpecula said, leading them back through the hallway. "They're only interested in achieving a specific biological goal in most of their surgical patients—such as observing the relationship between theta wave manipulation and sleep deprivation, to cite one of their more well-known experiments. They're notorious for disregarding the risks of transplant rejection: if a surgery works, fine; if it doesn't, dump the body and pick up another subject tomorrow.

"Even their more ambitious projects, such as making you a psionic and Orion a cybernetic, weren't handled with long-term sustainability in mind. It's why you experienced adverse side effects and collapsed during the attempt on Josiah Corvus's life."

Through another doorway, they entered a lab. More white-coated scientists labored at workstations: utilizing complex-looking equipment, sampling and cataloguing various solutions. Lyra gaped at the scope of the doctor's enterprise; despite being a hunted fugitive, Vulpecula had apparently put together a team of experts and a state-of-the-art facility for her purposes. How did she continue to evade capture? She supposed the people of Flagstaff were fiercely loyal to their patron, perhaps even unconsciously so. An operation of this sort would be uncovered in UCO territory, but the veneer of legitimacy granted as an augmentation clinic (even a back-alley one) in an outlander stronghold had thus far kept prying eyes away.

"The unfortunate subject you just saw expired from a variety of factors, most notably uncontrolled osmotic lysis. That's when the cell membrane breaks down due to a fluid imbalance in the blood. The increased metabolic demand of psionic activity uses all of the subject's energy stores, and is then forced to feed on muscle tissue—the same as what a starving, emaciated person experiences. Many of the internal organs don't get the nutrients necessary to power their basic functions, and hover at a near-shutdown state. The blood still circulates, but it isn't oxygenated or perfused—that means delivered to the needed tissues—at an effective level to fuel the body's cells. Especially the brain, which requires the most energy. The body as a whole loses functionality and potency, like an elderly person's. However, the decline is sharp, not gradual over time, as with normal aging. Do you follow me?"

"Yes, enough to know that this is really bad." Lyra was dizzy; whether from a sudden attack of premature aging or from more psychosomatic symptoms, she didn't know. "How long until…" she couldn't get the rest of the question out.

"So far, you've appeared able to handle the metabolic demand. Eat plenty, rest plenty, avoid stress and overexertion. These things will help."

"You're joking. You want me to go on bedrest? Does that sound remotely possible to you, considering everything that's going on?"

Vulpecula's smile was mirthless. "No, of course not. I was only telling you what a doctor should say to someone in your position. I think we both know more extreme measures will be needed."

Lyra couldn't catch her breath; a panic attack threatened to surface. "Will I have to have surgery again?"

"I hope not. I'll need to run some tests, but surgical intervention will be a last resort. No surgery in the world can reverse the aging process, and half-cocked experimental operations are what caused this problem in the first place."

"Then what can you do?"

"I have a good idea of the best approach, but it's too soon to go into the details…my dear, you'd better sit down and have some water. You're pale and shaking."

Lyra sank into a hard-backed plastic chair while Vulpecula brought her a glass of water and a handful of saltines.

"Eat these," the doctor said. "I don't want your blood sugar to drop; I'll need to draw a few vials from you."

Dismally, Lyra chewed the crackers and sipped the fluoride-tasting water. She hardly felt the pain when the doctor's needle pierced her skin; a strange sense of detachment filled her as her blood dripped into the waiting vials.

"By the way," Vulpecula said as she worked, "I'm sorry to bring this up so indelicately, but in one way or another, time is short for all of us. I have to ask you for a favor."

The first vial of blood was full, and the doctor capped it, then started drawing another. *This is it,* Lyra thought. *The reason why she wanted to speak to me badly enough to drop two million caps.* In that moment, watching her life-force trickle into the waiting container, Lyra wouldn't have been surprised if her host had dipped a quill pen into the vial and handed it to her with an unfurled scroll. Pavo looked on with concern, a silent witness to the contract unfolding between Lyra and the doctor.

"All right, let's hear it," Lyra said, although she could already feel the oncoming request.

Vulpecula's dark eyes rose from her work. "I want you to get a message to an old friend of ours."

Chapter 11

Harlow suffered through the prison's incoming security checks as best he could. Although his skull ached and his stomach lurched with queasiness, it wasn't the hangover that made his head spin. Unanswered questions from last night still rattled around in his brain, and he found himself slow to respond to the Protectorate guards' requests.

Harlow winced at the sharp squeal of the hand-held metal detector as one of the guards passed it along his arm. "Your watch, please, sir," the guard prompted, and Harlow unfastened the timepiece. He placed it in the proffered plastic tray, wondering that he'd forgotten to remove it before reaching clearance. He remembered the knife on his belt, too; the zirconium oxide blade and ceramic handle hadn't been picked up by the scanners. It joined his other belongings in the tray.

Another pass with the metal detector, and the guards cleared him—but Harlow caught the dubious look exchanged between the two senior officers just as he passed.

As Harlow headed to Death Row, every face among both the guards and inmates seemed familiar, but a leering parody of its former self. The prisoners stared at him, cold and accusatory; for the first time in his life, Harlow fought an odd compulsion to justify himself to the men behind bars. *Maybe things aren't as simple as I thought. Maybe I'm not any different from you. Maybe we're all prisoners, but I didn't realize it until now.*

He shuffled down the hallway, its bright lights intruding and painful to his eyes. The structured symmetry of the neat rows of bricks on either side unsettled him. A guard followed closely, loading carfentanil darts into a gleaming pistol. The mechanical actions of his escort made Harlow uneasy; he itched between the shoulder blades, as though one of the gun's projectiles would find a home there.

Auriga's cell was orderly and almost bare, the soon-to-be-vacated look of a domicile whose occupant had almost no worldly possessions, and would soon be leaving even those paltry things behind. The doomed man sat stiffly on the cot, staring at a book.

Seventeen days left.

Harlow had no folding chair or other reminder of his status, and didn't feel that he could put it to effective use if he did. In contrast to his last visit, he now pushed the crimson steel door shut, enclosing himself in the cell with Auriga. This isolation increased the odds that he'd be stonewalled by the prisoner—Auriga had now been on Death Row long enough to either become acclimatized to it, or be tempted into a final concession.

But Harlow needed privacy for this conversation. The guard out in the hall frowned at him just before the door slammed home.

He moved to the foot of the bed, seating himself a few feet from Auriga. Sharing the same fixture put them on an equal field, which was undesirable, but Harlow doubted he'd get any further with Auriga by employing the same understated authoritarian tactics as last time. He didn't know if he could even pull it off, anyway. What would Auriga say to him if he were quiet, and allowed the condemned man to speak first?

A moment passed, and Harlow reflected on the claustrophobic solitude of the cell. He studied the room's occupant, and now noticed that Auriga hadn't acknowledged him in the slightest. In fact, the man's eyes were staring *through* the book, not moving as they read the lines. Harlow took in the book's cover: *Semper Augustus: A Farewell to Beauty.*

"Sounds like somber reading," Harlow said.

The prisoner's eyes now came into focus, and he set the book aside. Auriga patted the cover, tracing his finger over the illustration of a white flower with vivid red streaks.

"It's quite illuminating," Auriga said. "Some people don't believe history is important. I used to be one of them, but now I know better."

Good, Harlow thought. *He must be in a talkative mood.* It would be advantageous for Harlow to learn what Auriga spent his copious free time thinking about. Identifying patterns and themes in the prisoner's thought process would prepare Harlow to communicate in more meaningful ways with him.

"'Always majestic,'" Harlow translated from the book's title. "A book about the history of a royal family, then?"

"No, the subject might surprise you," Auriga answered. "*Semper Augustus* was the name of a strain of tulips that became immensely popular in 17th-century Holland, at the height of the Dutch Tulip Craze."

Harlow frowned. "I'm not familiar, but something tells me you're not actually interested in gardening."

Auriga flashed his sharklike smile. "No, *caballero,* I'm not."

"History, then," Harlow prompted. "Please enlighten me."

The prisoner's stormy eyes moved over him, as if judging the Protectorate man's worthiness to discuss the topic. Harlow attempted to banish his headache and prepared to listen carefully.

"In the early 1600's, Dutch prosperity was soaring from a booming textile trade and an expansive merchant fleet," Auriga began. "Amsterdam was the envy of Europe, and its affluent citizens became enamored with the tulip. Tulip gardens were a symbol of wealth and prestige, and the prices for tulip bulbs skyrocketed—even to the point where they were traded on futures in one of the earliest known economic manias."

"And *Semper Augustus* was considered the best of the best," Harlow surmised. "A status symbol among the richest men of its time…they must have cost a fortune."

"You bet," Auriga said. "At one point, a single bulb sold for as much as a mansion."

Harlow whistled. "Hard to imagine giving up that kind of money for a flower."

"Not even a flower," the prisoner said. "Merely a bulb that may or may not produce the flower you want."

"So what made *Semper Augustus* so special?"

"All tulips were beautiful, and highly prized," came the answer. "Their colors were bold, and they were the subject of sensational paintings that still define the Renaissance era. But where most tulips displayed a solid chromatic scheme year after year, *Semper Augustus* bloomed with dramatic crimson streaks on its snow-white petals."

Harlow again contemplated the book's illustration. The flower was exquisite, no doubt. He imagined the glory of a living specimen, and the pride of a 17th-century merchant who owned such a trophy.

"What no one knew at the time was that a virus was responsible for the vivid markings," Auriga continued. "Specimens that were infected with this virus were more desirable than healthy ones. In attempting to cross-breed different varieties and introduce the beautiful red streaks to more strains, tulip enthusiasts were unwittingly spreading a virus through their carefully cultivated gardens."

Harlow's eyes left the book's cover, and traveled up to meet Auriga's. Chills raced through Harlow's body as the prisoner spoke.

"The intense red striations appeared near the end of the flower's life," The doomed man's expression was fierce, and barely controlled. "Its beauty flared, and then degenerated. A prominent botanist of the time noted that *Semper Augustus* was 'wanted only to delight its master's eyes with this variety of colours before dying, as if to bid him a last farewell.'"

Harlow's voice caught in his throat, and for a moment he couldn't speak. Tainer's description of the Perseus Agent came back to him again, mingling with phrases from Auriga's summary of the book.

The added ligands are accepted as an improved version...A sudden, blinding flash of brilliance at the end of the subject's life...Ordinary men and women transformed into heroes, capable of great feats...Infected specimens were more desirable than healthy ones...A last farewell...

"*Semper Augustus* is only a memory now," Auriga said. "It's immortalized in paintings and in history, but no one will ever hold one again. No one will ever trade his mansion and his entire life savings for the glory of owning a single coveted bulb. No one will watch it bloom year after year in a cycle of death and rebirth, until the virus finally takes hold once and for all."

Harlow's eyes sank again to the book's cover. *A Farewell to Beauty.*

"The men who owned these tulips must have gone on to change the world," Harlow said. "They'd have been the wealthiest people in the country for generations afterward—maybe even centuries. Even after they died, their wishes would have been known; their influence would have been felt."

"No, quite the opposite," said Auriga. "As with other economic bubbles, the value of tulips climbed sharply for years and then vanished overnight. Entire fortunes were lost. Wealthy traders who were holding an inventory of the bulbs when the end came were suddenly destitute. The tulip was once again just a flower: as beautiful as it had ever been, but no longer the master of its era."

"So *Semper Augustus* didn't change at all, but the world around it did." Harlow shivered. "Can you imagine seeing one at the height of its era: a beautiful, priceless object? And then the exact same flower, a year later—identical, but now almost worthless?"

"Something as simple as a flower, but in its time, it had the power to change so many lives forever. It made ordinary men into kings, and monarchs into peasants. Men changed, but it did not. The flower itself, alone, was…always majestic."

Stillness encapsulated the cell. Auriga's words seemed to hang in the air while Harlow summoned the nerve to broach his next topic. He cleared his throat, and hoped Auriga would be receptive.

"I need to find Dr. Vulpecula," Harlow said.

A derisive snort from the prisoner. Auriga smirked, and said nothing.

"I'm really serious," Harlow pressed, dropping his voice. "I know you don't believe me, but I need to talk to her."

"What a coincidence," Auriga chuckled. "I wouldn't mind having a little face-to-face with the good doctor, myself. But I thought *you* were the one I'd have to convince, and here you are asking *me* to arrange a meeting. How'd it get all scrambled up like this?"

"All I want to do is talk to her," Harlow insisted. "I'd go alone. I wouldn't try to arrest her. I wouldn't tell her you told me where to find her."

"If you actually did go alone, I assure you, you wouldn't be *able* to arrest her." Auriga began rolling a cigarillo.

"Okay, and she'd probably kill me, right?" Harlow said, utilizing what he hoped was a bluff. "Nice way to get me out of your hair. What have you got to lose?"

"It's not you I'm worried about, *caballero*. Let's say I actually believe that you want to speak to the doc, but not arrest her. Your UCO friends would follow you to her, whether you wanted them to or not."

This was true. Harlow had no immediate retort, so he asked a question that had been on his mind since his first meeting with Auriga. "You keep calling me '*caballero*'. That means 'gentleman', right? Why do you call me that?"

"Yes, it means 'gentleman,'" Auriga said, looking down at his tobacco. "It also means 'knight.'"

"Is that sarcasm?" Harlow believed the prisoner wasn't above using derogatory names for his foes. "As in, 'in shining armor'?"

Auriga shrugged. "As in chess."

Harlow considered this for a moment. "More effective than a pawn, versatile in movement, useful for offense at the beginning and defense in the middle of the game, and expendable near the end?"

Auriga's white-toothed smile told Harlow he was right on target.

Chapter 12

Harlow's office at the UCO skyscraper was small but not cramped, organized with the kind of care a disciplined man takes when he spends little time in a place that nonetheless holds great importance. He'd debated using the stage at such a heavily-monitored facility for what might turn out to be sensitive (if not restricted) research, but in the end, he had to accept that Auriga was likely right about Harlow's superiors. They'd have long since been watching and listening to every move he made, and any attempts to subvert their supervision would be effective only in rousing suspicion.

After donning the eyepiece, earpiece, and gloves, Harlow surveyed the desk containing the stage before seating himself at it. A small step forward could be irrevocable in its consequences. Once something was learned, it might never be forgotten.

As soon as you think something, your whole world changes.

Anyone can change the world with a thought.

I'm just not afraid to make it happen.

The terminal allowing access to the information superhighway—called the 'grid'—was a blank space with a prepared surface that allowed the user to manipulate screens and conceptual objects in augmented reality. Personal computers, with their idiosyncrasies and compatibility nightmares, had gone extinct immediately following the Greys' technological boon to mankind. By wearing the associated equipment and making a series of gestures, a user could employ the galactic supernet to access capital accounts, play video games, communicate with other users, and, of course, gather information.

It was well-known that the grid originated from Ios, the Greys' home...not a planet, but an immense space station that equaled the size and surpassed the grandeur of most natural planets. As such, he wondered about the potential for bias in the answers he was about to search for. This wasn't a concern for routine inquiries; Greys were rarely less than forthcoming with hard, empirical information—except when it came to information about themselves.

But Harlow couldn't shake the unease from last night's conversation with Carina, his daughter. Something she'd said had fractured the mirror of his perceptions: now, instead of a single, clear image, his view of the world seemed fragmented and distorted.

He used the AR glove to open a grid window for a Specialized Inquiry with Lodestar, the name given to the grid's virtual chaperone. *How can I help you?* it asked.

Do the Greys own Terra? he blocked out in type, and made the twisted-fist gesture for "Submit".

Instead of the lightning-fast response typical of Lodestar, there was a moment's hesitation in the software. The delay was slight, to be sure, but detectable, as a misstep in the cyberdance between man and machine caused his stage to regroup.

That inquiry concerns restricted information, Lodestar replied. *You do not have access.*

Stunned, Harlow sat back in his chair. In some ways, this was as good as an answer in itself. There would hardly be restricted access concerning the subject if there were no truth to what Circinus, his daughter's instructor, had said. And speaking of that, why tell a child something that wasn't common knowledge on the grid? Another step towards indoctrination, perhaps, for the trusted protégés of vassals in good standing. He wondered what other secrets his daughter had been entrusted with, and whether there were consequences to this knowledge.

Harlow, ever the Detective, knew what he would have to do to further his investigation. He was loath to take the next step, but...

There is always a price to pay for progress.

Where had he gotten that? Something Vulpecula had said? He resisted the impulse to shake her from his mind. It was a good thing that he was thinking like her; it would help him anticipate where she had gone, what she was doing. What she would do next.

Harlow removed the gloves and visor, and pushed away from the stage. Closing his office door, he headed through the UCO's crowded hallways toward the central elevator banks. On the way, Harlow passed office workers, errand runners for city officials, political appointees of varying degrees, other Protectorate men. He returned brief nods when necessary, dodging through the traffic with a quick gait that signaled his desire to avoid interruption. At the gleaming elevator bank, the first lift was filled to capacity and he had to wait for the second, jamming the call button impatiently with his thumb.

Why were there so many people here today? A holostacker in the small lobby recited the day's news, supplying Harlow with the answer: a Conscription was coming up, tomorrow or the next day. During these randomly-assigned events, usually two or three times a year, the Greys would select certain vassals—the given name for city-dwellers—to accompany them onto the ship over the city. The selection process appeared random to Harlow, who had witnessed his share of Conscriptions. The aliens didn't seem to favor young over old, or healthy over frail; whatever it was they were doing apparently required a diverse cross-section of subjects. Most of the nominees returned within a day or two, with indistinct recollections of what had happened on the craft; a small number did not come back. Even fewer were promoted to some position of authority within the UCO after the experience.

The last Conscription in New Zaragosa had been six months ago, just before the *Scout*-class ship had been boarded by outlanders, sabotaged, and destroyed. With the arrival of the *Principal*-class saucer, Harlow wondered if the procedure for these selections would vary. According to precedent, egress from the city was severely restricted when a Conscription was announced. The Protectorate would strengthen the border, preventing potentially disloyal vassals from draft-dodging. Things would quickly return to normal after the selections were complete.

Harlow didn't imagine that the program was enjoyed by the vassals, but he'd never heard an outright complaint against it. Conscription was simply the way things were—part of the cost of city life, with its miraculous technology, free healthcare, and protection from the murderous Lacertas. Those unwilling to make the trade lived in the wastelands outside the city walls, but Harlow wondered how happy the desert nomads were with their choice. Outlanders were always trying to get into New Zaragosa (a grueling legal process, but it could be done); however, vassals almost never wished to leave the city. Even right before a Conscription.

It was uncommon for Harlow to be only now discovering the upcoming event; ordinarily, he would be a part of the heightened security. He supposed that he hadn't been notified this time because of the priority case to which he was assigned. Meanwhile, the UCO skyscraper buzzed with city officials maneuvering to be helpful...or, failing that, to at least be seen. A potential shuffle in the power structure at the United Corporations Order had lackeys scrambling in anticipation, and supervisors scrambling with unease. Six months from now, he'd be watching the same circus act yet again, perhaps with different performers.

In the next lift, also crowded to its limit, Harlow waited until the other passengers dissipated among the upper floors before he held his ID card against the touchplate for access to the topmost levels. He pressed the button for the seventy-seventh floor, and stood rigid while the elevator's IFF scanners confirmed the identity and security status of its lone occupant.

The gentle green light that bathed the car, along with the synthetic announcement of his name and 'Access Granted', had originally brought a type of Pavlovian reinforcement to him. *Good job*, the light and the voice seemed to say. *You're one of the chosen few.* He'd received the coveted top-floor clearance only months ago, at the beginning of his priority investigation. Soon, though, the privileged feeling gave way to concern: hearing his name spoken aloud by a computer now served as a powerful reminder that he was watched and recognized. Files were compiled of his actions; aptitudes and statistics were discussed. Harlow held no illusions that this scrutiny had only now begun; what seemed most odd was rather the intangible expectation that he should take pride in it.

When the elevator doors parted, Harlow entered an opulent reception area. The seventy-seventh floor's attendant, a young man in a smart black tunic, would have been notified of the arriving visitor either by the elevator itself, or by his prodigious psionic abilities. The receptionist gestured Harlow towards the next room, meaning that the building's monarch had already approved the detective's visit.

Van de Kamp's office had curved, stylistic features in the Rococo style, albeit with a hypnotic, unearthly influence. Harlow locked eyes with a wall decoration framing a stern Grey alien in paisley relief, and suppressed a shudder. He turned away, facing the elaborate desk at the far end of the room, where Regent Strughold perched at van de Kamp's left hand. Van de Kamp was not alone, as Harlow had hoped, but at least the visitor wasn't Eridanus. The stern, perceptive alien plenipotentiary would be too much for the detective to handle at this uncertain time. It was critical that he keep his thoughts guarded.

"Come on over, Detective," van de Kamp said, beckoning him over the sound of the Regent's furtive mutterings.

As Harlow approached, the jowly, white-haired Regent continued murmuring in the Director's ear. Harlow fought a fresh wave of paranoia; surely the pair hadn't been talking about him before he arrived.

"Welcome, Detective, we were just talking about you," van de Kamp beamed, finally silencing his consultant. He didn't gesture for Harlow to sit down. So this would be a briefing, then. Harlow stood straight, and nodded once.

"Sir," Harlow said.

"If I may," the Regent spoke up, rising to his full height as well.

Harlow faltered. It was unheard of for someone to interrupt when the Director was clearly about to speak. Van de Kamp sat there, smiling quietly. What had changed? Then Harlow recalled the end of the meeting yesterday: Eridanus approaching Strughold, and the thickening of the air that signified the alien ship's transporters being put to use. He'd been in a rush to get out of there, and had missed a critical event. Strughold had been on board the Greys' *Harvester*, and was now different somehow. An early Conscription? Thinking about it in the Director's office, the nausea threatened to return.

"In your pursuit of Dr. Vulpecula, we're aware of your attempts at camaraderie with the condemned prisoner, Mr. Auriga," Strughold was saying. "The Protectorate men at the prison have informed us of your frequent visits."

"Yes, Regent," Harlow said. "Auriga doesn't have much time left, so I've prioritized him as a resource."

The man's fleshy face spread in a smile. "I didn't ask you to explain yourself, Detective. I'm well aware of the impending consequences of

Auriga's actions."

Harlow swallowed. This felt like a rebuke, but why? Had he lost so much favor in so short a time? He scanned the Regent's body language: fingertips splayed on the desk, opposite hand on the hip, leaning with one ankle crossed over the other. A listening posture, and mildly threatening. So Strughold was either interested in gaining information from him, or was waiting to pounce after Harlow hanged himself with the rope he'd been fed.

He'd have to offer them something before making his request. "At our last meeting," Harlow said, "I expressed the viewpoint that Vulpecula was likely planning an escape attempt to save her associate. My observations of Auriga are now leading me to reconsider that position."

Van de Kamp's eyebrows rose. "How so?"

"Auriga is spending more time thinking about his legacy. He isn't exercising regularly, like before, and his conversational tone is increasingly morbid. I'd say that in whatever correspondence he's had with the doctor, she's delivered the news that there won't be a rescue."

"But you're guessing," Strughold said. "We still haven't employed any concrete measures to find out what the prisoner knows."

"It's still too soon for that," Harlow said. "Enhanced interrogation should be a last resort, because you only get one shot with it. If we learn nothing from it, we can't go back to more amiable forms of gathering information."

"And yet, if we wait to apply this pressure until Auriga's final days, he has a better incentive to stonewall us," Strughold argued. "He would only have to hold out for the last couple days of his life without telling us anything. And I refuse to push the execution date back—the UCO would look foolish and uncertain."

"No one would ask you to delay justice, Regent," Harlow said, his disquiet growing. He didn't like disagreeing with Strughold, especially under the watchful gaze of the Supervising Director. Despite himself,

Harlow looked to van de Kamp for aid.

"I'm sure results are on the way," van de Kamp smiled blandly, but his eyes were predatory. "We're all eager to see how this develops. In the meantime, what can we assist you with, Detective?"

Harlow steadied himself. Asking for a favor from the UCO executive was no small task. What he was about to do would be remembered, and possibly held over his head, for an interminable eon. He could only redeem this sin by succeeding with flying colors: that is, by finding Vulpecula. And if he could accomplish that, it wouldn't matter what he'd had to do on the way there.

"Director," he said, "You may recall having mentioned the option of drawing support from the Office of Occult Occurrences. Although I'm loath to tap that resource directly, I believe there's a way of using the O3 to our benefit without imposing upon the Office too much."

A nod from van de Kamp, who spread his hands, inviting Harlow to continue.

"It's occurred to me that even when the doctor is laying low, certain high-profile events might manifest on her periphery. Vulpecula needs to surround herself with powerful people; providing the resources and security that she requires isn't a job for ordinary thugs and mercenaries.

"Therefore, she's likely to be the secondary and indirect cause of some extraordinary events—things like uncommonly well-organized robberies and thefts, especially those involving psionic expressions."

Van de Kamp nodded. "Events that the O3 would be interested in tracking and monitoring."

"Yes, but we volunteer to do it *for* them—at least in this vicinity, for a while. If I could be given O3 clearance on the grid, for example, I'd be able to review cases of this sort and form a hypothesis of Vulpecula's general whereabouts. We'd still need to zero in on her—she's too smart to sit in the middle of a firestorm, but it could be a way to pick up the trail. Her very nature dictates that anywhere she goes, trouble won't be far behind."

His pitch finished, Harlow kept his mind as blank as he could. The sky outside was pale blue, and he imagined his consciousness emptied of everything but that serene color, all the way to the edges of his thoughts. It worked, but not entirely, because he still sensed Strughold staring at him.

Van de Kamp grunted thoughtfully. "Couldn't hurt. I can get you a special dispensation for that access."

Strughold now spoke up. "Yes, Detective, we're confident in your ability to proceed here. In fact, I'm all the more pleased that you've found a way to pursue the doctor without relying too heavily upon the information supplied by the condemned prisoner. The man's untrustworthy, and consorting with him too much is...unbecoming." He appended this statement with folded arms and a frown.

So that's what the Regent's problem was. Harlow thanked the Director and withdrew, grateful when the men let him go without further questions.

On the way back down to his floor, Harlow's phone rang. Checking the incoming number, he realized he hadn't spoken to his wife in more than a day. Cass was as devoted to her job as Harlow was to his—one of the things he'd always appreciated about her—but it was unusual that they hadn't made time to talk. He chastised himself for the omission, and answered the call.

"Cass, sorry, I've been—"

"Guess who's got good news?" she crowed.

"Oh, great! What's up?" He could certainly use some.

"They're implementing my design for the new Plaza!" Cass, a developer with a city planning firm, had been focused on this project for months, starting before they'd wrapped on the Spaceport. Cass's plans for the combined park and amphitheater included a cultural monument: a statue of a guardian Grey atop a towering pedestal, in a nod to Mexico City's *Ángel de la Independencia*. Whenever Cass spoke about her role in what would be the city's first shrine to the extraterrestrials, her eyes shone.

Harlow listened distractedly as Cass related more details: the Plaza would be within walking distance of their condo, a perfect place for Carina to play and learn as she grew up. Important gatherings would be held there: speeches, political appointments and other demonstrations. He walked to his office, grunting at what he thought were appropriate times, half listening.

"But we've got so much to do here," Cass was saying. "I'm afraid it's going to be another late night. Are you home yet?"

"No, I'm still at HQ. Kind of in the middle of something big," he said.

"Well, that's okay. I'm sure Circinus can supervise Carina until you make it home. Did it tell you? Her VR went up another step this week!"

Harlow stopped at the door to his office. "Oh, it did?" Value Ratings were assigned to the children who were tutored by the Greys. Why had it never unsettled him before? The phrase itself was creepy. It seemed like everything bothered him these days. "Well, I saw her grades last night; they were terrific," he said.

"She likes studying," Cass agreed. "She's a good student, and obviously one of Circinus's favorites. Anyway, don't worry about going home. Nothing's more important than you catching that awful woman."

Harlow stared at his terminal, and then powered it down. "You know, I can do what I need from home. No need to bother the tutor."

"Don't feel like you have to. I'm sure it wouldn't mind staying with her."

"No, I'm sure it wouldn't." He put the gridvisor and gloves away. "But I'll just head on home. It would be nice to see Carina."

Somehow, he *did* feel like he had to.

Chapter 13

Carina met him at the door of his serene condo, and threw her arms around his waist. He returned the hug, not finding the need to speak for several moments. When she released him, Carina looked at his black tactical gear.

"You saw the bad guys today," she said.

He forced a smile, looking past her to where the stick-figure Grey with the bulbous head stood in the living room.

Well, I saw Auriga, and then van de Kamp and Strughold, and now the alien babysitter in my house. Which one are you talking about?

"Yes, honey," he said, picking her up. "It's so much better to see you than the bad guys."

Harlow spun the girl around, kissed her, and set her down. Walking into the next room, he performed a slight bow to Circinus, who returned the gesture—the approved greeting between the two species, since a handshake underlined the Greys' deficiencies in strength and size.

"Congratulations," the alien rasped. "At my recommendation, the prodigy has been promoted one rank in Value Rating." It sounded even more sinister than when Cass had said it.

"My deepest thanks," Harlow said. "We're so proud of her."

"Your pride is well placed," Circinus said. "This is an opportune time for advancement."

"Thank you," he repeated, not knowing what else to say.

After an awkward moment, the instructor bowed. "I withdraw," it said. "The prodigy's lessons continue in the morning."

When the alien had gone, Harlow set out a snack for Carina, and went to change clothes. He eyed the stage in the corner of the bedroom. Had his O3 clearance been approved yet? He'd log in just to check.

He tightened the gridvisor, fitting it to his temples, and thrust his hands into the AR gloves. The operative menu coalesced into view, and Lodestar offered its assistance.

»*How can I help you?*

Do the Greys own Terra?

»*Inquiries concerning planetary ownership must be directed to the Xenoplicity Foundation. A Xenoplicity agent will be in touch with you.*

He blinked, reading the words again. Planetary ownership? So there was such a thing. And there were people in charge of it—people who would now be aware that he was snooping around on the subject. What could he tell them? He sighed, removing the visor. He'd have to deal with that later. Placing the gridvisor back on its hook, though, he froze, thinking.

He'd had to tighten the visor on his head. Why? Cass was smaller than he, and Carina, who was much smaller, had her own child-restricted terminal. This one, in the bedroom, was private due to the increased UCO access granted to Harlow and his wife. He should have had to *loosen* the visor if it needed any adjustment.

Who had a larger head than him? There was only one possible answer.

He donned the visor again, and opened an Inquiry.

What did Circinus use this terminal for today?

»*That user accessed Administrative and Civic functions to place recommendations for promotion of members of this household.*

So that lined up with what the alien had told him. Harlow read the

122

sentence again, seeing the plural: *members of this household.*

Which persons received recommendations? he asked.

»Harlow, Carina; and Harlow, Cassiopeia, came the response.

Days ago, it would have been a source of pride to see his wife and daughter promoted in the ranks. Now, the morning's queasiness returned.

In the kitchen, Carina was standing on tiptoe to place her dish in the sink. He lifted her up again, and hugged her.

"I heard about your promotion," he smiled, feeling hollow. "I'm proud of you, honey."

Her grin stretched wide, summoning dimples to her cheeks. "My Value Rating is higher than Helen Tainer's now!"

He carried her to the couch, deposited her on a cushion, and sat next to her. "It's good to be proud of your achievements, Carina, but let's talk about something important."

"Okay. I like important conversations." God, she was so grown up. Harlow tried to keep the sadness out of his smile.

"What I want you to know is that you can be proud of yourself without comparing yourself to other people. It doesn't really matter if Helen's VR is higher or lower than yours."

Confusion crept into the girl's eyes. "But isn't that the point of Value Ratings? To compare people to each other?"

Harlow took a step out onto thin ice. "Yes, that's what the Greys use them for, but in all the ways that matter, all people have the same value."

She frowned at the idea. "That's not what Circinus—"

"I know it's not what Circinus says," he said, too quickly and with too much irritation. How had he allowed this surrogate to eclipse him in his own home? In his own daughter's head? "It doesn't know everything. It's not always right."

She recoiled at this blasphemy. Harlow cursed himself for his spontaneous words. If this were a standard interrogation with a normal prisoner, he'd never have lost control like that. He had to get her back; this was a sensitive conversation, and it was just starting.

He reached for her hand. She flinched when he took it, which broke his heart into a thousand pieces, but he continued gently.

"Look, honey. What I mean is that it's good to question things sometimes. Even things that people in authority tell you—it can be good to find out for yourself if you believe it and agree with it."

"But if they say it's true, you don't have to find out if it is," she protested. "And your Value Rating goes down if you're disobedient."

He squeezed her hand. "There's a difference between questioning and disobeying. And because I love you very much, your value can never go down with me. Do you know that? Even if you were to question me…even when you disobey me, which I don't want you to do. But your value to me can't be changed."

Carina was thinking, and her hand stayed entwined in his. "Circinus doesn't love me, so that's why my VR can go up and down."

Thank God, he'd gotten through with something important. "Yes, exactly right. But the way I see you is different—"

And then, in midsentence, something the Grey tutor had said struck him. He stopped, his thoughts frozen in shock.

An opportune time for advancement.

The aliens were going to conscript his little girl.

With that, the last thread of his lingering uncertainty snapped. He tried not to envision her taken from him, restrained on an operating table, poked and prodded by ashen fingers. Sliced open and rearranged. Returned to him a different child with a different body, a different brain…or not at all.

He gave a strangled gasp, and clutched her in a tight embrace. The sudden, frantic movement frightened her, and she whimpered, clinging to him in return but not knowing why. His tears were hot and instantaneous, and he wiped them quickly so they wouldn't fall on her head, so she wouldn't know he cried.

I won't allow it, he told himself, knowing it was a lie and there was no way to stop them from taking her. What could he do? Tell Circinus he didn't want her conscripted? They'd do it anyway, and Harlow would receive consequences for his disloyalty. Could he go to the top, and appeal to van de Kamp? How could he hope to convince the Director of a plausible reason for opting his daughter out of the selection? Weren't the UCO executives already beginning to suspect he wasn't entirely one of them anymore?

And what about running? Just taking Carina and fleeing the city. Where would he go with a seven-year-old girl? Dragging her through the perilous Outlands as a fugitive would get her killed or recaptured in short order. Could he explain it to Cass? Would she share his horror, and think of a way to get them out of this?

"What's wrong, Daddy?" Carina asked, confused and on the verge of tears as well.

Pull it together. He summoned his will, shutting the emotion down, putting it away to be processed later. "Nothing, sweetheart," he said. "I was just thinking about how much I love you." The words twisted the knife again, and he slammed the lid shut on his torn heart.

He released her, smoothing her soft hair. "Carina, I wanted to ask you something. I don't know anything about this, but maybe you can help your Daddy."

She smiled, reassured.

"Have you ever heard of the Xenoplicity Foundation?" he asked, still stroking her wavy locks. "Can you tell me anything about it?"

Just like that, the smile faltered, and was replaced with a facsimile. Harlow hated watching his daughter for clues, studying her kinesics like an interrogated prisoner. All parents did it, though: observing the little tells that indicated truth or evasion. With other parents, it was about missing cookies or crayon scribbles on the wall, though. And here was Harlow, asking his daughter to validate his suspicions about alien conspiracies.

Carina hesitated, looking from side to side. She kicked her legs nervously, and then stopped, self-aware. "I don't know," she said.

Harlow swallowed. She was being evasive. There would be no reason for this if she'd never heard of the thing. No, she knew something, and had been instructed not to share it.

"It's okay, Carina. You can tell me about it," he pressed.

Still she dawdled, not looking at him. Harlow waited, not repeating the request, leaving the ball in her court. When the silence got too uncomfortable for her, she would speak. Finally she mumbled a brief phrase.

"They don't want people to know about Xenoplicity," she said.

"But it's okay," he soothed. "If I already know about it, then we can talk about it. What did Circinus tell you about Xenoplicity?"

"The Greys are really fortunate," she said, repeating yesterday's benediction. "We are too, because we have each other."

Except that after the Conscription, they probably wouldn't.

"Yes, remember how we talked about the Greys owning Terra?" he waited for her wary nod. "What does the Xenoplicity Foundation have to do with that?"

"What's *your* Value Rating?" she asked, suddenly turning the tables. "It has to be pretty high to talk about this."

Harlow stopped, his mouth open, aghast. As he was formulating an answer to this insane riposte, the condo's front door chimed, announcing the arrival of one of the home's occupants. The brief melody it played was personalized to Cass. Normally Harlow would be overjoyed to see his wife, but today the chime made him wince. The conversation with Carina was over; when would he get a chance to resume it?

"Mommy!" the little girl jumped from the couch, meeting her mother as the door swung open.

Cass Harlow, smart and alluring in a slate-gray kurta, swept up the child in a hug without even setting down her briefcase. Harlow composed himself, and rose from the couch to go and put his arms around his family, somehow feeling like they might all be together, untouched and unchanged, for the final time. Feeling that even though he held them tightly, that they had already slipped away from him.

***

Later, in the bedroom, Harlow watched as his wife dressed for bed. They'd said goodnight to Carina an hour ago, but Cass had had so much to tell him about her project's approval that she'd scarcely slowed to let him get a word in. She gushed about the coming Plaza's aesthetic features and the cultural significance of its iconography.

"People will come from all the world over to see this landmark," she reveled. "And with the Spaceport open, they'll actually be able to! Oh, but that reminds me—security. The Plaza will be a tempting target for Vulpecula, don't you think? Tell me you're close to taking her down."

He climbed into bed, sagging like a deflated balloon. "Well, you know I can't talk about the investigation..."

This was a defense on his part. From time to time he'd shared little tidbits of things that were *technically* classified. Nothing sensitive, of course—he'd never put any job or person at risk with the things he divulged. Just interesting bits of gossip, really, but tonight he had no energy for it.

"But you got O3 clearance," she mused, studying her reflection in the vanity. "That's a pretty big deal. I'm glad something's moving forward."

He stared at her. How would she know that? She clearly had more access to the UCO's dealings than he'd realized. He was tempted to share the thing that weighed his thoughts down above all else. She couldn't possibly know about Carina—she'd have mentioned it if she had.

"Yes, the investigation's moving along, but there's something else on my mind at the moment," he said.

She turned to him, recognizing his serious tone, and raised a sympathetic eyebrow. "Yes, dear?"

Here it was. The time to speak his concerns out loud, and share the unthinkable burden with his partner. He wondered if she'd faint, or grow angry. She might cry, or slip into a catatonic state of shock. Harlow had been torn between all of these reactions since that afternoon.

He cleared his throat. "Something Circinus said today made me realize something. You know there will be a Conscription in the next day or two."

A leading statement, not a question. Cass nodded once; Harlow was right. She really did have knowledge that wasn't available to the public.

Deep breath. "I'm almost positive Carina's about to be conscripted," he said.

Cass's mouth formed a perfect 'O' as she gasped. She raised a hand to cover the lower half of her face, her wide eyes locked with his. So it was shock. He swung his legs out of bed, anticipating that she could sink to the floor, or simply fall. Instead she ran for him, crashing into his waiting embrace as her arms wrapped tight around his body. He stroked the back of her head, fighting tears again. There were no comforting words.

"That's *fantastic*," Cass said.

Harlow stiffened, and drew back his shoulders. "What?"

Her smile broke open in an elated chuckle. "I can't believe it! They want our little girl!"

Nausea swept him; beads of sweat erupted over his body. He dared not speak.

Cass hugged him harder. "They've selected her already—what great potential she must have! Can you imagine? There's no limit to what she could be. A UCO executive, a diplomat, an Illuminatus...one day she'll deliver great speeches in the amphitheater I'm going to build." She drew back from him at last, beaming from ear to ear. "Have you said anything to her yet?"

He shook his head, offering his best attempt at an excited smile. "No...I didn't want to mention it because I'm not completely sure. It's just something I believe is going to happen."

"Oh, I know! Can't be certain, but it's so hard not to get our hopes up, isn't it? She'll be so thrilled, but you're right, we'd better not mention it yet."

"I'm glad you agree," he said. "But I wanted to tell you and see what you thought."

She clasped her hands. "It's just amazing. Our family is going straight to the top! Me with my city project, and Carina, chosen by the Greys. And you, too: higher administrative access at the UCO, and when you find Vulpecula, you're sure to get a commendation and a promotion. A year from now, who knows where we could be?"

He sank back against the pillows, drained, thinking back to his first conversation with Auriga. *I'm the UCO's expert on cult behavior,* he'd said.

Yeah, you should be, he now told himself. *You're married to a cultist, and you're sacrificing your daughter to the Greys. And all without realizing it was happening until it was too late.* Once again, he allowed himself the fantasy of taking Carina and running, knowing they wouldn't get far, but running all the same. When they were caught, she'd be conscripted anyway, and he'd be executed—maybe sixteen days from now, alongside Auriga. He fought a grim smile at the morbid irony.

Cass placed a hand on his cheek, and kissed him. "You look tired," she said.

He came back to the moment. "I am. Think I'll get some rest." In

129

truth, he didn't know if he would sleep a wink that night, but the chance to be alone with his thoughts was better than fielding Cass's potential questions.

As he was reaching for the bedside lamp, a curious chime sounded from the grid terminal in the corner. These notifications were typically customized for each individual, so a user would know for whom the incoming message was intended. He'd never heard this chime before.

"Must be for you," Cass said, unconcerned.

Harlow rose, and went to the stage. Slipping on the visor and gloves, he logged in. The augmented-reality screens he manipulated were visible only through use of the equipment, so Cass wouldn't be able to look over his shoulder. As if she cared—she was sinking into the pillows on their bed, blissful and released.

After he logged in, his inbox flashed with a priority message.

To: Detective First Class Harlow, F.

Urgent notice. O3 Knight Commander Webb

HEREBY INFORMING YOU OF RECENT INCIDENTS INVOLVING PSIONIC EXPRESSIONS IN YOUR VICINITY.

10/25/36 37.189, -112.995 Altercation [singular/group]

10/25/36 37.161, -113.045 Summit [native/ET]

10/26/36 36.215, -112.057 Altercation [singular/anomaly]

10/26/36 31.7304841, -102.6415991 Summit [native/ET]

In the fourth entry, Harlow recognized the longitude and latitude of New Zaragosa. That was only yesterday, but he hadn't seen any major crimes in the headlines. He thought back to what he'd been doing: yes, it was his presentation with the senior board at UCO headquarters. After the meeting, when Eridanus had approached Strughold, he'd overheard the alien's invitation to the Regent, and then the air in the room had buzzed, warm and thick. Harlow had been nauseated with worry and a spectre of doubt—a spectre that had now materialized into the verge of solid rebellion—and he'd missed what was plainly in front of him.

'Summit', the report said. There'd been significant psionic activity immediately after Strughold had boarded the *Harvester*. And hadn't the Regent been scrutinizing him in van de Kamp's office today? Harlow's gloves froze in midair, halfway between manipulating two displays. How much could the man know about him? It was difficult for Harlow to conceal his thoughts from his wife; what about from a man with newly-acquired psionic gifts?

Harlow would have to assume he was compromised. Instead of sending sweat and prickles along his spine, though, the thought made him oddly calm, as though a difficult decision had been made for him. As though an entire world had been destroyed, and replaced with another.

But enough of that for now. He turned back to the earlier incidents and their coordinates, cross-referencing them, and found the names of the places as they'd existed when the United States was still sovereign. Springdale, Utah; and North Rim, Arizona, the sites of two 'alterations'. Assuming the events were related, the responsible party was traveling south. If Harlow moved fast, he could get to that area by tomorrow night. He'd pick up the trail in central Arizona—a psionic who got into fights every day wouldn't be hard to find, and would lead him to Vulpecula, either directly or indirectly. It was the best Harlow could do.

Pangs of guilt attacked him. Leave town now, with Carina surely about to be taken by the Greys? Now the calm dissipated, and his skin erupted in clamminess. It would happen regardless; nothing he could do would prevent her conscription. Cass would thwart him if she figured out his intentions. He'd blow whatever flimsy veneer was left of his cover, and gain nothing from it. In prison, his chances to find Vulpecula or save his daughter would evaporate altogether. He'd hate himself while he was doing it, but he had to leave Carina, and come back with help. If Vulpecula or her associates could even be persuaded to help him…if he wasn't beyond help completely.

He saved the O3 message to his portable datapad, and erased it from the home terminal. Taking off the gridvisor, he rose and went to the closet to retrieve a canvas rucksack.

"I just got a lead in the case," he told Cass as he packed the bag. "I've got to go. Should be back in a few days at the most."

She grunted in acknowledgement, already sinking into pleasant dreams. He envied her.

Down the hall, he stood in the doorway of a darkened room. Muted lights from the alien ship outside moved across Carina's face from left to right. For a long moment he watched her sleep before gently closing the door.

And several hundred miles away, Pavo stood in the doorway of a darkened room. Muted lights from medical scanners moved across Lyra's face from left to right. For a long moment he watched her sleep before gently closing the door.

Chapter 14

Harlow's rebreather filtered the sand out of the desert wind, but the air he sucked down was still stifling and hot. Sweat trickled around his goggles and mask; his eyes burned from lack of sleep, and from driving through the night.

He'd signed out one of the rugged black SUVs from the Protectorate's fleet, citing his destination as one of the outlander camps a few hours outside the city. The fleetmaster had recommended that he bring additional men if he was heading into the desert, but Harlow had anticipated this and countered by saying that the informant he was meeting would get skittish if Harlow didn't come alone.

He'd worried about being cleared to leave, with the restricted-egress protocols already in place for the imminent Conscription, but it turned out that appropriating the vehicle and leaving the city at night was simpler than it might have been during the day. Harlow outranked most of the men on night shift, who were more concerned about preventing ordinary vassals from draft-dodging. Harlow's family was still in the city, and recently-promoted at that; there was no reason to think he wouldn't be back. Besides, he suspected his elevated clearance still reflected that finding Vulpecula took priority over anything, even the Greys' experiments.

The sleek, air-conditioned SUV was a comfortable ride, but its location was tracked, of course. He'd traded it two hours later to one of the outlander caravans. No doubt they thought Harlow was crazy as he rattled away in an aged and growling Jeep that was worth a tenth of much as the Protectorate vehicle. He'd rounded out the deal a little bit by getting plenty of gas; the red plastic jugs were lashed in the cargo compartment in neat rows. By now, the desert traders had probably chopped up the SUV for parts, or sold it to *banditos* who didn't care if their new ride was obviously stolen.

Things were different out in the desert, for sure. Would Harlow be able to live among the outlanders, if it came to that? He balanced his thoughts on a razor's edge between loneliness and paranoia, roving over a devastated two-lane state route, chugging from a thermos of black coffee. He aimed the Jeep's spotlight with one hand and watched with bleary eyes for gaping cracks in the pavement…or bloodthirsty Lacertas. His rifle rested in the passenger seat, in arm's reach.

In the dead of night, a couple of hours after leaving the traders, the spotlight flashed on a horrifying, instantly-recognizable scene: a saucer-shaped UFO hung in the desert sky above stick-figure aliens with dead black eyes.

He was caught red-handed; they'd come to take him back. Harlow gave a muffled scream through the rebreather, swerving the Jeep in panic, fishtailing as he slammed the brakes. He'd be a sitting duck in the open-topped car—no way could he outrun the alien ship, even in open terrain. With the Jeep lurching to a stop, he leaned to grab the rifle. His foot slipped, he popped the clutch, and the engine died.

Harlow rose onto the back of the seat, bringing the rifle up with shaking hands. He steadied it on top of the windshield. *Don't let them see it coming. No time to aim. Get the first strike and surprise them; it's your only chance.*

He pumped the trigger. The gun kicked against his shoulder, sending a barrage of rounds that whistled in the night air.

Ka-ping, ka-ping, ka-ping.

The aliens didn't move as lead tore through them with metallic plinks. Standing frozen in time, one of them had an arm raised in greeting; the other two stood wooden and formal in mannequin postures. Harlow looked at the UFO: it was unilluminated, two-dimensional and flat. Attached to the alien craft, a highway sign read, "Welcome to Roswell, New Mexico!"

Paint flaked from the alien figures; the sign was sun-beaten and faded. Relics from a prior era, beckoning the motorists of yesteryear forward to a campy tourist destination. Harlow sagged, weary, unable to laugh. He chucked the rifle into the seat and started the Jeep again, then pulled forward onto a side route, circumventing the town.

**

When the sun rose, he rested in a dry-rotted shanty close to the state line of New Mexico and Arizona. Not that state lines meant anything anymore.

And not that sleep meant anything anymore, either. 'Rested' would be the word...but as the sun climbed over the desert, turning the splintered wooden shed into an oven, he gave up on tossing and turning with his thoughts of Carina at the mercy of her wicked abductors.

His discomfort heightened when an insistent throb began at the back of his neck. Had he slept on it wrong? Had he slept at all? It wasn't a muscular ache, though. Something insistent and weird ran through him. He rubbed the spot, massaging his muscles, and felt a lump at the nape, above the spot where his spine met his shoulders.

Inside his head, a click and a low-frequency beep sounded.

"Harlow, are you there?" the voice was feminine and familiar.

"Yes," he said cautiously. What on earth was happening?

"It's Vivienne. We got worried when your car was destroyed, so I needed to raise you on the Beacon. Are you all right?"

Vivienne Tainer, the deceptively youthful Secretary of the Human Health and Well-Being Office. She'd been working with him closely over the past month, and Harlow probably trusted her as much as anyone at the UCO. Admittedly, that wasn't much, but he'd guard his cover, and try to find out what she knew.

"Yes…I'm good," he said, not having to act much to feign confusion and fatigue. "I got hijacked by *banditos*, and they got away with the SUV, but I killed a few of them, and got an old truck…" he trailed off, not wanting to say more. They'd somehow implanted a chip in him without him even being aware of it. A *Beacon*, she had called it. Part of his training? Chills surrounded the foreign object at the base of his spine. He wanted to rip it out with his bare hands; instead, even though it was crazy, he forced himself to continue in civil conversation.

"I got a lead in the middle of the night, and had to move immediately," he said, feeling silly, like he was talking to no one. "I'm sorry, I had to sign out a car and take off."

"You got out just in time," Tainer said. "I hope your lead pays off."

"Just in time? What does that mean?" Again, he teetered on the edge of madness.

"The Conscription began this morning," Tainer said.

Harlow waited. Waited for the news that would punch him in the gut, knock the breath out of him, bring him to his knees and leave him gasping for sanity.

"They selected Cass," she said.

"What?" It was the stupidest thing he could say.

"Cass was selected," Tainer repeated. "They conscripted your wife."

He stared at a warped floorboard, fixing his eyes on the place where the smooth, burnished floor stuck askew at a crazy angle. Cass would be proud to have been selected. The Greys were doing gods-knew-what to her at this very moment, but she'd view it as an honor. Just like all the other sick vassals at the UCO.

When he saw her again—*if* he saw her again—she'd likely be a different person. His wife would be gone forever. One more part of his life crumbled away.

Harlow realized he hadn't said anything for a while, and this might be viewed as recalcitrance on his part. He'd best say something supportive, even though the lie burned his tongue worse than the sweltering cabin he'd hid in.

"That's great," he said. "I'm happy for her. What an honor."

"Yes, it's wonderful for her. But I'm afraid there's something else."

Oh, no. How much more bad news could he take?

"Tell me," he said.

"There was an attack," Tainer said. "Vulpecula hit the city with another attack. A lot of people who were lined up for Conscription got dosed with the Agent."

A minute passed. Harlow said nothing as sweat streamed down his face.

"Harlow?"

"Yes." He coughed, wiped his face, and cleared his throat.

"Harlow, your daughter was infected with the Agent."

His world plummeted. He had nothing to hold on to, and clawed at nothing in a free fall. He didn't remember sinking to his knees, but suddenly the floor was much closer.

"Where is she?" he finally whispered.

"She's with us. She's okay."

"I'm coming back," he said.

"No," Tainer said. "There's no sense in it. You don't have the cure. There's nothing you can accomplish by coming back here."

She was right, but he screamed aloud, not caring if she could hear.

"I don't care. I'm coming back," he said again, standing up.

"I've placed the city under quarantine," she said smoothly. "You can't get back in."

It was her decision. As Secretary, she had authority over anything related to public health and well-being. If she'd made the call to shut the city down, even van de Kamp would have a hard time getting the approval to lift the quarantine.

And after the briefing on the Agent with Eridanus two days ago, Harlow now knew exactly how serious the Greys were about viral contamination.

"No one gets in or out of the city," Tainer said. "It's locked down completely. The only way you can help your daughter now is to find Vulpecula."

A dull, low-frequency tone as she disconnected, and the stillness closed in on him again.

For a long time he stared at the floorboards in front of him, at the place where one departed its intended path to stick up above its fellows. A tripping hazard, unsightly and offensive. He tried to press it down, but it popped up again.

Harlow gathered his things and headed out to the desert.

***

The wind assaulted him as he flew through the dust with a speed born of helpless rage. It was all falling apart. If he'd stayed, what could he have done? Again he repeated the truth to himself, although it felt like a cheap excuse. There'd have been no stopping Cass's conscription or Carina's infection—and the rapidly diminishing part of his brain that was still capable of logic told him that he was better off removed from these twin tragedies. If he were still in New Zaragosa, he'd be paralyzed into inaction. At least out here, hunting for the mystery psionic operative, he was doing *something*. For now, perhaps it was better for him not to see his wife and daughter, and deal with the aftermath of this insanity however he could.

All well and good to say that, of course, but his hammering pulse refused to quiet. There was no one for miles around. The open desert mocked him, daring him to choose a course…but today would surely bring new revelations, setting him on a certain path. Auriga wasn't the only man who was one day closer to a time of reckoning.

The growling Jeep ate up the road. In time, a dusty smudge on the horizon sharpened. An enormous wall, standing sentinel above the sun-baked plains. These formidable barriers were a necessity against the marauding Lacertas, and an outpost of any real size wouldn't last long without them. The hottest part of the day was approaching; if there were people here, he could get off the road for a bit, trade some of his gasoline for supplies, maybe even gather some information and see about dealing with a previously unknown problem that had suddenly become a top priority.

The battered remains of the highway led to a tall stone gate. Harlow couldn't see anyone manning the iron bars in the archway, but perhaps that was the point. He stopped the Jeep a respectful distance away and got out. The rifle stayed in the passenger seat; Harlow's pistol was still in its holster, and he kept his hands in plain sight.

"Hello!" he called.

Seconds dragged by, along with a spinning tumbleweed that crossed the road in front of him.

"¡Hola!" he yelled again.

After a moment, someone within answered. "Heard ya the first time, mate."

"Okay." Harlow was twenty meters from the wall, and still no occupants were in evidence.

"We got about thirty guns on ya," the voice came. A young man, with a strong Australian accent. "Is it just you, then? Whaddaya want?"

"Yeah, I'm alone." Harlow turned in a slow circle, hands out at shoulder level. "I need a cutter."

"Well, now. A cutter, is it?" A colorfully-crested head peeked above the ramparts. Harlow locked eyes with a twentysomething rogue with lavender-tufted shocks of hair and a number of facial piercings. The outlander leapt from the wall, gliding down through the hot current to splash a smooth crater into the dust. Striding up to Harlow, he turned a critical gaze on the man's tactical gear.

"You're from the city, despite that ancient heap you rolled up in," the punk said. "They got doctors there as can take care of most anything—and for citizens it's free, too. But you come way out here instead."

"I need discretion," Harlow said gravely. "and I can pay." His eyes followed the scar slashed straight along the top of the younger man's skull.

His correspondent chuckled. "Right-o. Turn the clock back a bit? Or no, don't tell me—you're looking to get turned into the type-ah bloke who can slam a revolving door."

"Not quite." The outlander was close, and Harlow spoke in a low murmur. "I need something taken out."

A half-smirk was frozen on the punk's face. Lemon-yellow eyes appraised Harlow thoughtfully. After a moment, the punk mouthed the word, *Beacon?*

Harlow nodded.

Show me where, the younger man breathed.

Harlow pointed to the back of his neck, and lowered his chin as the black-lacquered nails prodded the skin at the top of his spine. After a brief examination, the outlander grunted. When he waved in the wall's direction, the rusty gate began to clank inward.

"This way, mate," the punk said.

Chapter 15

His host, who'd given his name as Pavo, pounded on a metal door in a steamy alley. Harlow stood to one side, and chilled air blasted over him when the door released with a loud buzz. Inside the cramped chamber, a plexiglass wall separated them from a cantankerous-looking woman in surgical scrubs. The door slammed behind Harlow.

"Got a referral for the good doctor," Pavo said, jerking his thumb in Harlow's direction.

"No appointments without prior notice. The doctor's very particular on this point—"

"Yeah, I know. Why d'ya always have to argy-bargy with me on everything? Most places would be over the moon about a client drummin' up some new business."

The attendant studied Harlow. "What's he need done?"

"Just go and say that it's me, and say my mate's got an itch to be scratched." The look with which Pavo accompanied this cryptic phrase reinforced Harlow's ongoing commitment to silence.

After spearing Harlow with an appraising stare, the receptionist exited through a door on her side of the barrier. Pavo turned to a small row of lockers, shrugged off his jacket, and removed two nickel-plated semiautomatics from their shoulder holsters.

"Check your iron, mate," he said. "Speed things up a bit when the old bird gets back. They'll not have any metal the other side of this foyer, except for what they've already got themselves, special controlled for electromagneticism." The last word was pronounced with an extra syllable. "Knives, guns, boots, zippers and such—the scanners'll pick it right up."

Harlow removed his jacket, belt, and holster. Then came his wedding band; a heavy pang of guilt bit into him, but he couldn't allow himself to process that now. He kicked off his boots, and examined his tactical cargo pants. The assorted side pockets were closed with velcro, and the fly's zipper was some sort of heavy polymer. The garment had been designed to pass through the sensitive security at spaceports; he was glad of it, unsure how he would have handled a proper introduction to a surgeon while wearing boxer shorts.

While he was piling his things into a locker, the attendant returned.

"She's agreed to the consultation," their host said in a bored voice. "Metal-free environment. Remove all weapons, jewelry, and garments with zippers, grommets…"

While the receptionist droned on, Harlow's hand froze inside the locker. *She* had agreed to the consultation. Female doctors weren't uncommon by any means, but what if…? The secrecy, the security… this clinic was a hideout in its own right.

He wrapped his fingers around his knife. The zirconium oxide blade was folded into the ceramic handle; neither would register on a metal detector. He covered the weapon with his hand as much as possible while slipping it back into his left hip pocket—the side that faced the corner of the room, blocked from view. Then he looked back to the reception area: the woman was watching him and Pavo, but didn't seem to have seen Harlow conceal the knife.

"Ready?" she asked.

"What about…?" he pointed to the back of his neck while stepping into the plexiglass chamber.

"If it's what I think it is, the implant uses a silicon-germanium alloy. Metal-free, low-voltage and high-frequency. The point is that the carrier doesn't know it's there, so if the device were able to set off a metal detector, that would be detrimental."

"Is it okay for us to talk about this?"

"We're scrambling the frequency. This building is like a giant Farraday cage—we want to stay off the grid as much as possible."

Yes, and I think I know why...

"I guess you're prepared for everything," Harlow said.

A sharp blast of air made him jump. Gusts of wind buffeted him, and he nearly lost his balance. He planted his feet as best as his thick socks would allow. When the torrent died, Harlow exited the enclosure, hoping the attendant wouldn't insist on a pat-down.

When she motioned for him to wait by the door before turning to Pavo, Harlow suppressed a sigh of relief. He still didn't have a plan for exactly why he'd smuggled a knife in—could he actually kill Vulpecula, if she was here? Didn't he need her—and didn't *Carina* need her? This brought a lump into his throat; he swallowed hard, but didn't push the thought of his daughter from his mind.

Keep her with you. You've got to make it back to her.

Pavo joined him on the other side of the decon chamber, and gestured for him to proceed. "Straight down the hall," he said.

The place was like a cross between a hospital and a bunker, Harlow observed as he paced the length of the hallway. The clinic was weighted with a mix of oppression and sterility. Ambient sounds were muffled, and there were no signs; it was difficult to tell how big the facility was, or which doors might lead to where.

Pavo shoved open a set of double doors, guiding him into a spacious room stocked with laboratory equipment. Harlow took in the white counters and cabinets housing esoteric instruments, the large operating table, the doctors clustered around a holoscreen that displayed three-dimensional graphs and images.

One doctor stood alone near a countertop across the room. Even before she turned to face him, Harlow's blood went cold. He'd steeled himself to look into those dark eyes without betraying himself, but their quiet ferocity gave him pause all the same. He recovered, though, and crossed the room to greet her.

"Welcome," Vulpecula said, offering a gripping handshake. "I don't typically find it necessary to ask for the names of my patients, but since yours is stitched onto your uniform, I assume it's safe for me to call you 'Harlow.'"

He nodded. There was no hiding his identity as a Protectorate officer, or hers as a wanted fugitive. Vulpecula's compelling face was etched into the memory of every law-enforcement officer in the territory. Seeing her in person, his mind threatened to crack. How could he have prepared for this? Here before him was the woman responsible for infecting his precious daughter with some demented virus; even hearing his own name escape her lips was an insufferable blasphemy.

"Good to meet you, doctor," he forced himself to say. "I believe you know why I've come to you."

"The biochip implanted beneath your skin allows the UCO to track your movements and communicate with you remotely. Since you've decided to part ways with them, it'll have to come out immediately."

Harlow shuddered at the thought of resigning himself to this mad-woman's surgical implements. He recalled Tainer's voice: *Vulpecula launched another attack. A lot of people lined up for Conscription got dosed with the Agent.*

"It's a simple procedure, right?" he asked.

"Yes. I can have it out in no time, and you'll be enjoying your new life before you know it." Her smile was thin and self-congratulatory.

A new life. It was too much. Was this what she'd say to the people she'd infected? Would she dose him with the Agent during the procedure, and expect his thanks afterward? His life was in shambles; no operation could give him a new one.

Carina, running to meet him at the door. His wonderful daughter, smoothing his tie with careful little hands.

His left hand shot to his pocket. Before Vulpecula could see what he was doing, he'd taken a step closer to her, flicked the knife open, and pressed the blade to her throat. He grabbed her shoulder with his right hand, forcing her back against the counter.

"Neither of us gets to have a new life," he growled.

"What do you think you're—" Pavo began.

"Shut up," Harlow barked. "The antidote for the Perseus Agent—there's got to be one. I want it."

He stared into the doctor's vulturine eyes. The dark orbs blazed, angry and fearless. Harlow pushed the blade harder against her windpipe. The skin felt leathery and tough somehow, but he'd be able to slice it with enough pressure.

"Idiot," she hissed. "You'll never make it out of here. Even if you managed to kill me, you can't undo what I've done."

Harlow stole a glance to the sidelines. The other doctors clustered at the far end of the lab, not wishing to interfere; Pavo crept forward.

"Back off," Harlow said. "I mean it." He pressed harder, until a thin trickle of blood appeared at Vulpecula's throat. The punk rocker stayed put.

Then Harlow flinched as a needle pricked his skin. Vulpecula had grabbed an injection pistol from the counter and pierced the side of Harlow's neck. Her finger rested on the device's trigger.

"Going to infect me with the Agent?" he asked. "What's the point?"

"There's no pathogen cartridge in this; just an empty chamber," she said. "If I pull the trigger, you'll be injected with air, and die from a pulmonary embolism."

"Not before I take you with me. Give me the antidote—it's the only way we both walk out of here."

"Let's say there *was* one—and I'm not saying there is," Vulpecula said. "It won't do you any good. By the time the UCO synthesizes enough of it for the whole populace, I'll have developed a new strain. I have too much of a headstart on you, and I'll always be one step ahead."

"I'm not giving it to the UCO. I don't need enough for the whole Human race...just enough for one person." The needle in the side of his neck burned with tension; he kept his own muscles taut. If he heard the *snap* of the injection pistol slamming home, he'd draw the blade across her throat with all his might.

"One person?" Vulpecula asked. "What one person?"

It didn't matter if he told her; Harlow found that he actually wanted Vulpecula to know the reason she was about to die. "My daughter was infected in your attack on the city this morning."

Her eyes narrowed. "What attack? I didn't do anything this morning."

Harlow shivered; sweat dripped into his eyes. "Don't lie to me."

"I'm about to kill you," Vulpecula spat. "So there's no reason to lie to you. I didn't attack the city."

Harlow swallowed hard. Tainer had lied, then...and he couldn't process why at the moment. Maybe Carina hadn't been exposed to the Agent. Or maybe she wasn't beyond help. His mind raced, adjusting to the unfolding catastrophe he'd dived into.

"You'd have had some kind of insurance policy if there were side effects that outweighed the intended ones," he said. "You're cold, but not as cruel as the Greys."

She held still: blade to her throat, needle in his neck. Was she about to pull the device's trigger?

"It's not an *antidote*, but I have an enzyme that would confound the Agent's progress," she finally said.

Harlow eased the pressure of the blade by just a bit, allowing her to speak more easily. Still, he kept her back against the countertop. Neither of them could move without considerable risk.

"Keep talking."

"I never tested the Agent on children, but they'd have been naturally resilient to it," the doctor continued.

"What do you mean? Could my daughter be infected, or not?"

"I'm not sure. The virus looks for the most efficient way to increase the body's myocyte and osteocyte output. It would be sidelined by the continuous muscle and bone growth already present in a healthy young person. The Human body wasn't designed to reach maturity as fast as other species, so a small child can't support the kind of muscular structure that the Agent would bestow on an adult."

"Get to the point," Harlow said. "What if she *was* exposed? What would happen?"

"Maybe nothing," Vulpecula shrugged. "Or maybe her muscle and bone growth would go into overdrive, at a metabolically unsustainable rate. She could become severely disabled, or experience an accelerated growth spurt. It's hard to say."

"But the enzyme you have would block the virus's antigens from identifying which cells to attach themselves to," Harlow guessed, recalling Tainer's summary at the UCO meeting two days before.

"That's right. I needed insurance against the possibility that the Agent wouldn't stop after reaching peak efficiency."

"Give it to me, and I walk," Harlow said. "Pure and simple."

The doctor sneered. "It's anything but simple. I already told you, you can't walk out of here—if for no other reason than the tracking device you have embedded. It'll recover its connection and transmit your location to the UCO as soon as you're out of the building. My lab will get raided before sundown."

"Then take out the Beacon and destroy it."

"Oh, I will. But I still don't see a reason to leave you alive when I do," she said.

Harlow stifled a breath. It was time to play his trump card.

"I'm your only chance at getting Auriga back alive," he said.

She glared. Not the reaction he'd hoped for.

When she spoke, the words dripped with menace. "He's a dead man, and so are you."

"Wait!" a new voice shouted.

Harlow couldn't turn to look, but the young woman who'd called out spoke again. "He's right—Auriga mentioned him to me."

When the teenage girl with the feathery blonde hair crossed into his peripheral vision, Harlow recognized the oval face and solemn gray eyes. Lyra Vaughn, another UCO fugitive. Was it surprising that she associated with the doctor? In a way, no.

"You wanted me to reach out to Auriga, and I managed to speak with him psionically," Lyra said to the doctor. "Harlow's been visiting him. He wanted help finding you."

Vulpecula's unyielding gaze still bored into Harlow's eyes.

"Both of you, just back away and let's talk about this," Lyra said in a soothing voice.

"Don't try to manipulate me," the doctor snapped.

"Both of you can still get what you want," Lyra continued. "We've all lost someone. We can still work together and save our loved ones."

Harlow wanted to pull his knife back, but the stalemate held him at bay. He'd impulsively hit a nerve with the doctor, and she was now a coiled snake.

Long moments passed as he sweated, unable to advance or retreat.

Then, Vulpecula spoke. "I want Auriga back, but I can't risk it. Breaking a condemned man out of prison is almost impossible."

"Not with my help," Harlow said. "Lyra's right. We can do this."

"Simply disabling the biochip in your body would probably still cause a response from the UCO," Vulpecula said. "Even though we've scrambled its signals, it's probably still transmitted your last known location, before you entered the lab, as somewhere inside Flagstaff."

"Then we have to tamper with it, not just disable it," Harlow said. "Make it report false information."

Vulpecula snorted, and rolled her eyes. "It's Grey technology. I'm a surgeon for Human bodies, not for alien computers."

"So you need someone like me," a raspy, robotic voice pronounced.

Vulpecula gasped, and withdrew the needle from Harlow's neck. When Harlow turned, lowering his knife, Lyra had spun towards the laboratory's entrance as well.

They all stared as the young man, dressed in cargo pants and combat boots, entered the room. The left sleeve of his black sweater, rolled up to the elbow, revealed a glowing cybercomputer.

"Orion," Lyra whispered, her face erupting into joy.

She ran for him, but when the double doors swung a second time, she stopped in her tracks, and stifled a shriek.

An imposing Grey, purple-robed and with a bulbous heart-shaped head, stepped into the room behind Orion.

Pyxis, the alien commander.

Chapter 16

"When we crashed the saucer, it came down in eastern Canada—a place called Rankin Inlet, near the Hudson Bay," Orion said.

"Yes, I know," said Lyra. "Every time I tried to contact you through the astral plane, Pyxis fought me off. But the last time, I finally managed to steal a glimpse of where you both were. I'd been trying to get to you, but Pavo and Vulpecula didn't make it easy."

They were gathered in a wide semicircle of chairs in the laboratory: Orion, Lyra, Harlow, Pavo, and the doctor. Pyxis, eschewing the Human furniture, stood nearby, a glower etched beneath its wide, wrinkled brow.

"I did say I was sorry about kidnapping you," Pavo cut in. "I was after that grand payday, for sure, but I'm making it right now."

"I understand," Lyra said. "It ended up being a good thing that I came to Vulpecula's lab."

Orion eyed the punk-rocker with suspicion, but continued his story. "I wasn't hurt in the crash; the Vinculum had teleported me, you, and Pyxis off the ship just before impact. But I was still in trouble; you were far away, and Pyxis and I were much closer together. Most of the Greys had abandoned ship, and were landing in escape pods all around. Humans from the nearby village were coming to investigate the crash, too. When we all joined up, though, Pyxis and the Greys

150

didn't attack."

"The only danger you were ever in was that of your own making," Pyxis sneered. "I told you that on the ship. I've only ever wanted what is best for your species."

Vulpecula's scowl rivaled that of the alien leader. Her angry eyes flashed, but she said nothing.

"There was already a small group of Greys living with the villagers," Orion said. "They'd shared their technology with the Humans. It was nothing like New Zaragosa or the other Great Cities in terms of actual advancement—but they were coexisting peacefully."

"Peacefully, as long as the Humans didn't object to being sliced up and used in experimental surgeries," Lyra guessed.

"No, there was nothing like that. Those Greys didn't harvest or abduct anyone. They were more interested in studying Human culture."

"Like the aliens from a long time ago, who made contact with mankind in ancient times," Harlow said.

"That's right," Orion answered. "I started using scavenged parts from the crashed ship to build a small flying saucer, hoping that I could return here...and as they saw what I was doing, they actually helped me."

"Crikey," Pavo said. "You've got your own saucer?"

"It's parked on the roof. That's how Pyxis and I got here."

Silence and shock from the assembled Humans. Orion continued.

"And imagine my surprise when I found out that Pyxis and Eridanus—the new Grey commander for New Zaragosa—don't exactly see eye-to-eye on a lot of things."

Once again, Harlow recalled the chilling UCO meeting with the impassive Grey. "Eridanus introduced itself as a 'plenipotentiary,'" he said. "As in a diplomat who has full authority to act on behalf of a society's leaders."

151

"This is correct," Pyxis said. "Our home, a space station called Ios, has invested great authority in Eridanus."

"Your home is a *space station*, not a planet?" Pavo asked.

"Ios is a colossal city in space: the capital of this galaxy, and the seat of its Galactic Council," Pyxis said. "Many different peoples now live there, having expanded from their own home planets, but my species is the only one native to Ios."

"In my research, I found evidence that the Greys are an artificially-engineered life form," Vulpecula now spoke up, although with apparent distaste to be addressing the alien. "As in, whoever built this city of Ios probably also created you."

"This is correct," Pyxis answered. "When early explorers discovered Ios, they found the Greys isolated in cryostasis. Other than that, the entire station was deserted, in a state of security lockdown. Our makers were nowhere to be found. The explorers deliberated for a long time before awakening us...my ancestors, that is. Even I do not know how long ago this was."

"The term 'ancestors' seems a bit inaccurate," Vulpecula said. "Greys are asexual, and reproduce themselves in a lab, don't they? I'd imagine those circumstances are strictly controlled. You'd know exactly how many generations there have been since coming out of cryostasis. You'd probably even know who and what it was that put you there."

Pyxis wore an intense frown, and said nothing.

"We all know that the Greys don't like to share any information about themselves," Orion intervened. "We're very lucky to be getting this much, doctor. Let Pyxis tell us as much or as little as it wants."

"Strange to see you on friendly terms with this creature," she said. "That's all."

"The last time I was in your lab, you ordered Auriga to kill me," Orion shot back. "But I'm not pounding your face in. Are *we* on friendly terms?"

"I haven't forgotten," Vulpecula said. "But I said that only in order to protect the Perseus Agent, while it was in a vulnerable stage."

Orion balled a fist in anger, but thought twice, and relaxed his hand. Lyra quickly took it in her own.

"My species is secretive, and with good reason," Pyxis said. "I would be stripped of my authority for disclosing such information with you—if I hadn't been already, for losing the ship I commanded."

"You got a demotion when your flying saucer was blown up?" Pavo chuckled. "Tough break, mate. I guess some things do work the same with the Greys and the Humans."

Harlow's expression was sober, though. "I've had a similar experience, Pyxis. I was a high-ranking Protectorate officer until today. I had money, status, a future…but I was on the wrong side. Now I don't know where I stand."

"That doesn't make you special," Vulpecula said. "I walked away from a lucrative career with the UCO to uphold my own principles. And I did it without holding anyone at knifepoint."

"The difference between me and you is that I'm not throwing away the people who mean the most to me," Harlow said, his temper rising. "I still have a wife and daughter in danger, and I'm going back for them no matter what. I'm not leaving them for dead, like you did with Auriga."

Vulpecula set her mouth in a furious grimace, but did not speak.

"No one here is leaving anyone," Lyra said. "That's the point. That's why we're going to work together."

Trying to regain his composure, Harlow turned to Pyxis. "Orion mentioned that you'd had disagreements with Eridanus. Could you please elaborate on that?"

Pyxis stared at the semicircle of Humans, and took a few tentative paces back and forth while watching them. It was obviously debating on whether to proceed with further disclosure. Silence blanketed the laboratory until it spoke in its dry rasp.

"As you know, the Greys are very interested in the actions of other species," it said. "Before we ever visited the Humans, we poured our efforts into uplifting the Lacertas. By endorsing a species, we have always intended to speed its advancement in a variety of ways: intellectual, technological, cultural, and so on."

Harlow nodded, reflecting on the leaps in Human achievement that had been attributed to visitors from the stars.

Lyra looked fascinated, as well. "But we know that the Lacertas didn't turn out like you'd hoped. They weren't a successful project, and so the Greys abandoned them in favor of Humanity."

"Yes," Pyxis said. "The Terrans, as we have called your species, exhibited much greater potential."

"Potential for *what?*" Vulpecula asked. "The dissections, the implantations...the endless experiments. Building a super-species, or an army, whatever it is. What is it that you're trying to accomplish with us? It's time to finally have the truth."

Pyxis's mouth became a straight line, and then vanished. It wouldn't speak.

Harlow, though, agreed with Vulpecula for once. His knowledge of Human kinesics was worthless in dealing with Pyxis; its mannerisms and thought process were, in a word, *alien*. Harlow decided to take a risk. He leaned forward, going on the attack. "It has to do with Xenoplicity, doesn't it?"

The glistening black eyes captured him. Pyxis's expression was something Harlow could never have imagined.

"The Greys own this planet," Harlow pressed, knowing his attack had landed. "Which means they must have bought it from someone. The Xenoplicity Foundation—it's like a galactic real estate market, isn't it?"

After a moment's pause, Pyxis nodded once in acquiescence. "You know more than I had supposed."

"How can you own a planet?" Orion asked. "It's ridiculous."

"Not so ridiculous to me, mate," Pavo laughed. "Sounds like a bloody good idea. If I had the cash—"

"But the people that live there—you can't own them too. The Greys don't own us. They don't have the right to do what they've done."

"Yes and no," Pavo said. "We buy and sell land all the time, don't we? Anyone ever think about the animals that live on it? You may not own them, but what difference does it make? You can do as you please, because it means nothing to them. Animals never think about who owns the land they're walking on."

"This is accurate," Pyxis said. "A planet is salable as long as none of its native species have achieved a level of self-awareness that we call 'the convergence'."

"And what's that?" Harlow asked.

"Convergence is when a species becomes aware of other life in the galaxy, and when it makes attempts to integrate into that larger society," Pyxis said. "Most often, it happens when a species reaches a level of technological advancement that brings it into contact with galactic society. But sometimes, a convergence can be thrust upon a species without its own direct action."

"That sounds like what happened to us," Lyra said. "An alien invasion that changed the course of the entire species."

"The Terrans are still not recognized as post-convergent." It sounded like an insult, but Pyxis was only stating a fact.

"What would it take for that to happen?" Vulpecula asked.

"A meeting of the members of the Galactic Imperium, at the galaxy's capital." Pyxis turned cold eyes upon the doctor. "Such a thing does not happen lightly."

"And yet, you were working towards this," Harlow said.

"It would benefit the Greys to sponsor a lesser species."

"By raising their status in galactic society," Lyra said.

"Correct."

"Is this what you and Eridanus differed on?"

"Yes. We had a disagreement regarding the Terrans' proper place in the galaxy."

Harlow swallowed, and his mind reeled. The aliens—even the very one he was speaking to—had argued over the fate of mankind. Everything he'd done during his life, and the ground he was standing on, was up for debate.

"You wanted to lift us up for your own benefit, and Eridanus wanted to use us as shock troops against an emerging enemy," Harlow said. Ice rose up his spine as he spoke.

Pyxis looked at him, and Harlow needed no reply. He knew he'd revealed the truth.

"Neither of those is a very altruistic motive," Vulpecula mused.

Harlow let the comment slide. He'd not be drawn into a further debate with the doctor and her twisted sense of morality.

"You knew that Humanity would never reach the convergence if we're simply enslaved and thrown into battle for the Greys' benefit," Harlow continued. "You fear that the Greys will lose their political status in the galaxy if they're viewed as the harbingers of collapse for the species they sponsor—your failure in elevating the Lacertas has already cost you one strike, and you don't want to risk being proven wrong about mankind's potential, as well."

"Correct." The single word, spoken by Pyxis, was chilling.

Orion's gravelly voice broke the brief silence. "All of us can still work together for what we want, though."

Lyra shot him a worried look. "You're talking about working with the *Greys*? What happened up there in Canada?"

The scavenger had a faraway look in his eyes. "It's complicated. I didn't judge you for being here with Vulpecula when I got back. Is she any better than them?"

"That's different. I have to tell you—"

"Let's try to focus on one thing at a time," the doctor cut in. "Lyra, there's time for that later."

The girl's large gray eyes narrowed, but she nodded. "Okay, you're right."

Even if Lyra hadn't known by other means, Orion's face told her that he'd agree to come back to this, but wouldn't pursue it at the moment.

"Orion's right, too," Vulpecula said. "I think we should clear the air."

"You mean about how, the last time I saw you, you ordered Auriga to kill me?" Orion said.

"Yes." The doctor kept her hands folded neatly in her lap. "When I said that, I was trying to protect the Perseus Agent—something more valuable than any individual life, including my own. Now that it's been released, however, I have nothing to gain by killing you. I want you to know that that was a situational defense which won't be repeated. I'm sorry."

Orion suspected that the last two words were something the doctor didn't say often.

Pyxis had been looking at Vulpecula. Now it spoke, choosing its words with distaste. "I must concede something to you. Your designs, however displeasing to us, nonetheless show great promise for the future of the Terran species."

Harlow swung in his seat to view the alien. "You can't be saying what I think you're about to say."

Pyxis maintained its otherworldly gaze upon the doctor. "If Eridanus is able to move forward with its plans, the Terrans will become little more than a group of pawns to be exploited at its whim."

Vulpecula's demeanor was every bit as even as the alien's. "I fail to see how that's any different from your own intentions."

"You've exploited people for your own agenda, too," Orion accused.

Lyra studied Orion. It was the second time he had come to Pyxis's defense. How much influence had the alien been able to exert upon him while they were away? Troubled, she resolved to speak to him alone as soon as she could.

"My reasoning is sound," Pyxis said. "And our goals can align, if we so choose. We both oppose Eridanus—why not benefit from this? We have a better chance of removing it from power by cooperating with each other."

Lyra's brain pounded. The idea was outrageous, but as she looked to Harlow and then Vulpecula, they were clearly considering it. Orion had apparently already aligned with the former Grey leader, and Pavo was easiest of all to read.

"Can hardly wait for the fireworks to start," the bounty hunter said with a grin.

***

After the meeting, Lyra followed after Orion, but he was drawn into a pre-op consultation with the doctor and Harlow. The one who engaged her was the last person she wanted to see.

Pyxis approached her, its purple robes flowing behind it.

"I wish to speak with you," it said.

She shook her head. "You could have spoken with me at any time."

"True."

"You're orchestrating this whole thing," she accused, her anger rising. "I can't believe I'm the only one who sees it."

Two black mirrors looked back at her. "What do you see?"

"You're manipulating us, the same as you always have been."

It stared at her. "Do you mean Humans generally, or you and Orion in particular?"

"You know exactly what I mean." Lyra was so angry that she was close to crying, but she wouldn't let this monster taste her tears with its inky eyes. "I don't believe anything you've said about being opposed to Eridanus. You'll sell us out."

"That was not a deception. I oppose Eridanus, and your thoughts are important to me," it said.

She scoffed. "Don't even try to tell me that you care."

"I don't," Pyxis said. "But you're about to die. The thoughts and actions of someone who realizes that fact are quite important."

"So why didn't you tell Orion?" she asked. "By that logic, you'd know more about his inner motives if you told him his upgrades were fatal."

"Because he would blame me for that, and rightfully so," the alien answered. "I oversaw both of your operations."

She couldn't respond right away. Not with words. Her only reply was an inner vision of herself taking this creature apart, limb from limb.

"Besides," Pyxis said, "As far as knowing his secret motives, I have you for that. You were already about to tell him that you're both dying. You'll read from him, and like it or not, I'll read from you."

Her face burned with anger, and she hated it, knowing that her inner fire was a welcome warmth to this demon.

"How can you be so shameless?" she spat. "You know that I'll tell them they're being used, and they'll believe me."

"With you here, my capacity for deception is compromised," it said. "But I can achieve my goals with the truth. They already know my intentions, but I seek the betterment of both Terrans and Greys. That's all it should take for them to join me—and if you're as insightful as you seem, you'll do the same."

Lyra broke away, and ran through the clinic's sterile halls. She no longer wanted to cry—her unshed tears were gone, replaced by a simmering emptiness. She stormed through the doors of a small operating room, disturbing the gathered assembly of Vulpecula, Harlow, and Orion.

"Surgery is one half of our problem," Vulpecula was saying. "I can

159

help you access the biochip, but after that, you're on your own."

"That's fine. I'll be able to circumvent—" Orion answered, and broke off at Lyra's sudden arrival.

Vulpecula likewise gave up her prodding at the back of Harlow's neck, and turned to stare at the newcomer.

Lyra broke the awkward silence with quick strides. "Come with me," she said, grabbing Orion's hand.

"Lyra, I thought we agreed—" Vulpecula began, but Lyra ignored her, all but pulling Orion from the room.

Outside, the hallway was empty, and she took him around the corner for more privacy. Again, stillness like the vacuum of space had hollowed her insides. In Orion's presence, the quiet was chilling. He didn't breathe, after all. Finally alone with him, her own breath caught, and she tried to begin just one of the things she had to say.

We're going to die. Our operations weren't sustainable. I don't trust Pyxis, or Vulpecula, or that Protectorate officer. Just you. But there's even something different about you, now.

She finally drew a breath, but it was shallow, weak. The words wouldn't come.

"Are you in there, Orion?" she whispered at last.

"Yes," he said in a raspy monotone. "Of course I am."

His eyes still had the faraway look she'd seen during the conference, though.

"What did you want to tell me?" he asked.

A long moment passed, and she touched her hand to his cheek. "I wanted to tell you that I promised you another kiss," she said.

She leaned in, and pressed her lips to his. But there was no life, no spark. Only a dull, wooden contact between their mouths. Lyra stepped back, despair overtaking her, and he looked at her with a sad little smile. His thin lips and muted aspect reminded her of an expression she'd seen so often on Pyxis's face.

Chapter 17

"Try to remain calm, and clear your mind. The chip is resetting its neurologic algorithms, and needs to establish a baseline in your brain wave patterns."

Easy for you to say, Harlow thought. *You have no idea how this feels.*

It was ironic that the biochip's original implantation, carried out without his knowledge or consent, didn't seem as invasive a process as what he'd just undergone. Of course, that was because he had no memory of it happening. But the fiery flashes of Vulpecula's scalpel, and her teenage assistant's cybernetic ministrations, promised to stay with him until his dying day.

It wasn't just the pain. They'd all agreed that putting Harlow under complete anesthesia was best avoided, and the local painkiller was taking *some* of the bite out of the incision. In a few days, that part would be over. But for the rest of his life, Harlow would live with the knowledge that his brain was somehow, somewhere, jacked into some*thing*. Alien technology inside his body was not an idea he could ever get used to.

Haven't you ever wanted to be more than one man?

Harlow studied Orion, who in turn concentrated on his cybercomputer's display. The young man was integrated with machinery at a level that left Harlow questioning the scavenger's Humanity. Orion had experienced deeper, more invasive trauma, and at a younger age.

At least Harlow had chosen to join the Protectorate…and chosen to leave it. It was inescapable that he'd been a part, however small, of what had happened to Orion—and this left Harlow questioning his *own* Humanity. Then he wondered if what he thought was empathy could in fact be some form of symbiosis with the scavenger's software. The idea made him shudder.

Sharing his brain with another Human being was somehow more frightening than sharing it with an alien.

"We're almost done," Orion croaked. "Just another minute."

Shocks and ripples crawled along Harlow's body. He willed himself to stay on the operating table, although it was torturous. Shadowy figures moved above him, exchanging bizarre utensils. He tried to focus.

At least it seemed he had reached a grudging truce with Vulpecula—at any rate, they'd stopped threatening to kill each other. Harlow fully intended to keep his promise to Auriga, as well: the doctor would remain a free woman for as long as he could help it.

But what of Auriga? Could Harlow make good on what he'd said to the doctor about getting him out? It seemed that Carina's salvation now depended on Auriga's—when Harlow returned to the city, it would be to rescue a hardened killer and an innocent child.

These might well be his final moments of sanity, before embarking on an irreversible course. And yet, Harlow felt that the path had been laid for him. What choice did he truly have?

"That should do it," came Orion's rasp. "Next, I want you to use the biochip to contact someone at the UCO. During the communication, I'll restructure the account to show a completely different GPS journey from the time you ended your last call, with, uh…Vivienne Tainer, several hours ago."

"You'll erase all evidence of his having come to Flagstaff?" Vulpecula asked.

"Yes. I'll take him north of the location of that call, instead—into what used to be the Navajo Nation. Not much is known about that area. There are still some sovereign territories around there, presumably with independent Native American people who have fought off the Lizzies and want to be left alone. It would be a believable place for Harlow to meet an informant, or to search for your hideout."

"If they find out the log's been tampered with, I go to prison," Harlow said. "I sure hope you know what you're doing."

"I know what I'm doing," Orion answered. "If they catch you, it won't be because of the digital logs. It'll be because they suspect you of lying if you act nervous and sketchy. Then they'll bring in a psionic to look into your memories, and you'll be in serious trouble. So worry about that, instead."

Harlow swallowed. His skills in uncovering deception in others would have to aid him in concealing the truth about himself. Was he a smooth enough liar? He thought so, but time would tell.

"When you're ready, we'll head to the roof to get a clear, unscrambled signal from outside this building. I'll come with you, and use my cybercomputer as a sort of VPN. Just make the call last at least a minute or two, and I'll handle the rest."

"Who do you want me to call? What should I say?" Harlow asked.

Orion shrugged. "That's up to you. Just make it believable."

And in an instant, Harlow knew who he'd need to contact on the Beacon.

***

If he wasn't already about to lose his mind, the sight of a flying saucer parked on the roof of Vulpecula's building threatened to unhinge his dwindling composure. It was perhaps fifteen meters across, and almost a miniature replica of the larger craft he was so familiar with as a resident of one of the Sanctuaries.

There were minor differences, though. Some of the metal was

scarred or burned in places, giving the craft a battered, veteran look. The contours of the craft and its tiny exterior components, while still sleek, were nowhere near as hypnotic as the awe-inspiring *Harvester* of New Zaragosa. Even so, knowing its origin, and the fact that it was built for Human use, instilled Harlow with an uneasy pride. One day, would men pilot such things to and from the spaceports of this world? And of other worlds?

Harlow sighed, trying to clear his mind for the dreaded task at hand.

"Let's get this over with," he said to Orion, who was standing by with his display.

His right hand found the biochip, now under a freshly bandaged incision at the nape of his neck. Thumping it twice with his finger brought a sharp pain from the tender flesh, but the resulting activation, a thick purr upward through his brain stem, was even more uncomfortable.

"Beacon, call Cass Harlow," he said.

Connecting, it whispered in return.

Until that moment he had merely suspected that his wife had a similar biochip installed. What he had yet to confirm—but strongly believed, all the same—was that the Greys had bestowed their gift only this morning, during her conscription.

A tick, and then he still wasn't ready for her voice in his mind. "Honey, is that you?"

"Yes," he mumbled, his voice catching. Then, stronger: "Hi, Cass. I thought maybe I could be the first to talk to you on the Beacon."

"How sweet! Did you know they were installing one for me?" Her tone was light, but each word pulled him down like the gravity of a hundred planets.

"Not for sure, but it seemed plausible."

"Always the Detective," she laughed. "I bet you weren't surprised about my conscription either, but I sure was. What a privilege!"

"What was it like? Tell me about it." It twisted the knife, but he had to know the moment when his dear wife, his partner and best friend, had been taken away from him.

"Oh, it's amazing. They beam you on board the ship—it just takes a second, you know, and everything's already prepared for you. I thought there might be a lot of paperwork or something to slog through, but that's not how they do it up here. Just one preliminary scan, and they get right to work. I'm in the post-op room now, still on the ship."

Harlow maintained his spirit: what he hoped sounded like cheerful interest and pride. "So, a Beacon installed. And was there anything else they did?"

"Oh, yes. Why, I feel like a new woman! But never mind me; there's time for all that later. Where are you now, honey?"

Orion, his eyes on the computer display, nodded at the question. The cybernetic seemed able to follow the conversation somehow, despite Cass's voice being conveyed into Harlow's brain. *Go with what I mentioned before*, he seemed to be coaching.

"Well, of course I can't tell you all the details," Harlow answered, "but I'm heading off the beaten path, into unknown territory. Listen, Cass: is Carina all right? Where is she?"

"Oh, she's fine," Cass said. "She's with the Tainer family. And about your mission: this might sound wild, but I've been raised several levels in security clearance. You can actually tell me the details of anything you have going on. What's your destination, exactly?"

"Something Vivienne said this morning about Carina made me uneasy," Harlow tried leading the conversation back. "Something about an attack. Are you absolutely sure everything is all right?"

"I said she's fine. Don't worry about Carina," Cass said, rather sharply. Then, gentler but with persistence: "Where do you think Vulpecula's safe house is? One of the old Navajo reservations? Are you heading there now?"

Harlow was in danger of losing control of the exchange. Trying to regroup and buy time, he cleared his throat and answered, "Really, I think I should wait until I get official notice of the security clearance before I discuss—"

"I told you, I have clearance," she broke in. "Do you think I'd lie about something like that? There are consequences for lying, you know."

Orion's mouth twisted, and he made adjustments on his cybercomputer.

"I didn't say anything about lying," Harlow said evenly. It was madness, sparring with his wife like a random interrogation subject. "It's just that this is so sensitive. One wrong move, and I won't get another chance at Vulpecula. I've got to be careful, and do this on my own a little longer."

That seemed to work a little. "Okay. I understand," she said. "But by the same token, I can help more than you might realize. Since you've only got the one shot, we have to move fast with whatever you uncover. Faster than you can do on your own. You need to tell me the moment you have something to report. We're all counting on you."

Feeling like he was now married to Findley van de Kamp, Harlow promised frequent progress reports, and disconnected.

"Good job," Orion said. "I got the logs altered. I've also changed the passive audit so it's no longer listening to everything you say and do. I've replaced that with a loop of background noise, feedback, and patches from previous conversations you've had over the past three years. It won't fool them forever, but it'll look normal until you do something crazy enough to put you under scrutiny."

Like breaking Auriga out of prison, Harlow thought. His cover would be already blown by that time, so nothing relating to the tampered Beacon could further incriminate him.

"So they don't listen in regularly? Just when there's a good reason?" he asked.

"Basically, yes. Someone else was monitoring that communication with Cass just now—probably a Grey technician on the *Harvester*—but I'm sure it was routine, to see that the newly-installed Beacon was performing."

For his part, Harlow didn't know whether the discussion had gone well or not. It was so hard to judge a simple discourse with Cass, and he was not a man who was used to lying to his wife.

I feel like a new woman, she'd said. Why was a city planner suddenly discussing details of a manhunt with a Protectorate Detective?

"I can't even process what just happened," he said.

"The Greys adapt quickly," Orion said. "We need to do the same. Let's get back down to the others."

***

Vulpecula was speaking to Lyra in the lab when Harlow and Orion rejoined them. Harlow sensed a somber conversation between the doctor and the psionic; of course, very little of what went on here could be described as lighthearted.

Pyxis stood several paces away, studying what looked like test results. Harlow couldn't tell if the habitual frown on the Grey's face was any more pronounced than usual.

An awkward silence enveloped the room after Orion reported their successful sabotage using the Beacon. Lyra and Vulpecula nodded, each seeming to wait for the other to speak; Pyxis merely offered a weighty stare.

Finally, Vulpecula drew a cylinder from the pocket of her lab coat. "Harlow, this is for you," she said, holding it out to him.

The Detective examined the object: a few milliliters of hazy liquid inside a curious plunger. He raised an eyebrow, holding it to the light.

"A token of good faith," the doctor said. "It's a single dose of the inoculator enzyme we talked about."

Harlow's fist closed around the vial, feeling its thickness, its latent potential.

"I want to repeat what I said before: any event in New Zaragosa this morning, if there even was one, was not planned and authorized by me," she said. "If your daughter is in jeopardy, it's because the UCO is using her as a bargaining chip to control you. Nevertheless, I believe she could be in some danger, and you'd better administer that enzyme to her as soon as you can."

"So you are planning another attack, then." Harlow accused. "What about other peoples' children?"

"Children aren't being targeted," Vulpecula said. "Take the spaceport, for example: that would be a logical place to plan an action with an airborne virus. There were no children present—the facility had been open less than a week, and all commissioned flights had to do with official city business. Dignitaries, military personnel—high profile targets. Nobody is flying their kids to the beach for vacation."

Harlow rolled his eyes, but conceded that she was right.

"As far as planning another action..." she continued, pointedly avoiding the word *attack*, "I'll have operatives in the right place when the time comes. That's all I'll say. I know you're going back, but do so at your own risk."

"Of course I'm going back," Harlow answered. "But as far as I know, the city really is quarantined. I don't know how I can get in."

At this, Pavo spoke up. "Where there's a will, there's a way, mate. I'll pose as your informant, the reason you came all the way out here. Someone who knows a bit about the good doctor. They can't turn that down, can they? They'll have to let us in, and me and you can do what needs doing."

Vulpecula gave the bounty hunter a sharp look. "Just make sure you don't actually give them any information. I'm not ready to abandon this lab yet."

"No wuckas."

Harlow thought it over. "Are you sure? This is going to put you at considerable risk. I can't guarantee your safety. They could even use aggressive tactics, against my recommendations; they're desperate to find Vulpecula."

Pavo shrugged. "We can't guarantee anyone's safety. And they've hardly got a chance of getting anything from me against my will. Giving the UCO a false lead can buy you a few extra days here—which would be quite a help, am I right, boss?"

The doctor nodded. "They're bound to find this place sooner or later, but pushing that certainty back by another three or four days is all I need."

"I'll take my pay up front this time, you don't mind," Pavo's tone was sly. "With a bit extra for hazard pay."

Harlow raised his eyebrows at the uncharacteristic smile on Vulpecula's face.

"Good. We can leave tonight," Orion said, but Lyra turned sad eyes to him, and the doctor's smile vanished.

"I'm afraid the two of you need to stay here," Vulpecula corrected him. "I'll have to tell you why I need that additional time."

Chapter 18

The midnight desert was cold and dark, and for each mile the snarling Jeep devoured, hundreds more lay ahead. They'd slept a few hours before getting back on the road. Harlow had hot coffee and plenty of gas; these two things were all that contributed to any sort of peace of mind. He'd reinstalled the convertible soft top, but the whistling wind and the rumbling engine seemed to inhibit conversation.

Harlow stole a glance at his passenger. In the gloom, the colors of Pavo's twin rooster-comb tufts of hair weren't recognizable, but the punk rocker seemed to be in a rare pensive mood.

Harlow was trapped with uneasy thoughts. The bounty hunter had come up with the plan to return to New Zaragosa awfully quickly; Harlow would be a fool to believe there was no ulterior motive.

What could Pavo—and by extension, Vulpecula—want, in addition to breaking Auriga out of prison? The answer seemed obvious: the bounty hunter had to be one of the "operatives" the doctor had mentioned. He was surely planning for another attack involving the Agent, like the one Harlow had thwarted at the spaceport.

He didn't want to dig too deep and be shut down, but Pavo was a potential wealth of information and was separated from his secretive boss. A journey by car, over the course of several hours, required little effort get to get most people to open up.

"I'd like to ask you a personal question," Harlow said. This tactic could put some people on their guard, but Harlow was betting that the colorful young man enjoyed talking about himself, and would be intrigued by such an opener.

Pavo turned from the passenger window and lifted a barbell-laced eyebrow in his direction.

"Have you been administered a dose of the Perseus Agent?" Harlow asked. Again, as with Auriga, he avoided the words "infected" or "virus".

A chuckle in response, and Pavo turned back to the window. It wasn't what Harlow expected, but he had to continue, even if it meant going out on a limb.

"I'm sorry if this is a private topic," Harlow continued. "I was just wondering if you'd found it to have such a positive effect on yourself that you were willing to share it with other people."

"A bloody weird way to ask for a dose," Pavo said. "You sound like you're asking for a hit of street candy."

"No, I don't mean for myself," Harlow said. "I mean: when we get to the city, do you know exactly what's going to happen to the people you give the Agent to?"

"I think you already know what my orders are," Pavo said. "Only give it to them that wants it. No children. Whoever takes it knows the risk and the rewards, and whatever happens, happens. There ain't no sure things in life, mate."

"You're certainly right there." Harlow thought of the changes in his own situation from a scant week ago, and then pushed those thoughts from his mind. "It just seems you'd be better off targeting people who are dissatisfied with the current arrangement with the Greys, so why go to the city? Why not offer it to outlanders?"

"Outlanders live in small groups, and want to be left alone. They're armed to the teeth, and can take care of themselves. They're satisfied, humble as they are, and ain't gonna trust a bloke showing up on their doorstep with a pack of syringes and a lot of lofty promises. But you take a bloke who's slaving away at a desk or a construction site, year after year for no reason at all, and give him a chance to be more than what he is? Vassals understand what climbing the ladder is about. They lose their Humanity while they're working for aliens. Being Human ain't no special treat for them—they know there's more to be had."

"So you're betting on a conflict simmering under the surface. Like a virus that's already building inside its host."

"Ain't you a clever one. The way I see it, the current conflict between the Humans and the Greys amounts to a war on the technological front," Pavo said. "It ain't a straight fight—they don't want that. They're using nanotechnology to change our species, and Vulpecula's using viral tech to do the same thing."

Harlow thought again of his eerie conversation with Cass earlier that day. Had she acquired 'gifts' similar to Strughold's? How different would she be when he next saw her? Could what the Greys had done possibly be undone?

"I believe you're right," he said to Pavo. "Being a normal Human isn't enough to make a difference anymore. The psionics, bionics, cybernetics...the ones exposed to Vulpecula's virus...those are the people who will decide this conflict. Whoever perfects not only the technology to create supermen, but also overcoming the public relations obstacles involved in doing so, is going to prevail."

"Right-o. It was all bombs and bullets when we took on the Lizzies, but this time the Human body *itself* is the battlefield where the struggle unfolds." Pavo's eyes glittered, ever so briefly, in the dark. "You either dose up, go under the knife, or for God's sake stay out of the way."

Haven't you ever wanted to be more than one man?

Point taken, Harlow thought. After spending so much time with augmented individuals over the past few weeks, he'd become strikingly aware of his own inadequacy. He pushed the pedal further, hammering the Jeep down the black highway.

***

From out of the night they came. First, a ghostly light in Harlow's rear view mirror. His first thought was of slender alien abductors, but his breath quickened as the pinpoint separated into a set of headlights, faint but gaining rapidly. Far ahead, another set of lamps winked on: a vehicle squarely in the road, flashing its high beams, signaling him to stop.

"*Banditos,*" Harlow said.

"At least it ain't Lizzies," Pavo sighed. "I hope they never learn to drive cars."

Harlow considered his options. It was an effective, if simple, ambush: if he sped up to outdistance the pursuers, the highwaymen up ahead would open fire, knowing he wouldn't stop at their roadblock. Ramming his way through would likely end in catastrophe; whatever they had prepared in front of him would be designed to easily stop a single unarmored vehicle. Likewise, stopping the Jeep would put them in the middle of a confrontation against what he could assume were drastically uneven odds.

Of course, he could turn the Jeep off-road and take to the desert; but what could he expect, bouncing along in rough terrain at high speed in the middle of the night? A single boulder would end the pursuit even if it didn't injure him and destroy his transportation in the process.

Wrecking the Jeep, whether at the roadblock or in the wilderness, would put him and Pavo on foot in the middle of the desert, waiting to see whether the Lacertas would get them before heat and thirst did.

Harlow eased off the gas. They'd have to take their chances with the outlaws and trust that they'd at least have their lives and a working vehicle when it was over.

Pavo didn't ask questions. Reaching into the backseat, he retrieved Harlow's carbine, racked the bolt, and passed it to the Detective.

173

"I'll see if they can be reasoned with," the punk rocker said. "If not, shoot their headlights first. Those high beams make it easy for them to see *us* and hard for us to see *them*."

Harlow stopped the Jeep a dozen meters before the blockade: a massive pickup truck flanked by small concrete barriers. Someone in the cab trained a blinding spotlight on them as Pavo swung the passenger door open, planting his boots on the pavement and raising his hands in the air. Harlow opened his own door, but remained sheltered in the driver's seat with the rifle in hand.

Walking to the front of the Jeep, Pavo called out, "Just passing through!"

Behind them, the pursuing vehicle rumbled up to the Jeep's bumper. Doors slammed, and a sunburned ruffian with a black bandana pulled down almost over his shifty eyes approached Pavo.

"There ain't no 'passing through'. It ain't your road. You're in Carnicero territory."

"I see," the Australian said. "Well, no reason we can't be chums here. How much is the toll?"

The gangbanger spat a brown streak of tobacco juice on Pavo's boots.

"Twenty-five thousand caps," Pavo said, smiling.

"Where do you think you are, a shopping mall? That don't count as money out here. We want the Jeep."

"Hard bargain, mate. Fifty thousand it is." Pavo held out his palm, offering two black capchits. The other man struck them into the dust.

"You want to play games with me?" he moved closer, flicking a switchblade open. Its tip sparkled only a centimeter away from Pavo's throat.

"That's a crackerjack idea," Pavo said, the smile never leaving his face. He snatched with a blur so fast that Harlow's eyes could barely register, and in the next instant, the switchblade was in Pavo's hand.

"How 'bout a round of Pinfinger?" With the criminal aghast, Pavo turned to the Jeep's hood and slammed his left hand down on the hot metal, fingers splayed. His right held the knife.

"You know how it goes, don'tcha? If I win, I go my merry way. And if you win—well, I go my merry way, but only driving a pair of Carhartts instead."

The Carnicero sported a yellow-toothed grin. "You first, *imbécil.*"

With no more words, Pavo began to stab the knife between his fingers, alternating back to the space next to his thumb after every stroke. *One-two-one-three-one-four-one-five*, and back in reverse order. The jabs fell with hypnotizing regularity, perforating the Jeep's hood with the smooth ticking of a steel metronome.

One-two-one-three-one-four-one-five. One-five-one-four-one-three-one-two-one.

"Have a go," Pavo said, handing over the knife. His opponent mimicked the motions, stabbing between his own fingers with continuous ticks. Harlow counted the clicks, slow and steady; the bandana rose a fraction as the yellow smile broadened.

"Nice work, mate. Let's take it up a notch."

OneTwoOneThreeOneFourOneFive.

OneFiveOneFourOneThreeOneTwoOne.

Now the knife rose and fell with the hurried clatter of a typewriter....Pavo made two perilous orbits of his fingers, ending his turn in only a few seconds. The switchblade went back to his opponent.

OneTwoOneThreeOneFourOneFive.

OneFiveOneFourOneThreeOneTwoOne.

Pavo took the blade, and his plunging fist was a blur, puncturing the Jeep's hood over and over. His untouched hand stayed motionless in a minefield of gouges. The bully watched, his eyes wide, a shocked frown evaporating his previous cocky smile.

"Your turn," Pavo said, but the man hesitated.

"Come on, mate, let's kick it up a bit more. Have a go," the Aussie insisted.

Gingerly his opponent took the offered knife, but continued to stall. His eyes fixed on the sundered sheet of metal before them.

"Don't stop now," Pavo said. "We ain't got a winner yet. Tell you what, I'll help out."

Pavo's left hand seized the man's wrist and slammed it down on the hood. With his right, he grabbed his opponent's knife hand, driving it into the steel again and again. The already-breakneck speed doubled, tripled, quadrupled. Pavo's pace was blinding; he directed the blade around the man's splayed fingers with a machine-gun staccato that climbed to a steady, incessant drumming. It was impossible to distinguish the number of repetitions as Pavo stabbed in an endless circuit. Sweat poured down the other man's face; he dared not move his hand. He struggled even to breathe until his nerve broke and the yellow grimace finally failed to bite back a panicked scream.

"STOP! STOP!!!" he cried, and the drumming instantly ceased. Pavo released his wrist, and the bully clutched his hands against his chest in disbelief. The Jeep's hood was a mangled mess of holes, but without a drop of blood anywhere.

"You lose, mate," Pavo snickered. "Ta."

***

After one more stop for food and rest, it was early afternoon when they reached New Zaragosa. The sturdy, towering walls, once such a source of safety and pride to Harlow, now reminded him only of incarceration.

Even at first glance, it was apparent that emergency protocols were in effect. The West Point Parade gate was crawling with Protectorate men, their faces all but invisible behind rebreathers. Spiky orange barricades blocked the road.

Harlow brought the Jeep to a stop before a dozen black-clad commandos. Their leader, a short and stocky man with a single orange stripe on his helmet, approached the driver's side. Harlow was surprised to see an IFF flag identify the guard as "PONT BARNARD E"—apparently an adjustment Orion had made to his Beacon now brought selected visual displays to his attention. As a Pontiff, the man outranked Harlow by two steps.

"Security checkpoint," the point man said. "This city is under quarantine. You'll have to turn around."

Harlow displayed his ID, although it was redundant; a dozen men had already scanned his profile in the same way he'd identified Barnard. "I'm on a special assignment from the top," he said. "The Director and the head of HHWB are waiting for me and my passenger. He's an informant."

He couldn't see Barnard's face through the shielded helmet, but a slight tilt of the head was akin to raising an eyebrow. Name-dropping van de Kamp and Tainer like he'd just done was an impressive claim, and easy to disprove if Harlow was lying. "Stand by for confirmation," the Pontiff said.

Meanwhile, guards had assembled near the Jeep's passenger side. "Keep your hands where we can see them," one of them said to Pavo.

"Careful, he's augmented," another observed. Several men turned their battle rifles in the punk rocker's direction.

Pavo responded by resting an elbow on the windowsill and batting his eyelashes. Flashes of color cycled through his hair and irises. "Kind of you to notice," he purred. "Ain't this the red-carpet treatment."

Harlow tried not to wince. He'd warned the bounty hunter not to make trouble, but it seemed the gregarious young man could hardly help drawing attention to himself.

Barnard was a few paces away, speaking in a low voice to someone via his comlink. Harlow waited patiently; meanwhile, Pavo drummed his fingers, whistled, and mugged for the officers.

"Take it easy," Harlow murmured. "Remember what I told you: play it cool."

"Cool as a cuke, mate." Pavo responded with an aqua-green shade for his hair and eyes, but it did little to lessen the tension.

Finally Barnard returned to the Jeep's window. "Before you can proceed, we need to search you and the vehicle. Step outside, please."

Harlow complied. Having been on the other end of this procedure countless times, he made slow movements while exiting the vehicle. The passive scanners at the gate would have already registered his face, weapon, and vehicle; a Protectorate officer with special clearance would need only a few minutes to get through such a barricade, but the outlander was clearly a wild card.

Pavo popped out of the passenger side and produced a .357 semi-automatic from nowhere. "Be a chum and hold this for me," he said, thrusting it into a surprised guard's hands. Other officers corralled him against the side of the car and began pulling out various other weapons. Assorted knives, guns, and melee instruments formed a dangerous collection on the heavily-perforated hood of the Jeep.

One officer pulled a canvas bag from the floorboard of the passenger's compartment. Within was a zippered case containing dozens of small vials filled with a pale blue fluid. In an instant, the very air seemed to change: the Protectorate men doubled in number, swarming around the vehicle.

"That's a special medication for me," Pavo explained, almost laughing. "I turn into one sour bloke if my blood sugar ain't on the mark."

A guard examined the case with a handheld scanner. "Doesn't match the signature of the Perseus Agent, but it's certainly a virus," he said. "Biohazard level 2."

Protectorate men shoved Pavo up against the vehicle's hood. "Easy there," he said, pushing back. "Take it slow, hey? It's only our first date."

Idiot, Harlow thought. *You didn't have a better way to smuggle something in?*

Barnard grabbed Harlow's wrist, hustling him away from the tense standoff. Officers barked orders to Pavo, demanding his compliance, but the bounty hunter continued to shove against the mob, flashing a cocky grin while his hands were positioned behind his back. The loud *clack* of powerbinders closing on his wrists cut through the shouting, and still Pavo bashed at the officers with his shoulders and lashed out with vicious kicks.

"Get off me, ya mongrels!" Some of the men wheeled backward, falling prone as if kicked by a horse, but others rushed to take their place.

There was no point in Harlow intervening, even if he could have made a difference in the melee. He'd only blow his cover and go down alongside the impetuous youth. Instead, he affected a grimace born of distaste and contempt; acting wasn't difficult, given the sheer stupidity of Pavo's ill-considered attempt to enter the city with biological weapons.

More commandos rushed into the fray, wielding batons and cattle prods. Pavo dished out enough kicks to keep some of his attackers at bay, but with his arms pinioned, the fight was over quickly.

Harlow sneered as the young man collapsed beneath a sea of clubs and fists. *Great. Now what are we going to do?* Pavo was supposed to be helping him, but had made the situation so much worse.

"You'd better come with me," Barnard said. "We're going to need a full statement from you."

At least he'd gotten past the quarantine and through the gate.

***

In a small security office built into the city's outer wall, they seated themselves on benches bolted to the floor. A solid metal table stood between him and Barnard, and Harlow folded his hands, leaned slightly forward with his shoulders squared, and got ready to lie.

Fortunately, Harlow was well prepared for Barnard's questions; he had spent much of the travel time with Pavo getting their story straight. There was a fair amount of truth to the account, too: Pavo was a bounty hunter who'd had surgery at Vulpecula's augmentation clinic, and presumably knew her current whereabouts. The major fabrications were that Harlow had found the outlander in Navajo territory and convinced him to accompany Harlow back to New Zaragosa, where he would spill his guts in return for a sizeable reward.

Of course, the possibility of a reward in exchange for a red herring was out of the question now—not that that was what Pavo had really come here for. But being caught with biological agents exposed him as one of Vulpecula's operatives, and made Harlow's position so much messier. The young man was already on his way to prison, and one way or another, the UCO would get the information they were after.

Thankfully, Harlow wasn't being treated as a fellow conspirator. The debriefing conducted by the Pontiff wasn't hostile or accusatory; on the other hand, it was tedious, involving a multitude of questions about Pavo and the circumstances by which the Detective had found him.

Orion had warned him about close scrutiny of his Beacon logs; Harlow hoped that the falsified travel history, combined with a convincing and seamless testimony, would pass inspection well enough to keep the Protectorate from delving too deep. If they did, he'd have to blame whatever they found on a malfunctioning biochip—and they would want to repair it. That thought alone threatened to induce cold chills, but Harlow locked the anxiety away and doggedly finished the interview.

At last, Barnard had no more questions, and Harlow was able to ask a few of his own.

"How is my daughter? Can I see her?"

Barnard consulted a datapad, and ran a hand over his buzz-cut scalp.

"She's quite ill, but not to worry. I see she's in the private care of Dr. Tainer," he said. "No better place for her to be, after what happened."

Harlow's mouth was dry. The antidote Vulpecula had given him was in his pocket, but he couldn't explain how he had come to have it. "The doctor has my deepest thanks, but please inform her that I'll reassume custody of Carina now."

The stocky officer shook his head. "I'm afraid the quarantine stands. Releasing her to you might put you both in substantial danger."

He had to try again, even if his persistence was frowned upon. "Please," he said. "I haven't seen her in days. She's been without me and her mother both. It's hard enough that she's sick, but to be alone will make it worse—"

"She's not alone," Barnard corrected him. "As I've said, she's receiving personal care from the Secretary of Human Health and Well-Being. That's better than anything you or her mother can do for her. Don't let emotion blind you to that fact, Detective."

Arguing further was pointless; Harlow would get no further with this man. He was grateful when the Pontiff dismissed him. Out in the street, he fetched his rucksack from the Jeep, leaving the vehicle for the Protectorate to do with as they pleased, and set off walking alone up the Thoroughfare.

***

He could have hailed a hovercab, but instead chose the brief walk to the elevated train that serviced his condo. By the time he reached the platform, though, Harlow still had no solutions. The maglev train carried him through the city in a daze; he stared dumbly out the window at featureless buildings and faceless pedestrians that scurried between them. And above it all, the gargantuan saucer revolved, inexorable, like the action of Terra itself.

As the train slowed, approaching his building, Harlow spied an open, empty space nestled among the city streets. Well, not exactly empty:

a newly-cleared lot was being terraformed by a handful of bustling robots. This was to be the new Plaza brought about by Cass's city planning firm.

Harlow shuffled off the train and into the residential building. From the polished lobby, a glass elevator shot him into the sky, to an altitude adjacent with the brooding *Harvester*.

Cass wasn't home; he hadn't expected her to be. No grinning little girl clapped her hands at his arrival. The condo was dark and silent.

He shrugged the rucksack onto the floor by the entrance, and walked woodenly to the huge bay windows in the living room. He gazed down at the construction site, a hallowed ground assembled before his eyes by mechanical marvels.

Far below, a vacant pedestal stood, awaiting its trophy.

Chapter 19

Five days crawled by. Five days of anguish without Carina—no matter who Harlow called, where he went, what approach he took, her quarantine stayed in force.

All his skills and resources as a Detective turned up nothing: on the first day, he found that no hospital in the city had her registered as a patient. Vivienne Tainer responded to none of his calls or messages. When he showed up at her office in UCO headquarters, she wasn't there.

On the way home, he passed the Plaza; clouds of terraforming dust obscured the site, but a ghostly silhouette could be seen atop the pedestal's tall spire.

On the second day, after visiting the Health and Well-Being office in the morning and afternoon and finding Dr. Tainer on neither occasion, Harlow was sharply warned by security officers not to continue harassing the Secretary.

On the way home, he passed the Plaza; the dust was gone, and the dull gray statue of an alien towered over him.

Undeterred, he went to the Tainer residence on the third day, and was shocked to see the video screen next to the door answered by Circinus, his daughter's tutor. It scowled at him; the door remained closed.

"The prodigy is not here," it said. "Your actions are becoming unseemly."

"Tell me where my daughter is, or so help me, you'll be sorry," Harlow growled. It was a serious transgression to threaten this being, but Harlow was long past caring.

The video screen went dark. Harlow pounded on the door with his fists.

Cease your actions and leave at once, an automated message recited. *The Protectorate is being notified.*

"I *am* the Protectorate!" he screamed, knowing that it was barely even true anymore.

On the way home, he passed the Plaza; polished marble gleamed from decorative tiles and benches, and the flat titanium finish of the sentinel Grey statue returned no reflection. Its black eyes bored into him, and he almost felt physical holes in his body to match the ones in his spirit.

On the fourth day, Findley van de Kamp told him he wasn't looking well, and reminded him to be early and wear his dress uniform the next day, and he didn't know why until on the way home when he passed the Plaza and saw semicircular rows of seats facing the amphitheater stage and a banner congratulating Millard H. Strughold as the newly-appointed Illuminatus of the city.

On the fifth day, bleary-eyed, he stood at attention onstage with dignitaries and VIPs while Strughold blabbered at a legion of broadly smiling faces. The speech lasted nearly an hour, and Harlow barely heard any of it.

He scanned the crowd for Cass, but wasn't certain where she was; he'd only spoken to her once this week, when she'd contacted him on the Beacon to say she was alternating between sleeping at the office and periodically returning to the *Harvester*. With Carina away from home, there was little reason for Cass to be there, either. When Harlow asked about their daughter, she said it was important to focus on bringing

Vulpecula to justice.

Security had been heightened at the inauguration; the outdoor venue was patrolled by countless officers, their sharp eyes on the lookout for signs of an attack that Harlow knew would never come. To him, the Protectorate looked like foolish pawns, playing a children's game. He thought of Auriga's nickname for him, *caballero*, and smiled. *More effective than a pawn, versatile in movement, useful for offense at the beginning and defense in the middle of the game, and expendable near the end.* Was it indeed near the end of the game?

After the ceremony, he tried to corner Vivienne Tainer, but Strughold, van de Kamp, and Eridanus were speaking to her. He edged his way into the group.

"...some valuable information," the Director was saying, and turned at Harlow's approach. "Welcome, Detective," he smiled. "What a time to be alive, eh?"

Harlow could barely describe himself with that word. "Dr. Tainer, you've been keeping my daughter from me," he said with as much force as he could correctly apply in his present company.

"I'm afraid that's the point of a quarantine," she said with a sad smile. "But never fear. She's responding to our treatments. You'll see her again soon."

"And what treatments are those?" Harlow said. "I need to approve whatever's being done to her."

Eridanus spoke up, each syllable hollow and staccato, like a pebble thrown at Harlow. "The treatments have been designed and implemented by me, and the child's mother has given her full approval. I hope this alleviates your concerns."

It did no such thing.

***

Harlow checked his weapons at the front security office, and proceeded to the sallyport. A corrections officer with a Detective insignia similar to his own accompanied him.

"He's definitely a tough nut to crack," the officer said. "Not from lack of talking, though. It's just that he won't give us any *helpful* information."

Harlow wasn't surprised to hear Pavo described in such a way. "What methods have you tried so far?"

"All of the standard interrogation tactics, of course. Then we moved to privilege removal and psionic scrutiny. That was really a dead end—whatever that brain surgery was, it prevents our agents from any sort of mind reading."

"How's his behavior?" Harlow asked.

"Funny you should ask. He does just fine with the other inmates, but he causes trouble with a lot of the guards. They call him the 'Sponge' because of how much tranq it takes to make him go down. I was considering taking him out of gen-pop and trying solitary, but that's not likely to make a stubborn subject open up."

"No, it wouldn't," Harlow agreed. "Isolation would reinforce his feelings of persecution, and cause him to withdraw further. He might talk when he's finally had enough, but that could be weeks or months from now. How about a mole? If he talks to the other prisoners, you might get something that way."

"We did that. He knows exactly who the snitches are, and they're beneath his contempt. I think the other inmates tell him everything that goes on—probably a few of the guards, too. He's integrated into prison society like someone who's years into his sentence."

The first security door opened, and Harlow was admitted; the other Detective remained in the sallyport when the buzzer sounded, the first door slammed home, and the second one was released.

"We'll get him talking, though," the officer said with a smirk. "Today it's going to be 'enhanced interrogation techniques.' Squeeze the Sponge hard enough, and it'll all come pouring out."

The brightly-lit halls were familiar now; even some of the faces giving him hard stares from between the bars seemed like old half-forgotten acquaintances. Ward Three, the mentally disturbed section, was painted a soothing lilac. Ordinarily a combative prisoner like Pavo would be housed in Ward Two for violent offenders, but there had been concerns of sensitive information finding its way back to him from Auriga's former friends and cellmates. Placing the augmented bounty hunter among the "crazies" was another not-so-subtle form of psychological warfare.

Pavo's head had been shaved at intake; the absence of his distinctive reverse mohawk further emphasized the shiny vertical scar along his crown. He looked all the more like a mental patient, and his eyes were a malevolent orange.

Harlow found the young man in the midst of a bartering transaction with his cellmates. Quickly he scanned the objects on display before they were scooped up and hidden: a pack of playing cards, a few loose cigarettes, a magazine pin-up girl—and a tiny cylinder that vanished the moment he laid eyes on it.

He'd not break whatever trust Pavo had built with the other inmates by revealing their connection. Instead, he banged on the bars unnecessarily, as a clumsy show of power.

"Let's go, punk," he said.

Pavo took his time getting up, came to the door, and placed his back against it. Harlow opened the small window in the cell door through which the food trays were given, and Pavo stuck his hands through. Once Harlow had applied electromagnetic powerbinders around the prisoner's wrists, the door was opened by a guard at the control station, and Pavo followed him to a table in the common area. When they were seated, Pavo lifted an eyebrow—now devoid of piercings—with a crafty smile.

Neither of them needed to remind the other that they were being watched and listened to.

"It's been, what, five days? Thought I'd see you sooner," Pavo opened.

"I've had other priorities."

A smirk. "What could be more important than me? I've had the star treatment around this joint." Pavo made a show of pretending to recline on the metal stool, even though there was nothing to lean back on.

"I'm afraid that ends today," Harlow said, remembering the other Detective's plans to torture the unwilling informant.

"You've got that right, mate."

A pause.

"What have you told them so far?" asked Harlow.

"That the food sucks, and orange isn't the new black."

Harlow allowed himself a tiny chuckle, but his heart wasn't in it.

"How's the sitch with your daughter, mate?"

The Detective shook his head; another weighted silence followed.

"Well, I was just stopping by to say hello," Harlow said. "If you don't want to talk, I can't make you."

Pavo's expression was diabolic. "Ta-ta, then."

Harlow pushed himself up from the table, and led the younger man back to his cell. The ritual was reversed: door closed from the remote console, slot opened, powerbinders released.

"Last chance before things get ugly," Harlow said.

No answer; he didn't expect one. The Detective turned, and headed up the hall. Instead of turning toward the exit, though, he took the branch toward Death Row.

***

Auriga's cell was neat as a pin, as always. The condemned man hung by his ankles from the exercise bar mounted high on the wall, doing inverted sit-ups. Harlow closed the cell door behind him and stood just inside, silent as the man exercised with the rhythm of clockwork.

Thirteen days left. In the face of death, Auriga could only be maintaining his callisthenic discipline for the sheer enjoyment of it, or out of boredom or force of habit.

"Mind if I sit?" Harlow asked.

Auriga grunted; it could be taken as permissive, neutral, or just part of the workout. Harlow seated himself on the cot. The prisoner disengaged himself from the exercise bar, flipped himself right-side-up, and slid down with his back to the wall, seating himself on the floor. It was the language of a man who was tired; Harlow suspected mentally, rather than physically. He'd probably do better to talk about himself, rather than ask questions of someone with a weary brain.

"I've had some time on my hands the past few days," Harlow said.

Auriga rolled his eyes.

"I'm sorry if that's an insensitive remark," Harlow went on. "It's just that I've figured some things out, and a lot's changed since the last time I saw you."

"Not for me, *caballero*."

"Maybe not. And speaking of that, I think you've known all along that Zubrin, the attacker at the spaceport, was never sent by Vulpecula in the first place."

Auriga's stormy eyes regained a glint of their mischief. Harlow went on.

"He was using the supernet when I walked into the security office, and after his cover was blown he didn't just release the virus in response—instead, he got away from me, found another stage, and logged back on. I realized he must have been receiving orders, coordinating with other operatives, or something similar."

An eyebrow raised above one of the steel-blue eyes.

"So I checked the logs on both of those stages. Zubrin didn't have time to cover his tracks. He was communicating with someone on board the *Harvester*. Definitely not Vulpecula."

An amused grunt from the prisoner.

"Zubrin wasn't allowed to disseminate the virus when it would put Greys at risk. Any Greys at the spaceport would have been killed by it, so he was waiting for some kind of go-ahead from the *Harvester*. He was checking the supernet to determine whether all the aliens were off the premises."

A silent smile from Auriga.

"I think you also know that the virus he tried to distribute wasn't the Perseus Agent," the Detective continued. "His was airborne; Vulpecula's is injected."

Auriga smiled, and said nothing.

"When you were working with her, Vulpecula explicitly said that she didn't want an airborne virus that would blanket the population. She wanted a volunteer army—if not real warriors and soldiers, then at least ordinary people who would step up, raise their potential, and choose to join the fight."

Silence, and a smile.

"When I spoke to Vulpecula, she spoke about the spaceport attack only theoretically, from the viewpoint of someone who had carried it out: *'Take the spaceport, for example: that would be a logical place to plan an action with an airborne virus.'* She spoke of how it would possibly make sense for her to choose that place as a target—but she never claimed responsibility for it, because she didn't do it. If we know one thing about the doctor, it's that she's brutally honest."

The smile became a full-blown grin.

Harlow continued. "Zubrin died by overexertion, the same way as most of the Greys' subjects. Vulpecula's derivative Agent, her current project, works to correct that problem."

Auriga was nodding.

"But the attack at the spaceport was blamed on Vulpecula, even though the people who recovered and analyzed that virus—or who created it in the first place—must surely have known it wasn't the Perseus Agent. And lastly, Zubrin didn't just have a high-quality fake ID; he was a *real* Protectorate officer, reassigned to the spaceport when it opened, less than a week before the attempted viral attack...and during the pursuit, I noticed that he was reluctant to use force against other officers. So who has experience in virology and epidemiology? Who has a reason to stir public sentiment against Vulpecula, apparently on orders from the Greys?"

"Human Health and Well-Being." The way Auriga spoke the words was acidic.

"Why didn't you tell me?" Harlow asked.

"Would you have believed me? It's better that you found it out for yourself, Detective."

It was true: Harlow was still stunned at the depth of this treachery, especially in view of what came next. "I found out that, and a lot more. If Vivienne Tainer ordered the attack at the spaceport, she'd have also caused the later one on the city streets. The one that enabled her to call for a lockdown. The one that infected my daughter and gives her leverage over me, in case I get out of line."

"Speaking of that, how are we even having this conversation? They can't do anything more to me, but aren't you putting your own daughter at risk right now if they're listening?"

"Before I came to the prison, I contacted Orion on my Beacon, and had him screw up everything that's going to happen here in the next couple of hours."

Auriga gave a quizzical look.

"Technologically speaking," Harlow clarified. "Don't get your hopes up—it's not like I'm able to break you out of here during a prison riot or something."

Auriga's face fell, but just slightly. Then he chuckled. "Clever *muchacho*. How's he doing?"

Harlow saw no reason to sugar-coat the news. "He's going to die from his operations. Probably soon after Lyra, who goes soon after you."

Auriga seemed to be worlds away. Mechanically, he rolled a cigarillo, his fingers deftly twisting the paper. "No stay of execution for anyone, then."

"Quite the opposite," Harlow said softly. "Your final appeal was denied this morning."

***

The guards locked Auriga away for the last time; it was Harlow's finishing visit to the condemned man. As far as the UCO was concerned, the prisoner was taking any information on Vulpecula to his grave, so there was no reason to drag out the process. They'd focus their efforts on Pavo, instead.

The Detective took his time retracing his steps back to the prison's entrance. Perhaps he'd be in Pavo's place soon enough—or Auriga's. How long would it be before the hammer came down? This awful place might soon become his home. How many of the men he saw were imprisoned here due to being petty criminals, or simply having defied the UCO in some way? Had they wanted to be outlaws, or were they only filling a role society had set for them?

He heard yelling from another part of the facility. Again, his thoughts drifted back to his conversation with Vulpecula.

Children aren't being targeted, she'd said.

I'll have operatives in the right place when the time comes, she'd said.

And suddenly Harlow knew.

The screaming built to a roar, and the harsh bark of an alarm answered it. Harlow broke into a run. Rounding a final corner, up ahead he could see the sallyport through which he'd arrived. It seemed miles away.

On his right, an inmate gripped the steel bars of his cell door, and wrenched the entire door off its track. On Harlow's left, a prisoner kicked another door so hard it burst from its hinges and out into the hallway.

As he shot down the hall, convicts on every side twisted steel bars, punched through locks, and charged through solid doors. The prison was a boiling storm. Harlow dodged inmates as they swarmed out of their cells. They weren't fighting each other; they were practically forming ranks, as organized soldiers.

A few Protectorate men tried to respond, and were lost under a swarm of fists. The mob wasn't a mob, but a force of orange-clad strength. The wiser guards retreated, rallying behind the sallyport. The door slammed when Harlow was ten meters away. On the other side, two rows of guards stood and kneeled in shoulder-to-shoulder formation, leveling shotguns at the advancing crowd. It was a stalemate; even with the prisoners' numbers and terrifying power, no one could approach the gatehouse without being blown to pieces.

Harlow spun with his back to the steel-barred wall. It was too late; he was trapped alone with an army of prisoners. He raised his hands, palms outward, and the crowd didn't close in.

"Don't kill him," someone said.

"Hostage," someone cried.

"Hostage!" The crowd roared, and closed in on him. Dozens of hands seized him; their strength was tremendous. Struggling against it was like fighting the ocean. Harlow bit back a scream as he was dragged away.

Chapter 20

He was carried into a cell and hurled against the far wall. Harlow clung to the bottom level of a bed bunk to stop from faceplanting onto the concrete, and tried to recompose himself before the door crashed.

He'd been relieved of his weapons before entering the prison, and had no keys to the cell. The doors were operated electronically at the guard station, and no one there would know Harlow was trapped in this particular one.

The bedlam was going in full force; convicts raced through the corridors, brandishing improvised weapons. Would they start a fire? The steel-and-concrete building couldn't be burned to the ground, but Harlow would surely asphyxiate in this locked room.

He paced; he rattled the bars; he shouted at passing prisoners. They jeered at him in reply. Exasperated, he finally flung himself on the bottom bunk, not knowing what else to do. He clutched his skull in both hands and fought the urge to ram himself headfirst into the wall.

Then two feet swung into view, hanging in the air above the side of his bed: orange pant cuffs, gray rubber prison-issue slip-on shoes. Someone was sitting on the bunk above him.

"Enjoying the festivities, mate?" an Australian voice queried.

Of course it was him. Harlow was somehow both relieved and annoyed. "You've certainly put a lot of preparation into this," he said.

"Too right. A party like this one doesn't just happen on its own."

Pavo hopped down from the top bunk, grinning at the chaos unfolding out in the corridors.

"This isn't even your cell," Harlow said.

Pavo leaned against the bars, his orange eyes dancing. "Nope. It's yours. I'm just stopping by for a visit."

"*Mine?* Are you really using me as a hostage? They'll never trade me for Auriga, if that's what you're thinking."

"I know that. Just want to have you out of the way for a while, Detective. Vulpecula doesn't trust you, you know. And me, I'd rather not kill you, but I can't have you running about loose, either. A bit of a troublemaker, you are."

Harlow rolled his eyes at the ironic pronouncement.

"You got arrested at the city gate on purpose," Harlow said. "You wanted to be here in prison to start all this. And the virus you failed to smuggle in—they said it didn't match the signature of the Perseus Agent, because *their* profile of the Agent, the one they've been working with and watching for since the spaceport, is really *Zubrin's* virus. You brought in the real thing, so they didn't recognize it."

"Hats off, Detective." Pavo tipped an imaginary cap atop his shorn head.

"And someone smuggled it in here for you. Over the past few days, you've dosed half the prison population with the Agent."

A grin flashed on Pavo's square jaw.

"They'd have been all too eager for it—a volunteer army of superhuman men, just like Vulpecula wanted," said Harlow.

Pavo laughed. "The best part is, we're recruiting." He stepped forward, stretching out his fist, and opened his black-lacquered fingertips. On his palm rested a makeshift syringe. "Saved you a dose, mate. It could be just the ticket."

Harlow took the improvised needle, but shook his head. "What are you expecting, for me to shoot this right here and sail into the fight? You think I'm ready to drop everything and fight the Protectorate this very minute? And who knows how long it might be before it takes effect?"

Pavo shrugged. "You'll never know until you find out." He produced a small electronic device and clicked a button; the cell door rumbled open by remote control. "In any case, I've got other fish to fry, so you'll have to excuse me."

"So this is how you plan to break Auriga out?" Harlow asked, incredulous. "Death Row is a separate facility within the prison. It'll have been locked down tight by now—shut off from the rest of the building. You're strong, but you're not going to tear through an eight-inch steel vault."

"We'll see," is all Pavo said. He stepped into the corridor, and pressed the button again. The gate slid shut, locking Harlow inside.

For a moment he stood dumbly, studying the syringe in his hand. The screams and blaring alarms which seemed deafening moments before had now faded into the background of his thoughts.

Harlow reached to the back of his neck, and double-tapped the Beacon. After the flat, neutral tone, he said, "Orion Danes." The young man didn't have a Beacon of his own, of course, but it was possible to contact him through his cybercomputer. Grey technology was designed to be much more compatible and universal than the Human variety.

After a few moments, the gravelly, artificial voice entered his head. "Things must be heating up there. It's getting tough for me to keep the place scrambled."

"Yeah, it's mayhem, but I really need some help. Can you open cell 26 in Ward Two?"

"It'll take a minute," Orion said. "I've got security countermeasures popping up all over. I won't be able to keep the cameras blacked out much longer."

"Please do the best you can. I'm in a tough spot here."

The next few minutes were a restless age. Pandemonium continued everywhere; Harlow smelled smoke, and heard blasts of gunfire over the angry shouting of the prisoners. As time ticked by, Harlow clung to a rapidly diminishing hope—and at last, the cell door clattered open. Harlow squeezed his body through the space at the earliest possible chance, and took off in a sprint in the direction of Death Row.

***

"The extent of the cyberattack was pretty severe," Barnard said. "Cameras were down throughout the entire facility for over two hours, so we'll have to rely on testimony from our officers, such as yourself, to piece it all together."

They were in a plain office room near the prison's visiting quarters. The pungent scent of smoke still hung in the air, and the hushed but urgent chatter in the halls marked the aftermath of a disaster. It was his second debriefing with the Pontiff in less than a week, and Harlow fought to keep the discomfort—no, the full-blown *paranoia*—at bay.

"Let's start with your visit to the prisoner called 'Pavo'. What was the purpose for your meeting with him today?"

"I was warning him that it was his last chance to talk before the interrogations became much more unpleasant for him. I was attempting a 'good cop' routine by leveraging any rapport that I had built."

"And how did he respond?"

"I got nothing. He snubbed me, so I didn't pursue the issue. I wanted to appear unconcerned to him, as though we would get the information no matter what."

Barnard grunted. "And during this interview, or at any time before it, were you aware of Pavo's impending plans for an uprising at this prison?"

"I was not," Harlow answered truthfully. "I became aware of that only when the trouble started."

"All right. And after leaving the prisoner, then what did you do?"

"I returned Pavo to his cell, and then paid a visit to Martín Auriga."

"And what was the purpose of that visit?" Barnard asked.

"To say goodbye. To tell him that his final appeal was denied, and that his sentence would be carried out."

"How did he respond to this news?"

"It was what I would describe as a normal reaction. He was disappointed, but tried not to show that it bothered him," Harlow said.

"Was there any indication that he knew of the impending riot?"

"None whatever. I'm confident that he wasn't a part of its planning or execution."

Barnard nodded. "And when you left Auriga's cell, what happened next?"

"I was in A Corridor when the alarm was raised and the prisoners began breaking out of their cells. I tried to make it to the guard station, but didn't get there in time. I was surrounded and overpowered; this was in view of the sallyport, and several officers there witnessed this."

"And then?"

"I was informed that I would be kept as a hostage, and was imprisoned in cell 26 in Ward Two."

"And did they in fact use you as a bargaining chip during the riot?"

"No, sir," replied Harlow. "I was left alone during the event, perhaps because it was over so quickly. I was not approached by any inmates and remained locked in the cell where Protectorate men later found me."

Barnard nodded again. Harlow willed his breathing to remain even, his body to remain wholly under his command.

"This informant of yours has caused quite a bit of trouble. Pavo was only imprisoned here for a matter of days," Barnard said. "How do you think he was so adept at staging an insurrection in that brief time?"

"He was popular among the inmates," said Harlow, recalling what the Detective at the entrance had told him. "And he was generous with the performance-enhancing serum that caused such dramatic results among the prisoners."

"Yes, the virus he had on him at the city quarantine checkpoint. Looks like he found a way to smuggle it in after all. I ask you point blank, Detective: did you assist him by sneaking in this contraband?"

"No, sir, I did not."

"Do you know who did?"

"I do not."

"Very well." Barnard grumbled. "What about disseminating the virus? How did he get it to so many prisoners? How did he administer all those injections?"

"With these," Harlow placed the makeshift syringe on the table in front of him. "Pavo would intentionally cause a stir with the guards, and get himself shot full of carfentanil. As a heavily augmented bionic, it would take such a high dosage to put him down that it was easy to hide a few of the darts away—the officers would lose count of how many they had to use. Then later, he'd use the tranq darts to make improvised syringes, and pass them out with doses of the Agent. Pretty soon, the inmates had several syringes circulating through gen-pop. Once the serum took effect, they could break out easily. They just waited for Pavo's word."

The Pontiff's large, square hands examined the dart. "And that just happened to be while you were here? Rather odd timing, don't you think?"

"I believe Pavo wanted me to see the breakout, as a show of power. I was the one tasked with getting information from him, and this was his way of highlighting my failure."

"Failure, indeed," Barnard set the syringe aside. "Not only did you lose the opportunity for valuable intel on Vulpecula, but you may have at least partly facilitated the debacle that took place here this morning. I'm aware that Ms. Tainer and Mr. van de Kamp simultaneously have great faith in you, and are placing great pressure upon you. As such, I'm inclined to attribute this to a lapse in judgment due to your eagerness for results."

"Yes, sir."

"Three inmates dead, and twenty-six escaped by breaking through the concrete roof," Barnard glowered. "It's fortunate that Auriga wasn't among them, and that no Protectorate men were injured."

"Yes, sir."

"But speaking of him, I'm petitioning to have Auriga's sentence carried out immediately. I'd rather not endure another escape attempt. It will require approval from the Illuminatus, but I'm confident that Mr. Strughold will agree there's no reason to keep the man around any longer."

Harlow swallowed, and nodded.

"One more thing, Detective," the Pontiff said. "In trying to reconstruct the events of the riot, I reviewed your Beacon logs and found them to be corrupted and illegible. Your biochip is obviously malfunctioning."

Harlow went cold. "Oh, I'm sorry about that, sir."

"I'm scheduling you for corrective procedures on board the *Harvester* at 1400 hours tomorrow. You'll have a brief consultation before your surgery; who knows? Perhaps they'll make a whole new man out of you."

Harlow faltered, nearly collapsing in his chair. From far away, he heard the Pontiff dismiss him, and weakly, he walked to the door.

Chapter 21

0600 hours.

Harlow stood at the back of the small salon, saving the two short rows of chairs for ranking dignitaries. He wore a black silk suit with a marengo shirt that matched his wet-concrete eyes. An emerald-gray silk tie was unfurled against his chest. A heavy tactical pistol rested in its holster beneath his left armpit.

"When you see the bad guys, you wear black and carry a gun. When you see the good guys, you wear a tie," Carina had said.

Ordinarily, weapons would not be allowed in the viewing area, just like anywhere else in the prison, but recent security concerns had overridden this rule. The Chief Warden wanted to avoid another fiasco at all costs; after yesterday's failed escape attempt, this already deeply-charged event had taken on even more urgency and significance. The execution would *not* be interrupted by a second uprising.

Harlow nodded darkly as Millard H. Strughold entered the room with a small entourage. As Illuminatus, the one and only man capable of legitimately stopping the execution was, in fact, its most ardent supporter. A grin stretched Strughold's fleshy jowls as he took his seat in the center of the front row. All he was missing was popcorn and a soda.

Yellowed linen curtains obscured the view beyond the reinforced plexiglass. Honeycombed wire from the window cast a pattern on the flimsy cloth, but deeper within Harlow could distinguish the apparatus of doom: faint outlines of a table offering a fatal rest.

Others filed into the chamber: mostly local political hustlers, a couple of reporters, and a few that Harlow didn't recognize. Barely twenty, in all. One woman controlled a drone camera for Trans-Galactic Communications; the demise of this notorious criminal was being broadcast to untold worlds.

At ten minutes after the hour, the Chief Warden entered the salon. Warden Gunay was a wiry ghost of a man with a bristly white mustache. He slouched when he walked, as though an invisible burden stooped him forward. When he faced the assembly, though, his red-rimmed eyes and thin, sneering lips commanded instant silence.

"Open the gallery," he said.

The curtains drew back, displaying a sterile room prepared for the act of death. On the far wall, a closed door next to a large one-way mirror divided the execution chamber from the control room, where ranking members of the prison staff would oversee the event.

On the injection table, a single flower stood in a narrow glass vase. The white tulip, with its vivid red markings, was striking. Some of the assembled members even gasped at its beauty. Harlow had paid a fortune to a local genome artist in recreating the legendary *Semper Augustus*; every fold of its delicate snow-white petals, streaked with the reddest crimson, was the herald of a glorious life coming to an end.

"Bring out the condemned."

A door on the viewers' right side unlocked, and admitted two Protectorate men with Auriga ushered between them. The prisoner wore a pristine orange jumpsuit; his dark hair was slicked back, and his salt-and-pepper stubble cleared almost down to the skin. His stormy eyes were somewhere far away until they came to rest on the brilliant flower; then, they regained their intensity. Auriga smiled a thin, wistful smile.

The condemned man had no family and no clergy present—his wife and young son had perished during the Lacertas' arrival ten years before. Knowing that Auriga was a Catholic, Harlow had made every effort to find a priest to officiate the execution, but had come up empty-handed. Religion was sorely outré in the Sanctuary Cities; the Greys strongly discouraged such unscientific pursuits among the vassals. Meanwhile, humble churches still dotted the outlands, although these were few and far between. Rather than the organized religions of yesteryear, however, these individual churches often merely espoused a hodgepodge variety of post-apocalyptic beliefs. Even if Harlow had found a Catholic priest to conduct Auriga's last rites and preside over his final moments, he could hardly have gotten the clergyman approved to enter or leave the city—especially during an active quarantine—or even guarantee his safety while there.

The result? Harlow himself had read the short, simple prayer to the condemned man yesterday, before leaving his cell and being swept up in the prison riot. Wine and Eucharist wafers were forbidden, but he had brought simpler icons: crackers and grape juice would have to do. At Harlow's behest, one other concession was made: Auriga had been permitted a small crucifix on a fragile chain. Harlow had never been a spiritual man, but found himself hoping that Auriga's deity would understand he was doing the best he could in the absence of actual clergy.

Harlow was not the only one standing in for a more qualified candidate. Executions were required to have a trained medical attendant as part of the staff. Herein lay a paradox: medical professionals such as doctors and nurses still adhered to the Hippocratic Oath, "First, do no harm." Since doctors were forbidden to intentionally kill people, the role was usually filled by anyone with "medical training", however broad that might be. In practice, this was someone who had the basic knowledge required to place an IV and monitor a heartbeat. True medical expertise was not required, and was not usually available. Stories of botched executions, in which the inmate suffered needlessly or took up to two hours to expire, were commonplace.

One of the Protectorate men removed the white-and-red tulip, and Auriga was restrained to the table. The attendant, wearing a blue paper gown and white surgical mask, entered the chamber from the control room. Gingerly, he placed an intravenous needle in each of Auriga's outstretched forearms. Two lines were required, in case one malfunctioned; both ran from the table through the wall and into the control room, where the drugs were loaded and administered.

The masked assistant nodded, and returned to the back room. One of the Protectorate men in the room manipulated levers on the table, and tilted it so that Auriga was nearly upright. In cruciform posture, his face was serene.

Gunay cleared his throat, and announced: "Martín Auriga, you have been sentenced to death by lethal injection for the murder of Josiah Corvus. The condemned is now permitted to speak his final words."

Stillness for a moment. And softly he said, *"¿Así esta el mundo?"*
So this is how the world is?

The table's levers were adjusted again, and the table reclined to its original position. The Warden signaled to the staff behind the one-way mirror, and the execution began. No one in the viewing gallery could see into the control room, but Harlow knew the procedure: an IV stand loaded with three separate vials containing three different drugs would be administered one at a time: first, sodium thiopental, a powerful sedative to render the prisoner unconscious. Next, pancuronium bromide to paralyze the muscles and stop breathing; and finally, potassium chloride to induce cardiac arrest.

Someone in the control room was now initiating the first IV drip by depressing a large plunger to send the sedative into the IV line. The observers waited, not daring to speak and ruin the buzz of excitement; Harlow watched the TGC reporter put away a small microphone and take notes on a datapad instead.

At length, Auriga's breathing slowed, and his body relaxed. The fluids continued their course; after a while, the medical associate entered the chamber again, and lifted Auriga's eyelids, then poked at his extremities with a needle.

"No response," the medic said. "Proceed to the second stage."

The process was repeated: someone in the far room issued the next dose. Harlow watched as pale blue fluid crawled through the line and into the dying man's arm. The attendant observed carefully as well; after a few moments, Auriga flinched once, and then returned to peace. Again, minutes ticked by. The medic frowned, and retreated to the control room.

Harlow stepped back to the gallery's corner, and used his radio earpiece to listen at a low volume:

"His breathing is shallow, but it hasn't stopped."

"How long has it been?"

"Long enough."

A pause.

"Just one more vial. Let's get it over with."

"The potassium chloride can cause a lot of pain if he's still conscious."

"He's unconscious. Look at him. Besides, nobody cares."

"Sir, I don't know—"

"I don't want to hear it. Just do it."

Clear fluid crept through the line. Auriga gasped, and flinched again. Harlow held his breath. Strughold leaned forward in excitement. Warden Gunay hurried out of the gallery.

The radio voices resumed.

"He's not all the way out—"

"Shut up."

"What's the problem?"

"Sometimes it takes a while, sir."

"Use a higher dosage, then."

"The dosage is set by legal guidelines, sir. We're not allowed to use our own discretion for this. Besides, the drugs are pre-measured and we've already given him well over a fatal amount. It just takes time."

Harlow exhaled quietly. Standing at the back of the room, he tried to remain unobtrusive, forgotten by the gallery's more distinguished witnesses. Fifteen minutes dragged past, then twenty, with no change in the prisoner's vital signs—only an occasional tremble or groan.

The crowd was restless now—except for Strughold, who Harlow had expected to be the most impatient. The newly-appointed Illuminatus was fixated on the prone figure, staring with an intense interest. Others in the gallery whispered about the prolonged interval before death, but none of them had an idea of what to expect. There was nothing to do but wait.

Out of nowhere, Auriga's words from his cell came back to him: *Sometimes I meditate, to pass the time.*

And so waiting is what they did. Over an hour progressed as the audience grew more and more ill at ease. At length, snatches of hushed conversation developed: Shouldn't it be over by now? Had something gone wrong? From his earpiece, Harlow heard the control room staff discussing dosage, toxicity and body chemistry, and hints of where to place the blame if the situation didn't resolve itself quickly. Through it all, the Illuminatus merely sat engrossed with a troubled half-smile on his lips.

Then, Auriga took a sudden, deep breath. Was it a dying gasp? The witnesses sprang to attention. Strughold rose from his seat, his scrutiny redoubled.

"He's not any weaker," the Illuminatus announced. "It's a trick—he's not dying at all."

Auriga's right hand clenched into a fist, and with a sudden effort, tore the restraint free of the table. He reached over, plucked the IV from his left arm, and wrenched the other pinion open. Sitting up, he'd removed the right IV line and discarded the metal bangle rolling free around his right wrist before the two Protectorate men could react.

The ankle shackles snapped as if they were made of tin when the prisoner swung his legs to the floor. One guard produced a powerful taser, but Auriga wrested the entire table off its mooring and deflected the two electric darts with the oversized shield. He swung the corner of the heavy steel table into the plexiglass window separating the death chamber from the viewing room; with a colossal cracking noise, the barrier dislodged but did not shatter. Auriga peeled one layer of the plastic-coated glass away, and jerked out the wide rectangle of hexagonal chain link. In a flash, he wrapped it around the pair of astonished Protectorate men, forming a tight metal confinement that squeezed them together.

It had all happened in a couple of seconds. The convict's movements were fluid, and blurry with quickness; when his arms or legs moved, they repositioned almost invisibly. It nearly gave Harlow's senses the impression that the man was teleporting—almost, but not quite, stepping from one place to another without occupying the spaces in between.

Auriga was back at the destroyed window, and with a flick of his hand, the last layer of plexiglass, already askew, crashed out of its frame. The assemblage of spectators, recently so eager to witness death, now fled in panic. Harlow opened a door leading to the hallway, and ducked aside to be free of the stampede. One man did not join the frantic exit: in the center of the gallery, Millard Strughold stood his ground.

Auriga's action of vaulting over the sill and into the room seemed instantaneous. Another blink, and he'd closed the distance to the defiant Illuminatus. His fist drew back for a devastating blow...but the punch never came. Auriga hesitated, held in some unknown abeyance. Then his fist lowered, his head bowed, and he sank to one knee, grimacing.

"Idiot," Strughold seethed. "Weak-minded imbecile."

From the corner, Harlow crept forward a scant couple of paces, enough to view the scene closer and from a better angle. Strughold's face came into view, imperious, furious. The older man radiated a twisted grandeur; something at Harlow's core tugged at him, demanding that he kneel before this awesome, unworldly might. He dared come no closer, yet he was powerless to retreat. Attacking—or even simply disobeying—the man was inconceivable.

The Illuminatus turned to him. "And do you waver in your duty, Detective? Now I see what you've done. Your duplicitous acts, your foolish unfaithfulness, your *treason*. Your wife and daughter will serve the masters of this world far better than you have done, but your usefulness has not ended yet. Perhaps the Greys will bestow gifts despite your unworthiness—or perhaps you'll be better used as an example, a warning to others. But first: take out your weapon, and kill Auriga."

Auriga knelt at the man's feet, struggling to move, but he was rooted to the spot. His teeth ground together, and he snarled, but could not force words out. The heavy semiautomatic was in Harlow's hand; he did not recall drawing it from its holster. In wonder, without thought or will, he moved it to aim at the prisoner's head. He thumbed the safety off with a click. His trigger finger began to squeeze.

He would not watch what was about to happen. Harlow's eyes rose from the doomed man; staring ahead, he found himself locking eyes with his own reflection in the one-way glass on the opposite side of the death room. The mirror image beguiled him: his desperate, red-rimmed eyes blazed from a slack-jawed, dopey face. A couple of meters away, Strughold grinned—but his majesty was gone in the reflection.

Instead of an intimidating sovereign, Harlow saw only the leering old man himself.

Using the mirror to guide his hand, moving only the weapon and not his eyes, Harlow shifted his aim from Auriga to the glowering Illuminatus.

"No, stop—" Strughold's eyes went wide, and he reached for the gun just as Harlow squeezed off a shot.

Blood splashed, and Strughold reeled backward. As he collapsed on his back, Auriga leapt from his kneeling position. In an instant, he was astride the fallen man, and Auriga's fist drove with the force of a meteor through the fleshy face, shattering it into pulp.

Harlow stared as Auriga rose from the floor, shaking the gore from his dripping fist. Then his gaze moved to rest on the corpse, its clothing matted with blood, its face a red ruin. White streaked with deepest crimson. *Semper Augustus.*

He pulled out the radio earpiece, tossed it aside. Harlow felt no remorse, only a singular detachment. He thought of his daughter; what would become of her if he were imprisoned and executed? He would find her and flee. There would be no stopping him, no matter what.

A weighty hand gripped his shoulder. He turned, and found the eyes with the turmoil of a hurricane. "It was you, wasn't it?" Auriga said.

"Yes," Harlow cleared his throat, and nodded. "Pavo gave me a dose of the Perseus Agent during the riot, and I got into the control room. I switched vial number two with the virus, and the first and third with saline solution."

"*Muchas gracias*, my friend."

The tranquility of the demolished gallery was fading. An alarm blared, but it seemed far away. Harlow strode with Auriga to the open door and into the corridor. On the short walk to the front of the prison, they passed only a few scattered Protectorate men, who stepped aside and flattened themselves against the wall. No one interfered as Harlow unlocked the final set of doors and exited with Auriga through the front gate.

Chapter 22

"There is no reason, scientifically speaking, that the Human body should ever die," Vulpecula said. "At least, not from what is commonly called 'natural causes.' Throughout recorded history, people have considered death to be inevitable, a necessary end. I myself do not."

Although Lyra had been resting for much of the past few days, she still found her body and mind sluggish. The fatigue was like a spiderweb wrapped around her whole body, clinging fast despite every effort to shake it off.

Days of tests administered by the doctor; days of waiting while Vulpecula worked away in her lab. She hadn't seen much of Orion, either; sometimes he was receiving his own consultations with the doctor, and at others he was deeply engaged with some cryptic task requiring feverish input on his cybercomputer. She'd approached him when she was able, but he retained that faraway manner: stilted somehow, familiar and yet not quite himself. Now, in the laboratory, they sat adjacent and held hands during the meeting Vulpecula had called. The shared gesture lacked vigor, lacked meaning.

During her five-day hiatus, Lyra had slept and ate frequently, but it did her little good. A persistent headache was blossoming in the center of her skull. She tried to brush the pain aside and listen to the doctor.

"The cells that make up our bodies have all the equipment needed to reproduce themselves," Vulpecula continued. "Old cells die, and new ones constantly take their place. You may have heard the old saying that the Human body replaces itself every seven years—this is untrue, it's more complicated than that, but the question remains: if we're getting new cells all the time, why do we age and die?"

From her seat in the laboratory, Lyra stole a glance at Pyxis, who was still foregoing the use of Human furniture and standing to one side. However, the alien listened with rapt attention, also foregoing its pride and its disdain for Human science; Lyra sensed that it was fascinated by the topic, despite itself.

"The answer," Vulpecula said, "is that with every copy of itself a cell makes, the DNA contained within deteriorates a bit. It's a given that copies of copies of copies never possess the same quality as the original—this applies to nearly any medium you care to name. In the case of cell reproduction, this is exactly what leads to aging: bones become thinner, muscles atrophy, and metabolic processes decline.

"This is a highly significant problem for you and Orion—your conditions are exacerbated due to the increased metabolic demands resulting from your surgical gifts. However, it's not unique to the two of you. Since much of my research focuses on the potential bridges between Human and Grey physiology, I formed a hypothesis that Grey cell division is similarly affected—but that the Greys have some method of combatting these degenerative effects. After all, their use of psychokinetic and telekinetic powers far exceed the abilities granted by their slender bodies and meager caloric intake."

Pyxis frowned. Wrinkles ran deep through the rubbery skin of its face.

"We don't know what would be considered 'old age' for a Grey," Vulpecula said. "Humanity has only had close contact with their species for about ten years; that's not long enough to observe the complete life cycle of one, even if we were allowed total access to this information—which, of course, we are not. The Greys only contact us with emissaries of their choosing. Age likely plays a factor in this, as it does with Humans...we don't send the very young or the very old on important missions of diplomacy or negotiation. And Greys, of course, won't respond to questions such as 'how old are you?' or 'how long do members of your species live?'"

"I strongly object to this line of research," said Pyxis.

"Trust me, you're going to want to hear this," the doctor answered. "During my time with the UCO, I worked with a limited number of Grey scientists. My contact with them was sporadic—I could only make casual observations, without drawing definite conclusions. I discreetly collected tissue samples when I could: mostly trace amounts of skin, oils, or saliva from equipment they'd used or containers they'd drunk from—"

"*How dare you.*" Pyxis was furious, but Vulpecula did not react to its anger.

"—and combined with the knowledge I gained later while developing the Agent, I managed to figure a few things out."

Lyra's headache throbbed, and her skin prickled. Orion's hand, clasped in hers, thrummed with tension. Pyxis was moments away from responding to this provocation; Lyra couldn't guess what the alien might do, but its displeasure radiated through the room with an awesome gravity. She attempted a soothing response, knowing that she could hardly influence Pyxis directly with her psionic powers, but she had to try and defuse the strained atmosphere in the room.

Let's all stay calm. No need to be angry, she thought. Vulpecula's face was set, a hint of challenge on her features. She was satisfied, enjoying some personal victory. Orion shifted in his chair with unease, but was spellbound in anticipation. The glare on Pyxis's wrinkled face was fearsome, but she perceived that even it was eager to share in whatever knowledge the doctor had gleaned. Vulpecula knew she would not be threatened or interrupted.

"The Greys' cell structure and genetic coding are quite different from that of Humans, but their stem cells are compatible—even *complementary* to each other, making the Greys' cells an effective vehicle to introduce desirable catalysts to the Human body. This was the basis of my research that led to the creation of the Perseus Agent.

"In Humans, the Perseus Agent can be compared to the Seneca Valley Virus, which has selective tropism for certain cancers. While it benefits Humans, Senecavirus is detrimental to its natural hosts: pigs and perhaps cows. In the case of Perseus, its source and natural host is the Grey aliens. This would be equally true for whatever it is the UCO is doing to corrupt my own work: the alternate pathogen Harlow mentioned in the spaceport attack."

"They're trying to make their own Perseus Agent—only for the Greys?" Orion asked. "Something based on your designs, but not perfected yet?"

"I believe so. Human Health and Well-Being is blaming me for something that they made—something that harms the Greys, and has an as-yet-unknown effect on Humans.

"The Greys are an artificially-engineered species, created by some other beings," the doctor said. "Since we know that they were purposefully engineered to be the way they are, we can infer that they were designed for cerebral and psionic function. Gödel's Incompleteness Theorem states in part that a system can never fully understand itself. No machine can fully explain its own workings. He was referring to man's inability to reach certainty in pure mathematics, but I'll apply it to biology: a Human brain can understand a frog's brain, but not a Human one. For that you would need a superhuman brain. We use simple tools to build more complex tools; we use computers to build more advanced supercomputers. Why not use our brains to build more advanced brains?"

Lyra swallowed with a dry mouth, and then spoke. "So the Greys' creators made them in order to understand more about themselves—more about *all* living things, probably. The abductions, the dissections, the experiments…it explains a lot. The Greys were designed to gather information, and to keep secrets."

"What *is* this other species, Pyxis?" Orion rasped. "Who built Ios, and made you?"

"They are gone," the alien said. "I do not know of them."

"Whoever it was, they intended for the Greys to be a long-lived race—I can tell that much from the cellular biology I've studied," Vulpecula said. "They exhibit slow metabolic function and cell division, which makes sense: the Greys were apparently tasked with acquiring and preserving knowledge through the ages—even sharing it with others, if they were worthy of it. A sort of living, constantly developing super-encyclopedia.

"The problem is that the Greys suffer from the very same problem as their experimental subjects: their synthetic DNA is susceptible to corruption during mitosis. I believe their natural lifespans are comparable to that of Humans—or perhaps shorter. If they could utilize my research, but go in a different direction to address this problem, they would."

Again Lyra studied Pyxis's stern countenance. The wrinkles carved into its forehead and jaw—had they always been there? Or had it visibly aged even in the six months since she'd crashed the first alien ship? Then it turned its knitted brows to her, and she looked back to Vulpecula.

"So maybe fixing the problem of DNA corruption during cellular division would help us *and* them," Lyra realized. "Can you do something about it?"

Vulpecula shook her head. "There's very little I can do. Remember, you're talking about halting or reversing the aging process—something the collective efforts of Human science has dreamed of and worked toward for thousands of years. I'm not going to solve that problem alone, in a clandestine aug clinic, in a matter of a few days."

Lyra's face fell. She was going to die, after all. How could any part of her mind ever have avoided that conclusion? Sooner or later, the Greys' attentions were invariably fatal.

"However," the doctor said, and Lyra's heart leapt for hope yet again. "There is something that I think can help.

"The Greys must be aware of their own weakness, and must have attempted to address it somehow. The answer is obvious: their 'food', which is not a solid food at all but a sort of nutrient-rich, enzymatic broth. I've never obtained a sample of it, but it seems clear that they've developed an enzyme that protects or repairs damaged DNA during the cell-division process."

Orion's eyebrows raised. "Is this true, Pyxis?"

A pause, while the alien considered what to tell them. Apparently, it was time to be forthcoming. "Yes, this is correct. We engineered an induced-fit model enzyme that performs the appropriate chemical action, as you suggest. But I have none of this food, and am now in need of it."

Orion nodded. "We crashed your ship, and your supplies were lost. You may have gotten some from the Greys at Rankin Inlet, where we landed, but you've probably had none of it since we left there, is that right?"

"Correct."

"But there would be plenty of it on board the *Harvester*," Orion said.

Lyra wanted to scream. How could she ever return to one of those fiendish killing grounds? The horrors inflicted on her and so many others in the floating slaughterhouse over New Zaragosa would stay with her until her last day...which evidently wasn't long from now.

"Not again. Never again," she said.

"Lyra, we have to," Orion said, turning to her. "I don't want to either, but this is life and death."

"Can't Pyxis just go and get some of this stuff from them?"

"If I returned to the *Harvester*," the alien said, "in so doing I would place myself under the command of Eridanus. I would be compelled to acknowledge its authority, and could not leave again without its approval. I would likely be given tasks that conflict with our designs here."

"So if you return to the ship, it needs to be with the purpose of removing Eridanus from power, which we've agreed needs to be done anyway," Orion finished. "We have the small saucer and the Vinculum; we can make this work. And we need to go now, before we get weaker."

***

The saucer would fit three occupants: Orion, Lyra, and Pyxis. Vulpecula would stay behind, dismantling the lab and preparing to evacuate Flagstaff. She'd stayed in one spot for long enough; it was time to cover her tracks once again. She'd given Orion a small parcel of supplies, but they were traveling light and fast; Lyra changed back into her beige button-up blouse and ripped blue jeans, and climbed the stairs to the roof to find Orion, back in his baggy black sweater and combat boots, already finished loading the peculiar little craft.

"Pyxis will be here in a minute," he croaked. "It said it had one last thing to take care of."

***

Downstairs in the lab, Vulpecula was packing away samples and equipment when the door behind her swung inward. The footfalls were very light, made by a diminutive being.

Slowly she turned around. Pyxis stood across the room, its wrinkled, ashen face a neutral mask.

Vulpecula charged, closing the distance in half a second, but it was

217

not fast enough. Just as she leapt forward, drawing back to strike, the alien lashed out with psionic force. Shimmering spears of raw energy impaled her, then exploded in dazzling displays. Her skin sizzled and blistered. Caught in midair, she was flung against the far wall. Concrete blocks cracked from the force, and she collapsed in agony.

"As I told you before," Pyxis rasped, coming forward, "your designs show great promise for the Terrans of the future. But if they are implemented, it will be without you."

Fighting a world of pain, she clutched the countertop above her, and hauled herself upright. She dug through the counter with her hands: a pair of hemostats, a supernet camera, a roll of cloth bandage, a striker for igniting Bunsen burners. Nothing was useful. What could she use as a weapon against a psionic entity?

Pyxis gestured, and an unseen hand, as hard and strong as a stone giant's, gripped her and bashed her face into the counter, leaving a bloody imprint. She fell back, her face gushing, and then the hand hurled her into the corner. She crashed into a group of heavy oxygen tanks, and wailed in suffering. Facedown on the floor, she raised her head as the alien approached. The giant green cylinders toppled around her.

"You have a meddlesome nature," Pyxis said. "And your intrusiveness cannot be tolerated. Your gifts in science have led you to a wretched Human hallmark: curiosity."

It stabbed her again and again with that wicked psionic lance, piercing her flesh as with a stiletto. Now, blood pooled under her limp body. One of the fallen cylinders hissed, leaking oxygen from its nozzle. Vulpecula grabbed the nozzle of a second cylinder and twisted it all the way open. With a roar, oxygen flooded the room.

In her other hand, she held the flint striker. Defiantly meeting the alien's black eyes, she clenched the metal prongs; simply squeezing her hand shut would produce a spark. Pyxis took a step back from the cold rush of flammable gas, then another. It grimaced at Vulpecula, tempted to finish her off, but knowing that every further second spent in this room was unwise.

Pyxis turned to the exit, leaving her to bleed out. After the double doors swung shut behind the alien, pain and blood claimed Vulpecula, and she collapsed.

Chapter 23

Harlow climbed over the waist-high concrete barricade erected in the street; Auriga hopped over it with ease.

During the morning rush hour, hovercars zipped to and fro, maglev trains ferried workers to their jobs, and the streets were filled with foot and vehicle traffic. People turned to gawk at the escapee in the orange jumpsuit; then, as their faces registered disbelief and fear, Harlow and Auriga were given a comfortable amount of elbow room on the busy street.

"That train goes straight to my building," Harlow said. "We've got to get to my condo; we can get you some clothes and get ready to leave the city for good—*after* we get my daughter."

"I don't want to sound ungrateful, but couldn't you have brought me a change of clothes when you broke me out?"

"I didn't really expect it to work," Harlow said. "I kind of thought you'd be dead and I'd be in prison right now."

"Fair enough."

They bolted for the elevated platform. The crowds parted before them; Harlow also spotted several Protectorate officers, who eyed them from a healthy distance—there was obviously an order not to engage Auriga directly. Wise, Harlow thought, since that would be pure suicide.

Harlow double-tapped his Beacon and called up Orion. He skipped the pleasantries. "Public transport around here is shut down. How are you with trains?" he asked.

"I'll get the closest one going. On the way to your place?" the cybernetic asked.

"Yup. He's with me."

"Okay, we're inbound. Meet you there." Orion clicked off.

It was a short run to the train. They bounded up the metal staircase, and halted before the entry gate. The massive barred door remained shut before them, and the facial-recognition terminal beside it flashed Auriga's face and then Harlow's, proclaiming "DENIED ACCESS" in angry red letters. Auriga kicked the gate open with a crash.

Ahead, the train waited at the platform. Crowds streamed into the open doors, but jumped back at the barking alarms. Harlow and Auriga rushed in; the other commuters gave them a wide berth, and they found two seats on a side-facing bench.

"Wish it was always this easy to get seats—" Harlow began, but was cut off by the holostacker displays that blazed to life above the cabin windows. The train doors closed.

"Now hear this. A wanted fugitive has been sighted."

"Here we go again," Auriga sighed.

The monitors showed Auriga's face with the caption "FUGITIVE", and then switched to Harlow's, with the same word emblazoned. He knew it was coming, but it shocked him anyway—the last shred of his life as a Protectorate officer, now gone forever.

Soon, though, Orion's override took effect. The flashing lights stopped, and the train accelerated out of the station. The holostackers reverted from the emergency message to their usual broadcast, which was the morning news; again, photos of Auriga's and Harlow's faces were displayed.

"—in a horrific scene at the thwarted execution of Martín Auriga. The convicted murderer has escaped and is currently wanted dead or alive in New Zaragosa. We urge you, if you see this man, do not confront him as he is extremely dangerous. We have confirmed that the newly-appointed Illuminatus, Millard H. Strughold, was ki—"

The display went black for a moment, and static flashed briefly before switching to a new scene. "That's enough of that," spoke an Australian-accented voice. Then a bobbing field of view appeared: a handheld camera, in a dimly lit concrete corridor. It looked like an underground bunker.

As Harlow and Auriga stared, the train picked up speed, racing along the track.

The camera swung, and centered on Pavo at close range. His shaved head and jet-black eyes were fearsome in the murky light. His teeth were bared and his mouth lifted at the corners, but the expression could not be called a smile.

"G'day, everyone," he said. "I'm Pavo, your field correspondent for an emerging story. We're here at a brand-new facility right under your feet, chasing down the truth behind the recent attacks supposedly involving Dr. Vulpecula's notorious Perseus Agent."

The cameraman panned out to show Pavo near a large steel double door. Above it was stenciled "HHWB 04-A" in yellow paint.

"What's this? Human Health and Well-Being, eh?" Pavo delivered the faux newscast with a theatrical flourish. "Must be a mighty exclusive club they've got tucked away down here. Maybe a day spa or an aug clinic? Let's have a look."

Harlow's skin prickled with an almost physical jolt.

Behind Pavo, several of the escaped cons from yesterday's prison riot were visible in the gloom. With their rugged clothing and broken noses, they looked like a gang of street toughs. Harlow thought he saw a few black-clad Protectorate men facedown on the concrete, but the camera centered back on Pavo before he could be sure. Two of the bruisers pulled the heavy doors open. Inside a cavernous chamber, overhead lights buzzed to life. They marched into the room, the cameraman going last. Inside, rows of hospital beds lined the walls in each direction—several dozen of them, at least. The screen focused on a few of the pitiful, emaciated figures: ashen skin, thin lips, protruding eyes, and then mercifully pulled away.

"These are the victims of the viral attack, eh? Doesn't look like they're receiving much treatment," Pavo said, perusing a datapad that hung at the foot of one of the beds. "'Subject administered HHWB Pathogen 04 on 05/05/32.' Sounds more like they're being experimented on. I don't remember the UCO saying anything about that. Why, I bet some of you's got loved ones down here, been wondering whatever became of them."

Harlow clenched his fists, gritted his teeth.

"But here's the best part, mates," Pavo said, crossing the chamber to a large metal cabinet. With another dramatic gesture, one of the cons opened it. Rows of neon green metal cylinders filled the shelves; Pavo selected one and held it out for the camera. It was slightly larger than a can of soda, with a pressurized nozzle sticking at a 45-degree angle from the top, and a complicated-looking assembly of buttons and safety switches near it. He turned the canister in his hands, showing the symbols and writing around the sides.

"'HHWB Pathogen 04,'" he read aloud. "Caution: extremely trans-mittable. Airborne pathogen." Pavo clicked his tongue, tapping the warning symbol with a black fingernail: the inverted pear-shaped head and almond eyes of a Grey, with crossbones beneath it. "Why, this ain't the Perseus Agent at all…"

As Pavo paced through the bunker, continuing his indictment of the UCO, Harlow's quick eyes caught a figure in the background. Only for a moment, in one of the hospital beds, he spied Carina: sickly and wan, his little girl caught on the precipice of an awful sleep.

"NO!" Harlow screamed, rising to his feet on the train.

"…but how's about we see what Dr. Vulpecula has to say about all this? She's been busy packing up so's to stay on the move, but she's going to spare us a couple minutes for an important message," Pavo continued onscreen. "I'd best be going now, anyway. Ta-ta, lovelies! Now over to you, doc…"

The display shifted with a burst of static and distortion, then returned with a confusing image. Still reeling in shock, it took Harlow a few moments to decipher what he was seeing: Vulpecula's lab in Flagstaff, but in wild disarray. Scuffed linoleum filled the left side of the screen, and Harlow now saw that the camera was lying on the floor, on its side.

"Doc? You with me?" Pavo was saying. "Doc?"

Through the train car's windows, Harlow's building loomed large up ahead. The track curved to meet it, and the monorail began to decelerate—but before his eyes, the elevated track exploded in a shower of fire and dust two hundred yards ahead. The maglev's automatic safety feature kicked in, braking the train with a massive lurch, and Harlow grabbed the steel pole next to him just in time to prevent being pitched all the way to the front of the car.

Outside, in the cleared street outside the new Plaza's entrance, a sleek black Demistrider shifted its torso to center its aim at the train. As he watched with wide eyes, missiles racked from deeper within its spheroid chest, refilling the empty bays that had just fired. The ten-meter-tall war machine's arms were equipped with energy cannons and colossal ballistic weapons. Its mammoth legs had backwards-bending knees and an array of three flexible circular bases for each foot. Atop its shoulders, on either side of the armored vault housing the cockpit, broad red slashes signified the pilot's officer rank.

"It's Barnard," Harlow said, identifying the Pontiff by the strider's markings.

They were in serious trouble. The walking tank had more than enough firepower to annihilate the entire vehicle they were in; Harlow supposed that the certainty of slaughtering the innocents on board the train would keep Barnard's finger hovering over the trigger, but who knew for how long? Collateral damage could be easily glossed over when eliminating a high-profile target like Auriga.

"We've got to get out of here," he said.

Harlow wrenched the doors open, and they vaulted onto the service walkway. The elevated track was a narrow concrete beam some fifteen meters above the street; a single steel rail ran slightly raised above the center. This was no better place to be—they'd be sitting ducks anywhere on the track, and it was too high to jump. Harlow raced down the walkway back in the direction the train had come from, away from the strider. A concrete pylon was farther back, twenty meters behind the train's last car. The support pillar had metal rungs fixed in the side for maintenance workers to climb up and down. As he ran, he heard the mechanized stomping of the strider closing the distance to them. They'd be out in the open, no matter what.

Auriga passed him like he was standing still, and bounded down the first third of the ladder before leaping off. Using his legs to shove off from the pillar, Auriga sprang sideways, hitting the ground and rolling far away from the pylon. The 'mech swiveled, strafing his path with a storm of large-caliber bullets from the heavy machinegun on its arm. Auriga ducked and tumbled, drawing its fire away from the pylon while Harlow climbed down. He jumped the last few meters just in time; Barnard had turned back in his direction, and hot lead chewed up the concrete where he'd been only a second before.

Harlow ducked down behind the pylon; his cover was degrading fast, exposing the steel reinforcement bars within, but he dared not move. In no time, the pillar was barely wide enough for him to hide behind, but then the dry click of empty chambers sounded, and he broke from concealment, trying to sprint to the next pylon, knowing it was hopelessly far away.

There was nowhere to run. The monorail bordered the town square, a deadly playground for the Demistrider. His residential building was over half a kilometer from where he stood, with zero cover on the way. Not even Auriga would be able to outrun those long-range weapons. Behind Harlow, the 'mech took two steps to reposition, and leveled the arm with the energy cannon directly at him. Barnard had him dead to rights. He filled his lungs one last time; his last thought would be of his daughter.

I'm sorry, Carina. Daddy loves you.

And like the wrath of heaven, twin bolts of white-hot fire streaked from the sky, pummeling the strider, knocking it off center; the walking tank took one step backward to steady itself. Harlow's face and arms reddened and cooked with an instant sunburn. Shielding his eyes, he spun, looking up and behind him: Orion's small craft was diving from high in the air towards the Plaza. A second volley unleashed from the saucer's cannons, striking the energy weapon on the strider's arm. That gun exploded with a sunburst of giant sparks, each flare the size of a basketball as the superheated coils cooked off.

Barnard twisted the 'mech to meet the airborne challenger, and loosed a salvo of missiles; coming in fast, Orion swooped the saucer above the ground in a shallow arc and then banked sharply up, turning the craft on its side in the air. Missiles streaked after him, weaving long tails of smoke that twisted together like the serpents of Medusa's hair. The agile little saucer shot for a loop and then skirted the vertical surface of a skyscraper before turning on a razor's edge and disappearing around the building. The missiles blossomed into flame along the skyscraper: thunderous detonations accompanied broken glass that rained like confetti.

The saucer wheeled around the other edge of the building, coming back in for the kill. As it bore down on the crippled Demistrider,

Harlow took off in a vicious sprint, trying to get as far away as possible. He heard and felt the hollow *whump* of Barnard ejecting just before the airborne assault began again. Orion peppered the chassis with fiery streams that boiled its armor away and scorched the skeleton underneath. The strider's core was exposed, and twin bolts found it with a flare that lit up the city square like the birth of a tiny sun. Energy unleashed in a shockwave that knocked Harlow sprawling, and bits of molten metal and detritus cascaded over the Plaza.

Harlow climbed to his feet, seeing that ten meters away, Auriga was doing the same. He was battered and burned, but hardly felt it; seeing Carina in that bed somewhere in the murky gloom beneath his feet had renewed his purpose, his desperation.

As they jogged toward Harlow's building, the small saucer set down in a wide expanse of pavement. A door on the craft's side folded outward and down, creating a short ramp to the ground, and out came Orion, Lyra, and Pyxis. When they were clear of the craft, the ramp raised to its original position, and a shimmering bubble of shield encased the ship.

Auriga exchanged awkward greetings with Orion and Lyra, and seemed at a loss with Pyxis; he managed a wide-eyed nod at the stoic alien leader.

Protectorate men were converging around the Plaza's perimeter, albeit keeping a healthy distance and eying the blackened crater where the Demistrider's smoldering wreckage lay.

"Let's get upstairs," Harlow said. "They're waiting for reinforcements, and who knows what will show up next."

As if on cue, the maglev train now pulled into view, coming from the opposite direction as the one that was still stalled before the broken track. The arriving train slowed as well, coming to rest well ahead of the destroyed section. After a few moments, the doors were forced open in one of the passenger cars, and to Harlow's disbelief, dozens of figures came pouring out.

They jumped the prodigious distance from the track to the street: Pavo's new coterie, led by the gregarious punk rocker. The cons fanned out, swarming the square, heading towards the Protectorate men. At the sight of Pavo, though, Harlow broke into a run, wincing as his blistered muscles challenged the effort.

He collided with Pavo, his hands bunching up double fistfuls of the younger man's jacket. *"Where is she?"* he screamed. *"Where is that bunker?"*

Pavo's hands remained at his sides, not resisting as Harlow shook him with unthinking rage. "That facility is right under us, mate," he said calmly. "There's entrances all over. We took to the city tunnels after the escape, and ran right on top of it."

Now the others were hustling Harlow into the residential building. "It's about to get ugly," Auriga said, noting the outlaws and guardsmen beginning to square off. It seemed Pavo's men would keep the Protectorate from entering the building for a time, but they had to hurry.

Through the lobby with its marble floor and high mirrored ceilings, they packed into the elevator and shot into the sky. Made of glass and positioned on the building's exterior, it offered an expansive view of the street below and the great ominous spacecraft above. On the way up, Lyra explained: "Orion, Pyxis and I need to get on board the *Harvester*. Their supplies might be the only thing that can save all three of our lives. From your condo, we ought to be close enough."

"And I've got to get to Vulpecula's lab," Auriga said. "Something's wrong—she never answered on that broadcast."

"You can take the saucer," Orion said. "Fastest way to get there."

"Are you crazy, *muchacho*? I can't fly that thing."

"I'll enter the coordinates and set it to autopilot," the cybernetic answered. "It'll take off, fly, and land itself. You won't have to do

228

anything."

The elevator gave a gentle *ding*, and the doors opened on a plush, spacious hall. The six fugitives charged down the corridor, and Harlow unlocked the door to his condo. It was empty as usual; through the floor-to-ceiling windows in the open living room, the *Harvester* turned in pensive revolutions. It was fifty or sixty meters away, close enough to distinguish the odd antennae and irregular grooves in the surface. His condo was even with the saucer's rim; at the widest part of the craft, ridges and lights pulsed in the morning sun.

From Harlow's closet, Auriga hurriedly changed into a short-sleeved shirt, which was tight at the chest and biceps, and tough work pants, which he had to roll up at the cuffs. Meanwhile, Orion fine-tuned the settings on the Vinculum, the device he'd built from scavenged Grey technology that allowed him to access the functions of nearby alien ships. The wand-shaped object was thirty-five centimeters long, tapering to a point at one end and a scepter-like knob at the other. Twin displays, reminiscent of bat wings, splayed from the center, and curious glyphs crawled over the entire surface of the gadget.

After attempting for several minutes to sync its applications with those of the spacecraft, Orion shook his head in frustration. "This ship's systems are a thousand times harder to hijack than the last one. I can't just beam us on board with the biotransporters like before."

Lyra stared at the great saucer. "So what do we do?" she asked, in a voice that made plain she already suspected the answer.

"I have an idea," Orion said, "But you're not going to like it."

The uneasy hush was broken by a brief electronic melody from the front door: a personalized chime announcing one of the condominium's residents.

Cass Harlow was home.

Chapter 24

The front door swung open, and Harlow spun to meet his wife. *I feel like a new woman...*

His raven-haired beauty, always so savvy and charming, was now captivating in a truly horrid manner. Her smooth, tawny skin was now the mottled bluish-silver of a waterlogged corpse. Her eyes bobbled and shone like mercury; her dark hair was butchered in a radical hatchet job that exposed one side of her head. She wore a powder blue kurta, wrinkled and ragged; her fingers twitched, her head jerked. Harlow swallowed a scream at the sight of her.

He'd not dare to approach her. It tore his heart out, but he would not rush to her, would not wrap his arms around her. Would not press his lips to that drowned mouth or gaze into those quicksilver eyes. He'd already known the Greys had stolen her away; knowing that the creature before him had ceased to be his wife sickened him, but he would not deceive himself. He would only say her name.

"Cass," he murmured.

Her liquid eyes were large. Again her body spasmed, as if it was struggling to remain still.

"How could you?" she asked. Her voice was icy and brittle. "How could you join them?"

This time when she trembled, a sudden distortion seized her form. Cass seemed to phase out of reality, replaced by a fuzzy silhouette wrapped in static and delusion. It lasted a split second, and when Cass returned, she was half a pace away from where she had stood a moment before. She'd made no conscious movement with her body, but had shifted in space in an instant.

The Humans in the room gave a collective gasp.

"You're a traitor," Cass said, her voice cavernous, as though she were speaking in a tunnel. "But they can fix you. I'll tell them you didn't mean to do it. You thought you didn't have a choice. Maybe they'll take you back. You still have a surgical appointment on the ship. You still have a chance to make it right."

Again the distorted form blinked into view: a whisper of an outline sharing her place, and gone as soon as Harlow saw it. Now Cass was two meters closer to him. Alarmed, he took a step back. Orion had drawn a pistol, and was holding it discreetly by his side.

"That woman is stepping between dimensions," he heard Pyxis say. "We are watching her manipulate space-time to traverse alternate planes of existence. By leaving this dimension at one place, she moves through overlapping layers of space-time and reenters here somewhere else. The effect takes place at normal speed to her, but is akin to teleportation from our perspective."

"She's doing *what?*" Auriga said.

"Guns ain't gonna work," Pavo translated. "She won't be at the same place as the bullet when it gets to her."

"Nobody is shooting my wife," Harlow said softly. "Orion, put that away."

"It's not for her," the cybernetic said. He turned to the large bay windows, raised the gun, and fired several times, fracturing the safety glass into ragged white spiderwebs. He kicked the window free of its frame; the whole rectangle fell in one piece out into the empty air. Across a dizzying gulf, the *Harvester* was a silent sentinel.

"What are you doing?" Cass demanded.

231

"Do not interfere with us," Pyxis said, stepping forward.

Orion holstered the weapon, and gripped the Vinculum tight in his left hand. Thrumming blue waves of energy fed into it from the cybercomputer on his forearm. The device was absorbing power, becoming supercharged. The sigils on the Vinculum's displays turned violet, scrolling upwards in a torrent. Orion made a final few adjustments to it; the wand was now glowing with a blurry aura of imprisoned force.

Orion drew his arm back, raced to the very threshold of the missing window, and launched the mechanism like a javelin. It sailed in an arc through the sky, leaving an indigo tracer like an artificial rainbow. The Vinculum pierced the bubble of the great saucer's shields, and jammed into its hull a couple of meters above the ship's rim. Now the violet waves rippled, eating a gaping hole in the layer of shields large enough to drive a truck through. Seeing this, the Detective understood: the resourceful young man had set the supercharged device to cancel the ship's shield frequency within its immediate vicinity. It was a small portion in relation to the titanic craft, but around the Vinculum, the breach was more than adequate for them to get onto the *Harvester's* surface. They'd have to find, or create, a way in from there.

The plan was obvious to Cass, as well. She gave no further warning, but pulsed directly to Harlow. He threw up his hands from shocked instinct, and felt a painful gash on his forearm. Blood dripped from his elbow, and his eyes widened at the large chef's knife in Cass's hand. She'd retrieved it from the kitchen without him even seeing. Only his involuntary defensive posture had kept her from thrusting the blade into his heart. Already she was stabbing again with the knife, but this time he caught her wrist. Somehow she was difficult to hold on to; when she jerked backwards, he got a nasty laceration on the heel of his right hand, just missing the veins of his wrist.

Then the blade flew from her fingers, spinning behind her; from the forceful and unseen rush of its deflection, either Pyxis or Lyra had to have disarmed her. But in an instant she'd rebounded, darting back and neatly snatching the knife from its whirling trajectory as if everything around her were moving in slow motion. Harlow supposed that from her perspective, partially outside of this dimension's time, it was. Before he knew it, she'd flung the knife at him, but Auriga crashed into his side, knocking him down. He landed painfully on his injured arm, but the projectile missed. Laying on his side, another instant alarm seized him: his shoulder holster was empty. Cass had taken the gun from under his arm in an invisible instant. Now ten paces away, she aimed it at him, but Auriga burst through the open space to intercept her. They wrestled with the gun, and it fired once, bringing a thunderclap to the room and a puff of white dust from the ceiling.

Cass wasn't a trained fighter; the Greys' operations hadn't transformed the city-planning careerwoman into a fearsome combatant. Her gift was a deadly one, though—even with a layman's knowledge of weaponry, she had the upper hand against anyone moving at a normal Human's pace. Only Auriga was able to approach her level of celerity, but his flurries of punches and clinches still never landed as she remained one step ahead of his attacks. She fired again, but he'd turned the gun at an angle just in time—the bullet grazed Auriga's side, and pounded into the hardwood floor centimeters from Harlow's chin.

Harlow needed to get up, but he was bleeding, hurting. His other companions were jumping out the window. Pyxis alone was coming to help him...but as the alien stretched its slender hand forth, Harlow's eyes moved to the small cylinder that had rolled from his pocket when he'd fallen. The inoculator enzyme, the single dose of antidote that Vulpecula had given him for his suffering daughter. Carina's only hope for staving off the infectious agent in her weakening body. Pyxis snatched it up, and with one skinny digit pushing down the plunger, injected itself in the arm.

Harlow screamed with rage as Pyxis turned back to the window and the whistling wind outside.

***

"You've got to get me over to the ship," Orion said.

Lyra stared at the chasm between the condo and the spaceship. It seemed deceptively close, but a misjudgment would send him falling sixty-five stories to the street. Far below, Pavo's fellow escapees skirmished with Protectorate men in the Plaza. The faint pops of gunfire sounded like pressure building in her ears.

"Don't think about it, Lyra," Orion said. "Just hurry."

Pavo took a deep breath with a gesture that said, *I'll do my best...*

"Alright, mate," he said. "If you're ready, let's give you a boost."

He picked up the youth with both arms, like one would hold a large dog. With a couple of steps for momentum, he hurled Orion out the window with all his might.

Lyra's heart skipped a beat as the young man soared over the abyss. Pavo's strength had given him plenty of momentum, and he was more or less headed for the breach in the shields, but she could see that he'd never make it all the way to the ship. Orion was two-thirds of the way there when gravity caught up to him, and Lyra reached out with her gift, buoying him up, guiding his body through the barrier's hole. With his arm outstretched, he seized hold of the embedded Vinculum and clambered onto the ship's hull.

Lyra exhaled, and sagged a bit. Even that amount of effort had been taxing; she'd not have had the strength to bring him the entire distance, and was grateful for Pavo's teamwork. Now the bionic Aussie lifted an eyebrow at her, extending his hand.

"Ready, love?" he asked.

"Just a moment," she answered. "I'm not sure I'm—"

Then a gunshot sounded, both of them ducked and glanced back to Auriga and Cass still grappling with the firearm, and Lyra remembered she didn't have enough time to be a hundred per cent ready.

"Okay," she said. Pavo took her in his arms. He was so strong; his face was close to hers for a moment, and oddly Lyra found herself thinking of Cass's ability to seemingly slow time—not really, not for everyone, but only for herself and the way she perceived it. Thinking of other dimensions, other possibilities, other places where things were not the same as they were here, on this planet, in this time.

As soon as you think something, your whole world changes.

Anyone can change the world with a thought.

I'm just not afraid to make it happen.

Then two bounds jostled her, his arms lifted and quickly fell, and she was flying, facing backwards and viewing the building with Pavo in the missing window. Cold wind whipped her and she swiveled towards the ship, waiting for the instant when she started falling to the street, and then lifted herself up, floating to her target and coming to an enervated rest on the ledge next to Orion. Pavo came next, leaping from the window until she caught and carried him the remainder of the way, and finally Pyxis, who made the journey entirely on its own. Although it must have been strenuous to fly the whole way, Lyra suspected Pyxis had objected to being picked up and thrown like a rag doll.

The four of them stood on the upper surface of the great saucer; away from the edge, the exterior sloped upward in a curve that was sharper and more arduous than it had appeared from a distance. Walking as though up a steep hill was possible in most places, but now and then a radiant canyon appeared, flashing vivid lights in kaleidoscopic patterns at the bottom of a trench. Some of these they could jump across, but others had to be climbed down, crossed, and climbed out of again. Then, too, were the odd arrays of antennae-like apparatus that

235

bristled at odd angles from the surface; proximity to these produced a nauseating, bone-jarring sensation that was quite unpleasant. They learned to give these antennae a wide berth, only to encounter other obstacles: narrow bands of the expanse that spun so fast as to give no sense of motion. A careless foot placed here would upend the unwary traveler like a rug being pulled out from beneath them. And above it all, the dreamlike ambience of the great ship's shield formation swirled and evanesced in disorienting rhythms like aurora borealis.

A shapeless aperture followed overhead as they traversed this maddening landscape—followed Orion and the Vinculum, more accurately, as he carried the device that prevented the shields' bubble from closing, trapping them inside, or perhaps even expelling them from the ship's façade altogether. Lyra tried not to think about that possibility, and from time to time stole glances at the bright blue sky through that shifting gap. The heavens seemed close, a cerulean pool into which she could dive and never be seen again.

It was a bewildering realm in which to wander, and the bizarre surroundings sapped her concentration as surely as the grueling terrain drained her strength.

The body as a whole loses functionality and potency, like an elderly person's.

Alongside her, Orion stumbled and fell. She helped him to his feet, finding it difficult to do so. She glanced at Pyxis, whose ashen face was wrinkled. Lyra suspected the alien was making an effort to hide its fatigue, but it slouched a bit when walking, and its deep, measured breaths were labored.

However, the decline is sharp, not gradual over time, as with normal aging.

"We won't have to go all the way to the saucer's center to get on board, will we?" Lyra asked. "That would be quite a walk."

"Be on the lookout for a hatch or something where we can enter," Orion said. "This is harder than I thought; it could be disguised with the surface very well."

"We are not looking for a hatch," Pyxis said, the mesmerizing colors of their surroundings mirrored in its onyx eyes. "I will know what I seek when I see it."

Behind Lyra, Pavo muttered something about 'bloody mystic tour guides', and she reached back for his hand, gripping it for balance as she stepped around what looked like a skylight. Another prismatic gulf lay ahead; on the far side, the ground was ten meters higher, creating a wall that they faced at their current height. At regular intervals in the wall, massive fans whirled behind protective housings that could be automatically opened or shut as the ship entered or left atmosphere.

"We can climb up between the fans," Orion said. "Let's go two at a time; Lyra, you can get on my back. Then Pavo and Pyxis can follow together."

Lyra would have objected, but thought it best to save what little strength she had remaining. Even the idea of using her psionic powers was taxing. Again Orion heaved the Vinculum with as much force as he could muster. The device plunged into the wall, creating an anchor like a piton embedded in a slope.

Lyra wrapped her arms around Orion's neck, piggyback-style, and held fast, bracing herself as a running leap off the edge carried him to the embankment where he seized hold of the wand's handle. For a harrowing moment they dangled over the trench below; then Orion found purchase and pulled himself up the surface, catching a handhold in the grooved metal. Orion wrenched the Vinculum free and stabbed it higher above them, dragging them up after it, using the apparatus to climb like a mountaineer's pickaxe.

After several repetitions of this process, they had nearly gained the summit, but Orion's stamina was wholly gone. With a furious effort, Lyra launched herself to the top, grasping the edge with both hands. When she had rolled over onto the surface, she reached back down along the wall to pull Orion up. Spent, they sprawled at the wall's vertex; her body ached with exhaustion, but looking down and seeing Pavo's encouraging grin, she already felt a little better.

"Now you two come on," Orion called, tossing the wand down to Pavo. Pyxis directed the bounty hunter where to aim with one spindly digit, and he rocketed the Vinculum into the wall as Orion had done.

Instead of piggybacking on the Aussie, though, Pyxis floated unsteadily to the makeshift anchor by itself, grasping the Vinculum with a bony hand. Lyra frowned, watching the alien force an access panel open and rummage through the guts of the ship. Her viewing angle wasn't good enough to see much else.

"Yes, this is it," Pyxis said, hooking an elbow over the wand's handle and unscrewing a flexible cable inside the panel. It locked eyes with Pavo, standing at the gulf's edge. "Give me the canister."

"What are you doing?" Lyra asked.

"But it's supposed to be for Vulpecula to study," Pavo objected, producing a metal container from his jacket pocket nonetheless. Lyra squinted at the neon green canister, its side emblazoned with a skull-and-crossbones featuring an alien head instead of the traditional warning symbol. 'HHWB Pathogen 04' was just legible on the side.

The Perseus Agent can be compared to the Seneca Valley Virus. While it benefits Humans, Senecavirus is detrimental to its natural hosts. In the case of Perseus, its source and natural host is the Grey aliens. This would be equally true for whatever it is the UCO is doing to corrupt my own work: the alternate pathogen Harlow mentioned in the spaceport attack.

"Pavo, no—don't give it to Pyxis," Lyra pleaded, realizing the awful plan. "It will kill everyone on the ship—"

Pavo turned the cylinder in his hands, tracing the warnings with a finger like a child learning to read. "I'm supposed to bring it to the doctor."

"I am the doctor. You are supposed to give it to *me*," the alien repeated in a patient tone.

"If the ship is infected with the pathogen, we can't board it and get what we need—" Lyra shouted, horrified and desperate. But Pavo paid no attention.

Pavo threw the canister to Pyxis, who threaded its nozzle into the flexible cable. Its long, skinny fingers manipulated the series of switches and safeties on the container, and then pressed firmly on the trigger mechanism. With a hiss, the pathogen flooded into the vessel's air supply. It was done—nothing Lyra could do would prevent the deadly virus from circulating through the ship.

Emptying the canister took several seconds, and Pyxis replaced the hose and closed the panel. At once, the ship responded with a throbbing vibration that would have knocked Lyra off her feet, had she not already been lying at the top of the barrier. She gripped the ledge with both hands, fearful of the quake tossing her over the edge. All the *Harvester's* myriad lights shifted to a baleful magenta; the colors of the Vinculum changed with it, matching the monochromatic alert signal.

Pyxis then turned its inky eyes to the Vinculum, still partially embedded in the wall. It made swift adjustments to the odd device, and the outline of the alien's body grew ultradistinct, contrasting with its weird, nebulous surroundings. It had accessed the ship's biotransporters and was beaming itself aboard. Lights swallowed Pyxis's form, and it was gone.

Chapter 25

*H*aven't you ever wanted to be more than one man?

How long had he been out? Apparently just for a few minutes.

Harlow left slick smears of blood on the polished wood floor as he heaved himself to his feet. Auriga and Cass darted about the condo in a delirious struggle. Furniture seemed to fling itself about as if a furious poltergeist were demolishing the home. In the brief flashes that were visible to Harlow's eyes, the combatants wrestled in a variety of places and positions; Auriga maintained the advantage in hand-to-hand combat, but Cass escaped from every clinch, slipping away to retrieve a fallen weapon to even the score and force Auriga into defense for another round.

"Cass, think of Carina," Harlow said, gritting his teeth. "Our daughter, she's sick, she needs help—"

The rest of his sentence was choked off by a massive bass reverberation. Windows splintered throughout the building, snapping into opacity; except for the one pane that was entirely gone, the condo was reborn with the appearance of a tomb lined with icy sheets that obscured the sky. Harlow staggered to the missing window and viewed the *Harvester*. Before his eyes, the wheeling ship darkened, turning to a deep purple. An angry magenta disc hovered over the city.

Harlow turned back to his destroyed condo. Auriga was on his back, then atop Cass as she struggled beneath him.

Harlow retrieved his gun and leveled it at his wife, feeling the stab in his heart as the sights lined up with her pretty head. It was unbelievable to point a gun at her. He'd never be able to pull the trigger.

"Cass."

The buzzing from the ship ran through them all: a violent shudder, as if Harlow were being shaken by a giant who was angry with his playthings.

Cass was pinioned by the ship's lowing. The bass note held her captive, and she reached for the nape of her neck where the Beacon had been implanted by the Greys.

Harlow dropped the weapon, and seized the back of his neck, as well.

"NOW HEAR THIS. THE HARVESTER *HAS BEEN COMPROMISED AND IS WITHDRAWING FROM TERRAN ATMOSPHERE."*

Cass's eyes were wide, her mouth open in disbelief.

"THIS IS A STATE OF EMERGENCY. NO PERSONNEL, HUMAN OR GREY, IS PERMITTED TO BOARD OR DISEMBARK FROM THE SHIP DURING THIS SELF-IMPOSED QUARANTINE."

And with that last word, it was clear what had happened. Somehow, a virus had been unleashed on the *Harvester*—Zubrin's agent, he speculated, since it was airborne and more transmissible. The Greys were following some protocol that dictated a return to orbit, so as not to jeopardize any aliens on the ground or risk the continued spread of the pathogen. Harlow gaped at the massive saucer as the magenta deepened to a perilous crimson. Had Orion and the others made it on board? If so, they'd be trapped; but if they hadn't gotten on the ship, they were probably dead by now.

He came back to the moment just in time to see Cass flee the condo without a backward glance.

***

The surface of the *Harvester* was a wrathful red world. Lyra turned to Orion, his face cast in the sanguine blush of the ship's alert.

"We can't board now," he said, close to panic. "I don't even know if we can get away from here in time."

"In time for what?" Lyra asked.

He showed her schematics on his cybercomputer; the figures and diagrams meant nothing to her, but Orion seemed sure of their significance. "They're preparing to leave atmosphere, and return to orbit."

On the ledge below them, Pavo blinked. "That bloody no-good double-crosser."

"Pyxis manipulated you," Lyra said. "It's done that to Orion too. I just hope it's too busy or too far away from us now to keep it up."

"I think it's gotten what it wanted," Orion said. "We've got bigger problems than Pyxis. If we get on the *Harvester*, we'll be infected with the HHWB virus. Even if we get the supplies we need, we'll probably die. And if we don't get on board…"

The shuddering of the ship finished the rest of his sentence. They'd never survive the return to orbit; the only chance was to flee the *Harvester's* surface and get back to the ground—but even if they did, without the aliens' food, they would die in a matter of days.

Lyra nodded sternly. "We can't stay here and think about it, either. Right now the only choice we have is to get out of here."

"Let's move it," Orion said, bounding down the side of the precipice to where the Vinculum was still embedded in the wall. He seized the wand with both hands and thrust against the wall with a powerful kick that carried him to the lower deck where Pavo stood.

The Australian looked up at Lyra, holding out his arms. "I'll catch you," he said.

She leapt from the edge, thinking of another panicked flight many days ago off of the forest cliff. Then, she'd been infuriated, abandoned by Pavo and yet averse to his attentions; now, his presence was a comfort.

Lyra tumbled into his arms, and though the moment was dire, he did not put her down right away. They lingered for an instant before she drew her fingers along his cheek; then, suddenly conscious of their surroundings and of Orion nearby, she hopped to the ground.

Orion was intent on the Vinculum's displays and hadn't seen... whatever it was that had just transpired between her and Pavo.

"The ship's triggering an action potential," Orion said. "If we're not out of here by the time it reaches full power, we're going to be vaporized."

"How long is that?" Pavo asked as the trio broke into a run.

"There's no way for me to know. I'm using the Vinculum as a power sink to draw energy off the *Harvester* and slow down its charge, but it still won't be long. Maybe a minute."

Their flight through the hellish landscape was torture to both body and mind. Now they stumbled downhill, running headlong over and around the alien obstacles. The distorted aperture pursued above them, ragged and shrinking, shutting out by degrees an azure window that Lyra doubted she would ever see again. The wand in Orion's hand was a blazing beacon of otherworldly insanity; it seared her eyes to look at the thing, and the scavenger grimaced as if it scalded his flesh to hold it.

Sprinting, they took a flying leap over a pulsing red chasm. Lyra crash-landed on the opposite side, skidding on the ship's blistering surface that tore and bruised and burned her all at once. Then she was up and running again, half-blind and exhausted, her legs unsteady but unable to stop, moving from a desperate terror. A sickening fizzle had begun in her chest, a dreadful disintegration, not eating her alive from the inside but rather...canceling her out at the core.

Ahead lay the rim of the saucer, the outer edge of the world, a boundary between agony and oblivion. It was futile; she could only hurl herself from this place of suffering and be lost to nothingness.

Next to her, Orion could hold the Vinculum no longer and flung it away with a shriek, a fiery javelin that coursed through the blasted sky. It burst like a meteor entering atmosphere, a crimson fracture of the crimson heavens. Thunder overtook all her senses. She was tumbling in a void; reaching out, her fingers clenched something rigid, inanimate and yet hateful. When her vision returned, red and raw, she was dangling from the saucer's edge by her left hand. Below them, the skyscrapers were like matchsticks, a dizzying final vista. Orion clung to the craft's rim a meter away. Pavo fell past her and she stretched her other hand out.

I'll catch you...

Their fingertips brushed and Pavo plummeted into the empty sky. Orion lost his grip and dropped after him. Her hand burned and slipped from the edge, and she plunged into oblivion.

***

Harlow raced with Auriga down the hall. Here, too, the windows were a whiteout ruin, shutting out the city, and he strangely recalled his time locked away from the world during the prison riot. When they reached the elevator, its reinforced plexiglass hadn't shattered and the panorama of a different New Zaragosa made his breath catch in his throat.

The *Harvester* was gone. The brooding spacecraft had abandoned the troubled city, its conspicuous absence leaving the skies exposed as if to invite judgment from above. The surfaces of the surrounding skyscrapers were battered and broken from the ship's parting shock-wave, and Harlow wondered if the elevator was operational. When he jammed the button for the lobby with his thumb, though, it began a smooth decline.

Below them, the city square boiled. The fugitives had been joined by a multitude of angry citizens in their clash against the Protectorate, and Harlow supposed that Pavo's renegade broadcast had found a sympathetic audience. Gliding down towards the street, he watched the officers falling back amid the onslaught—but then movement above caught his eye.

Three figures fell from the sky, helpless ragdoll forms that mirrored his own controlled descent. Harlow jolted forward, pressing to the glass, and groaned in dismay.

"*Dios mío,*" Auriga whispered, bringing the crucifix to his lips.

Harlow was every bit as powerless as the three plummeting victims, and could only watch, horrified, as they fell hapless to the pavement.

∗∗∗

They burst onto the Thoroughfare where a crowd gathered around the site of the impact. Harlow saw only vassals; the Protectorate men had apparently retreated. He elbowed his way to the front, hoping he wouldn't be mistaken for an officer.

"Let me through. Let me through!"

In the small clearing, Orion and Lyra melded in a fierce embrace, on their knees in the street, heads buried in each other and shoulders heaving. Nearby, Orion's scavenged saucer rested, although the gleaming bubble of protection was gone from it. Still the Detective, Harlow gathered the truth: the pair had fallen onto the craft's shields, which had absorbed and dissipated the force of the collision.

Then Harlow's eyes moved to the wreckage a few meters away: the granite monument and pedestal smashed into rubble, the pulverized gray and black mingled with liquid crimson that coursed through the cracks in the pavement. The shattered body sprawled amid the debris of the guardian Grey statue.

He knelt with Lyra and Orion, placing his hands on their shaking shoulders. He could find no words, or will to speak them if he had. The crowd's low murmur droned in his ears. Somewhere far away, shouts and gunfire rang, but here, time had stopped.

Then Auriga spoke. *"Mira…look here."*

Harlow raised his head, trying to avoid the sight of Pavo's broken form. Auriga hefted a jagged fragment of the pedestal; beneath, a cavity opened beneath the Thoroughfare. Rubble cluttered a stone staircase descending into the gloom.

That facility is right under us, mate. There's entrances all over.

Astounded, Harlow stumbled to the entrance. Cass's designs for the Plaza had included an entrance to the bunker—she must have been aware of the structure, but surely could not have known that it would come to imprison her own daughter.

One simple thought of Carina was all it took. He dashed into the shadows, pounding down the staircase into subterranean depths where he would challenge the very underworld itself.

In the long concrete corridor, infrequent LED lamps battled the darkness. Harlow was bruised and burned, and the gash on his wrist had begun to throb, but he would not let any of it slow his pace. He paused only once, to smash open a wall-mounted cabinet containing personal protective equipment and don a rebreather over his face; then, he redoubled his headlong race beneath the city.

He passed a massive set of double doors. Above them, stenciled in yellow paint: "HHWB 04-C". A hundred meters down and on the opposite side of the tunnel, "HHWB 04-B". Then Harlow reached the final portal, wide open and guarded only by the facedown dead men he'd seen on Pavo's broadcast.

The lights were still on in the yawning chamber. He careened around the corner, and stopped in his tracks right in the doorway.

Vivienne Tainer, the vigorous Secretary of Human Health and Well-Being, was fleeing the hospice with Carina in her arms. The girl was sallow and listless, but conscious; her eyes brightened at the sight of Harlow, and his threatened to overflow with tears.

Behind Tainer was Carina's empty bed; before her, Harlow blocked the room's exit.

"Put her down," he hissed at the Secretary. Tainer's ageless face froze in shock, but for no more than a second. Her mind and body were quick; she set Carina down, and although the child wobbled on her feet, Tainer crouched behind her, literally holding her upright as a shield.

The spineless maneuver shocked Harlow, but even if his shoulder holster hadn't been empty, there was no way he could point a gun at his own daughter. Having had to do such a thing to Cass would stay with him forever as it was. Tainer wouldn't know he was unarmed, though, and appeared to be weaponless herself. It didn't matter; he would take this fiend apart with his bare hands. Harlow moved forward.

"Let her go, Harlow," Tainer said.

It stopped him short, hearing the same demand from the Secretary that he had been about to issue to her.

"Please, let her go. The Greys need her," she continued. "I don't know all of it, but somehow, she's exactly what they need."

What's your *Value Rating?*

"No. It's too late for that," Harlow answered. "Even if I wanted to help those monsters—and believe me, I don't—the ship is gone. Give me back my daughter."

"That's just one ship. There are other facilities, and there will be other ships. There may not be another Carina."

Harlow advanced another two steps, and Tainer tightened her grip on the child. Would the Secretary go so far as to harm the girl rather than give her up?

"She'll be cared for," Tainer said. "No more experiments, none of this." She indicated their horrid surroundings. "Cass would understand, she would make the sacrifice. The Greys will show their gratitude, believe me. And she needs treatment—what can you do for her? If you take her back, it will be only to watch her waste away and die. They won't let any harm come to her, they need her alive and well. They have the knowledge and the technology to care for her; you don't. Please, put your feelings aside and consider what's best for everyone here."

Despite himself, Harlow faltered. Could it be true?

Because I love you very much, your value can never go down with me. Do you know that?

"You've lied about everything: the origin of the virus, the attacks on the city, you blamed it all on Vulpecula."

"Yes, to keep her away from here and prevent her from interfering with these trials." The Secretary avoided the word *experiments*. "Swaying public opinion against Vulpecula was necessary to safeguard our privacy here. But we're past that now—I don't care about her, just like I don't care about Auriga or that idiot puppet Strughold who you helped kill." Tainer's voice had gained an edge. "You either get full immunity and make powerful friends of the Greys, or you watch your daughter die before going on the run for the rest of your life. Don't be a fool, Harlow."

Thunder sounded in the corridor: the beating of footsteps as an army approached. Pavo's augmented bunch of convicts, joined by other vassals from the streets above, rounded the corner and poured into the room. In no time, Tainer was surrounded. The hard-faced men kept just enough distance, watching Harlow for cues.

Harlow tossed the rebreather aside, then stepped forward and knelt, holding out his arms. Carina rushed to him, and he melted against her with an embrace, squeezing her more tightly than ever in his life. He kissed her clammy face over and over, stroked her grimy hair. Tears poured from his eyes, and he shuddered, scarcely able to breathe.

"I love you so much," he choked. The girl clung to him, and he could bear no more. He rose, lifting her in trembling arms, and walked two impossible steps to the Secretary. He placed his daughter in Tainer's arms.

"Let her go," he whispered to the waiting crowd.

The men parted before Tainer as she walked to the door through a narrow path. The echo of her steps gradually faded, along with Carina's hopeless sobbing. Then Harlow collapsed, doubling over on the frigid concrete, and fully abandoned himself to his grief.

Chapter 26

A multitude filled the Plaza's amphitheater. The crowd contained people from every conceivable station: rich vassals from the high-rises, poor citizens from the slums, street toughs from the rapidly emptying prisons. Even some desert-dwelling outlanders were here, brazenly entering the city during the drastic decrease in perimeter security.

Protectorate men were absent here in the public square, despite the massive gathering; their numbers had dwindled from desertion and attrition, and the remaining loyalists had been positioned to fortify the UCO headquarters building. The skyscraper—last bastion of Findley van de Kamp—was impossible to approach, now surrounded by black-clad enforcers in full riot gear and encircled by Demistriders and Hoverwings.

Much of New Zaragosa was now effectively lawless, but peace settled the disparate citizens here today. The message anticipated from the promised speaker was far too important to be eclipsed by petty squabbles.

For now, though, the crowd would have to wait. Lyra Vaughn stood a stone's throw from the stage, pensive before the demolished site where Pavo had crashed back to earth. The broken granite had been cleared away, but a hollow crater in the pavement remained. She stared, holding her breath, reliving the calamity with tortuous clarity:

her curse, as a psionic and an empath. How many times would she see the corona of her blistered vision sharpening just in time to see him plummet past her? How many times, the ghostly grazing of his fingertips against hers?

For all her insight into the human mind, all her acumen in matters of the heart, Lyra would never decipher the final moments she'd shared with Pavo. Cradled in his arms, seeing the tenderness in his eyes and feeling the slowness of time while all around them, the world hammered to a final crescendo—what would have happened if just one thing had been different? How might her world, even the *whole* world, have changed?

Anyone can change the world with a thought...

She tried now, with a sudden ferocity that pounded her brain until her eyes overflowed with tears: tried to envision a world where he wasn't gone, where the things she saw and felt were simple—how had he said it?

An emotional response to pain—what bloody good does that do you?

But this wasn't the kind of pain Pavo was talking about.

It ain't the pain itself that draws most people up short; it's the emotional part.

But for Lyra, there was no distinction between the two.

The only relief she found was that as Pavo was gone, Orion had miraculously come back to her. With the *Harvester's* vanishing, Pyxis's influence on the young scavenger had melted away. Softly he approached her now; his left arm circled her, his hand found hers and squeezed, bringing a steady reassurance.

"It's time," he whispered.

Lyra strode to the dais's center. Her tousled blonde locks fluttered above the shiny halo scar. She wore a lavender kurta and leggings with high black boots, and an earpiece with a stalk mike. Her face was haggard, her steps were slow; but her eyes were not weary, her breath was calm, and she conserved her energy for the coming address.

She would not use her gifts to manipulate the audience. It would not be appropriate to use psionic influence on their emotions, and drawing upon her powers had become far too burdensome besides. The simple truth was all that was needed.

When she spoke, her voice was thin but clear. "Thank you all for coming. My remarks will be brief and straight to the point. This is not a political speech or an ideological sermon—merely a factual report of the recent events in New Zaragosa, as you will not hear them on UCO broadcasts. My only goal is to share the truth, and leave it to you what to do afterwards."

As she described the happenings of the past few days: the prison riot, Strughold's death and Auriga's escape, the revelations regarding the Perseus Agent and the HHWB-04 pathogen, and the contamination and retreat of the *Harvester*, the audience was still. When she reached the more lurid details of Human experimentation carried out beneath the city, some groans of disquiet could be heard. Murmurs of approval met her announcement that the destroyed statue of the guardian Grey alien would be rebuilt as a monument to Pavo. Mixed reactions followed the news that the Perseus Agent—the *real* virus, designed and working as Vulpecula intended—was being reproduced and made available at the city's aug clinics for any who were willing. Already, hundreds of people had taken the dose to gain enhanced strength and speed; many others were not as trusting, but Lyra emphasized that the decision was a personal one, with no expectations for those who did or did not pursue it.

She shared the revelations from Pyxis's own mouth regarding the Xenoplicity Foundation and the engineering of a Human army of shock troops bent to the Greys' purposes. When the wave of horrified anger had run its course through the crowd, she continued.

"Finally, and worst of all, there is one last thing I must show you.

Brace yourselves, please, and watch this."

Orion, similarly fatigued but determined, used his cybercomputer to cast a video feed to the holostacker terminals positioned throughout the Plaza. Lyra left the stage to join him; as they clasped hands, a spark branched at their touch, and they shared a silent kiss.

On video, the scenes flicked through various bird's-eye views of the *Harvester's* interior, and were timestamped from only an hour before. On every shot, the bodies of emaciated Greys littered the glossy decks, twisted and tranquil; stations everywhere were deserted, and the ship rested with the serenity of death.

At length, the vista came to rest on the ship's bridge. Here among the quiet bodies, one figure moved with laborious intent: Eridanus slumped at a computer panel, moving one feeble hand with agonizing slowness across the controls. The wheezing rasps of its breath filled the speakers with the regularity of a ticking clock.

Now the display before the alien flashed a message in multiple languages; in English, it read:

[OMEGA PROTOCOL] CONFIRMATION REQUIRED.

From offscreen, Pyxis entered the bridge, purple-robed and regal. Eridanus did not acknowledge the newcomer, keeping its attention on its ponderous task. It gasped for breath, punching keys one at a time.

"So, you are signaling Ios that the Terran experiment is over, and summoning an armada to vaporize this planet," Pyxis observed. "This is your final wish? To destroy the Terrans, out of spite?"

Eridanus's hand slipped from the terminal, dangling by its side. Its massive head lolled back; its strained gasps slowed. Its lipless mouth opened.

"Would that I could...destroy you...with them."

Eridanus toppled from the chair; with a last rattle, its breath ceased. On the screen, the message changed:

OMEGA PROTOCOL CONFIRMED.

Pyxis approached the panel, and entered a command. The message blinked, unchanging.

OMEGA PROTOCOL CONFIRMED.

Frowning, it continued to type. The screen refreshed, with the same statement.

OMEGA PROTOCOL CONFIRMED.

Pyxis hammered at the keys, typing furiously.

OMEGA PROTOCOL CONFIRMED. YOU DO NOT HAVE ACCESS TO RESCIND THIS COMMAND. OMEGA PROTOCOL CONFIRMED.

The screen went dark; the other terminals across the bridge deactivated. Pyxis backed away from the console, scowling, and stood motionless, surveying the room, sovereign over a realm of death in a metal coffin orbiting the globe.

Epilogue

Auriga bashed the metal door with his shoulder, sending it flying from its hinges. He sprinted to the staircase, leaving the roof where the saucer had parked itself on autopilot.

He descended the stairs with one leap, denting the metal platform when he landed. Another locked door, which he kicked open.

"Doc!" he shouted.

The halls were a dismal, dimly-lit maze of white. His steps pounded on the linoleum floor. The facility was deserted; ducking into room after room, he found empty offices, vacant operating suites and supply closets.

"Noreen!"

No response.

Another long hallway headed toward the rear of the clinic. He burst through the swinging doors to survey a ruined laboratory. Broken equipment was strewn all over; here and there, the white cabinets and counters were stained with red.

He found her in a corner, where a sputtering medibot had tried to minister to her. Now, the damaged bot was bumping stupidly against the wall, its job half finished; Vulpecula lay unconscious, her breathing shallow, hovering between life and death.

Auriga knelt on the blood-slicked floor to lift her mangled body. With one elbow, he swept an operating table clear of debris, then deposited her on it. Rummaging through the lab, he gathered medical supplies, fighting back the panic, forcing up a calm endurance. With a whispered prayer, he bent over the table and frantically worked to save her life.

THE END

Afterword

When I began writing *Scavenged*, I didn't know at first that I was creating a full-length novel. The early versions of Chapter One were first an intro for a character with which to playtest a developing role-playing game, and then later the narrative introduction for that game's core rulebook—but I found that those places weren't the correct home for the story. (By the way, the revised edition of *Xenoplicity* is now available from DH Publishing, and you can read two of my short stories included as the game's Prologue and Epilogue. You'll even find the backstory for a familiar character...) As I continued adding to Orion's struggle, it slowly became apparent that I was writing a book instead of a short story.

I doubt that I'd have consciously chosen to do so if it hadn't happened organically—you see, I was already working about 60 hours a week at a demanding job as well as contributing to *Xenoplicity* as a creative developer, and writing is a time-consuming endeavor all by itself. Over the course of a year, I wrote a paragraph at a time, mostly using a word-processing app on my phone in the parking lot before work or during my lunch breaks. Needless to say, it was a wild year, but I've always liked to stay busy!

After the book was released, I knew I'd have to find my way back into that zone and do it all over again; however, I found that writing a sequel was more difficult than I anticipated. My heartfelt thanks are owed to the fans of *Scavenged* who inspired me to continue writing. When friends would ask, "When's the next one coming out? I'm looking forward to it!" that helped to push me forward an inch at a time through the challenging process of working overtime, writing the second book, and promoting the first—all simultaneously. Thank you so much to Annette Simpson, Judy Gardner, Michelle Dimos, Aundrea Schippers, and Amanda Ahrens for your words of support and encouragement! Thank you to my writer friends Kelly Creagh, Cal P. Logan, de de Cox, and Ishmael A. Soledad: you are uplifting and invigorating when it is so much easier to be indifferent and unsupportive. Also, blessings to the late Paul Antony Jones, who even while battling a terminal illness continued to support other writers such as myself.

Thanks so much to my cover artist, Sandra Tubiera. You are a joy to work with!

A special thanks to Matt Muccigrosso, the lead developer of *Xenoplicity* and the master of its impressive domain. Without you, there would be no *Scavenged* trilogy! (And yes, dear readers, I said "trilogy". Stay tuned on Twitter @Starbuckle81 and my website, www.scottarbuckle.com)

Last but not least, endless thanks to my beautiful, wonderful wife, London. Your love and support makes me reach to be the best version of myself.

About the Author

Scott Arbuckle was born in Louisville, Kentucky in 1981. His debut novel, *Scavenged*, won the Best Indie Book Award for 2019 in the Young Adult category. His horror short story *The Show Must Go On* appeared in the Halloween 2021 edition of *Lovecraftiana* magazine. This is his second novel.